"WHAT HAVE WE HERE, NORAA?"

"Entertainment," the man farthest back said.

"Or not," Vale said, withdrawing her phaser with complete nonchalance.

The men paused, looking at the weapon, and then the man called Noraa laughed. At that, all five rapidly withdrew their own weapons, ranging from some form of energy pistol to a multibladed knife.

"It doesn't have to get ugly," Vale said casually. "I don't want to hurt you."

"Hurt us?" And the men laughed.

"Five against two, all with weapons. I like our odds," Noraa said.

Current books in this series:

A Time to Be Born by John Vornholt
A Time to Die by John Vornholt
A Time to Sow by Dayton Ward & Kevin Dilmore
A Time to Harvest by Dayton Ward & Kevin Dilmore
A Time to Love by Robert Greenberger
A Time to Hate by Robert Greenberger

Forthcoming books in this series:

A Time to Kill by David Mack
A Time to Heal by David Mack
A Time for War, A Time for Peace
by Keith R.A. DeCandido

STAR TREK®

A Time to Hate

ROBERT GREENBERGER

Based on
STAR TREK: THE NEXT GENERATION®
created by Gene Roddenberry

POCKET BOOKS
New York London Toronto Sydney

An *Original* Publication of POCKET BOOKS

POCKET BOOKS, a division of Simon & Schuster, Inc.
1230 Avenue of the Americas, New York, NY 10020

ISBN: 0-7434-6289-0

First Pocket Books printing July 2004

10 9 8 7 6 5 4 3 2 1

Manufactured in the United States of America

This one's for Kate and Robbie, the two who round out my life, filling it with love.

A Time to Hate

Chapter One

THERE WAS A REAL BITE in the air, but Will Riker liked watching his exhalations waft through the mostly still air. He and his father had been up before the sun, hiking at least five kilometers to get to this particular spot. The night before, his father, Kyle, had told him they would have to get up that early to stake out the spot for themselves ahead of the competition. It never occurred to the fifteen-year-old that people competed for coveted spots, but it made sense.

His father had rustled him awake and shoved a mug of hot cocoa into his hand. It felt good cupped in both hands, but he couldn't savor it very long because they had to get moving. Will had put on several layers of clothing, all the while hearing his father bang around the house, getting the last of the gear ready.

They didn't speak much during the hike; Will was tired and excited but knew Kyle preferred not to disturb nature if at all possible.

When they arrived at the site, Kyle beamed, thrilled to get there ahead of the other area fishers. It was a small, naturally clear semicircle, obscured from the path by trees. A circle of stones in one corner indicated that many a fisherman had not only caught his dinner, but had cooked it at that spot. The view from the location was spectacular. Will was impressed, even though he had grown up appreciating the natural beauty of Alaska. He let out a low whistle, earning him a broad smile from his father, although it lasted only a moment. Will quickly set up folding chairs, assembled their poles, and found the container with his father's patented bait. Kyle, meantime, set up the makings for a campfire, something they might need later. He also set up a container for their catch and a small transceiver. Will had grown accustomed to the sight of the device. After all, his father worked for the United Federation of Planets and his tactical skills might be needed without advance notice. All too often Will would arrive home from school to a note from his father.

It had been relatively calm the last few months, so Will was anxious, convinced that his father would be called away any moment.

They sat side by side, casting and reeling in their lines, neither saying much. As the sun peeked up over the horizon, it painted the lake's surface in dazzling colors. Once the sun cleared the horizon, his father decided it was time for breakfast. He pulled out a few wrapped meal bars, bottles of water, and a bunch of grapes. They ate in continued silence, his father very content with the slow passage of time. Will desperately wished to use the time to start talking, to have a real man-to-man conversation about the years ahead. He was doing well in school and was beginning to seriously consider Starfleet. His father's missions had captured his imagination, and Will was beginning to yearn to see what was beyond this land's snow-capped mountains. Will considered his grades to be good enough, and he wanted his father's perspective. But every time Will wanted to have this conversation, something came up. He had grown frustrated and more than a little angry. Kyle Riker, it seemed to the boy, was just not interested in his future.

Watching his line, Will grew impatient, and he felt himself starting to fidget. If he was going to spend the day in the chill air, he could at least have a decent conversation with his father. But every time he started to talk, Kyle shushed him. The teen finally gave up and cast at a much faster pace than his father, earning nothing but a scowl.

As the sun neared its zenith, Will finally felt a tug. It had some force behind it, and he imagined it to be a large fish, easily more than five kilos. He didn't say anything, ready to impress his father with the first catch of the day. Slowly, he reeled in the struggling fish, his pole bending in an impressive arc. Finally, Kyle noticed Will's effort and spoke encouragingly, breaking the uncomfortable silence that had grown over the hours.

The line, which he had cast out at least twenty-seven meters, was now half that distance, but Will's reeling had slowed. The fish seemed to be winning the struggle. Unwilling to lose his prize, the teen dug in his heels, gritted his teeth, and yanked a bit on the pole to show dinner who was the boss. The prey responded by yanking back, and it was large enough to gain back some distance.

And that was when Kyle grabbed the pole, his huge hands covering Will's. He used several sharp tugs and then reeled in quickly for several meters before tugging again. Ignoring Will's protests, he took command of the situation. The teen's hands remained trapped. Finally, the catch seemed to give up, and the last few meters were effortless.

Not again, Will thought. His father had done the same thing to him six years ago, and here he was, taking control of the situation again. Dammit, he was fifteen and he was going to bring in the fish or not—on his own.

"It's a beauty, Willy," Kyle said as the sheefish came out of the water. Its silver-and-blue body wriggled as Will reached down to remove the hook from its protruding jaw. "Make us a fine dinner."

Will didn't say a word as he finished removing the hook and dumped the fish into the storage container. The youth seethed, and didn't say anything to his father for the rest of the day. Not that Kyle noticed. He never picked up on Will's anger, or if he did, he never reacted. Once again, his father hadn't let Will complete a task on his own. He was still taking charge and refusing to let the boy grow up.

Will swore it was the last time he was going to let Kyle Riker control his actions.

Christine Vale ran a hand through her thick auburn hair, smoothing it down. She had already washed up from her last visit to the surface and changed into a fresh uniform. She refused to beam back down with Aiken's blood splattered all over her. It was their first casualty on Delta Sigma IV and she wanted it to be the last one. She knew, though, that was not likely.

Leaving her quarters, she refused to acknowledge how tired she felt. Vale would have to exist on adrenaline and caffeine for the moment, since she was needed down below. Sure, she could get some sleep and send down her second-in-command, Jim Peart, but she was their leader. Captain Picard had specifically asked her to oversee the deployment. She didn't want to let the man down. If they were going to suffer, she was going to suffer right beside them. And if she fell, Vale knew Peart was eager to step in and complete the mission.

The mission. She laughed mirthlessly to herself. Vale sent down her teams of security guards to augment the meager numbers of peace officers that were all the police or military support the planet had needed until this week. Her teams had been detailed to help maintain order while the public was panicked over the planet's first murder in a century. That homicide had quickly turned into a string of murders, and then a wave of madness had engulfed the populace. Vale's people were suddenly endangered on all fronts, and she hated it.

She preferred things to have reasons, patterns she could see and react to. Instead, the citizens of Delta Sigma IV were rapidly losing their inhibitions, acting out without rhyme or reason, and her people were managing, at best, merely a holding action. There was no victory to be had here; they could only minimize the damage.

Christine took the turbolift to engineering and, emerging, practically walked into the chief engineer himself.

"Sorry, Geordi," she said, stepping aside. They were approximately the same height, and she looked right into his eyes, which were augmented with cybernetic implants. Their irises narrowed, adjusting the focus, and she found herself staring and quickly looked away.

"I'm fine, but I think you need some rest," La Forge responded, unperturbed by the penetrating look.

"Later. I have to get back to the surface. Listen, the people have escalated the violence. It's also become destructive, and I'm going to need some of your people down there. I'm afraid of infrastructure problems, and the last thing we need is to incite further troubles because people can't get fresh water."

La Forge stroked his bearded chin and nodded in understanding. He turned around and led her to a workstation where he called up duty rosters. Names rolled upward on one screen, color coded by shift. "I'll alert my damage control teams, equip them for general-purpose needs, and have them on standby. You call, they'll come running."

"And my people will be with them, providing protection. Still, captain's orders are they beam down with sidearms."

La Forge nodded again, not surprised, but also not pleased that his people would be facing danger. His features softened a bit and he added, "Hey, I'm sorry about Aiken. He was a great kid."

"Yeah, he was." A kid, fresh out of the Academy, and all his promise snuffed out. The pain refused to budge.

And she could tell from La Forge's expression that he understood why she was pushing herself to get back below. He'd do the same thing if it were strictly an engineering problem.

"Listen, I think we need to start by restoring water to Testani."

"That's the city that burned first," he said, clearly having stayed current despite remaining aboard ship during the mission.

"Right. The fire in the capital was smaller and was extinguished pretty quickly."

La Forge went back to studying the roster, his hand back to his beard. "Have you heard from the captain?"

"Not since he and Counselor Troi returned to the planet," Vale said. She felt herself growing anxious and got ready to leave. But first, she had to get something out in the open.

"I know you're working with him, but if Nafir screws up and costs me time, I'm going to use him to clean the armory."

La Forge frowned at that, thought a moment, and responded, "Look, I know he's not at the top of anyone's competency list, Chief, but T'Bonz and I are working with him. He's gotten better since he transferred over. He won't fail you. You have my word on it."

"Good." She turned to leave and could hear La Forge already ordering his alpha team to go on standby. Vale couldn't help but grin at Geordi's attitude. He worked hard and was easy to get along with. He was one of the people who made her feel most welcome when she had transferred aboard a few years back.

Vale exited the deck and headed to the main transporter room, ready to return to her people. Along the way she mused on the difficulties many department heads experienced with recent crew assignments. At one point, the *Enterprise* was the number one choice of all graduating cadets. For the last several months, because of its tarnished reputation, the ship had been receiving fewer requests on and many more off. As a result, people were rotating aboard who would not normally fit the crew profile for the best ship in the fleet.

Fortunately, her recent recruits were young and still moldable, and she recognized her luck. Still, the eager-to-please smile on Aiken's face haunted her as the lift slowed to a stop. She tried to concentrate on the next assignment as she determinedly strode down the corridor. At no point did Vale notice crewmembers get out of her way.

Gripping her phaser, Vale stepped onto the platform and nodded toward Nafir, a tall Gallamite. She bit her tongue as he activated the controls and gave her a small wave with his pale hand. Within moments she was on her way back to the troubled world.

The Council had been relocated to an adjacent office building after the riot broke out just hours before. When Jean-Luc Picard materialized in the Council's new center of operations, he was impressed by the sounds of activity. Maybe being forced to move had finally shaken the people out of their torpor. At first, the captain thought they were so far in over their heads that they would remain paralyzed with inaction. Now, aides of both the Bader and Dorset races were scurrying between a set of rooms, many carrying wires and isolinear chips. They were clearly trying to turn these rooms into a functional seat of government. What concerned the captain, though, was that only the Dorset councillors were present in this room.

He exchanged curious glances with Deanna Troi and then stepped forward, making his presence known. El

Rodak El noticed him first and came gliding over, a small smile on her face.

"Captain, you've come just in time."

"Have I?"

"Yes." She paused, gesturing with a sweep of her arm to take in the entire room. "The Bader have chosen to set up a separate facility until things can be calmed down."

Picard was alarmed to see the Council, whose members he tried to protect from the spread of the contagion, suddenly split along racial lines. Troi seemed to share both his confusion and concern.

"Why is this better?" Troi asked.

"We've lost too much time to petty bickering," Rodak replied. "We feel we can split the planet in two, each of us concentrating on relief efforts for our respective continents."

While the woman had a point, the conclusion was not one Picard agreed with. "That may sound like a good plan to you," he said in a measured tone. "I, though, do not think it helps anyone in the long term."

"Aren't all four continents mixed race?" Troi asked.

"But predominantly Bader or Dorset, Counselor," Rodak replied. "We argued about it and then decided to stop arguing. It's what our ancestors did."

"Yes, stopped arguing to unite a world. Now you've stopped arguing and have effectively divided it." He keenly felt the need for Ambassador Colton Morrow, who was still in sickbay, recovering from injuries sustained during the riot that had forced the Council to relocate. If the Council was split, at least Picard would have someone he could trust in the other room.

"And what have you accomplished since this 'enlightened' plan of yours?"

Rodak's smile faded. "We're still rebuilding our communications network so we can track the problems and communicate with peace officers in the afflicted areas."

In other words, Picard concluded, nothing had changed. No one seemed to be working with any sense of urgency while the contagion spread across the planet. He was tempted to seek out the Bader, but suspected they would be in much the same situation.

He turned to ask Troi a question, but noticed his counselor was by a door, speaking with a Dorset aide. They were having a conversation he suspected was no more productive than the one he just concluded, but he decided to let it run its course rather than interrupt. Instead, the captain turned his attention to the monitor screen. It had snapped to life moments earlier and someone was fine-tuning the controls. Blurred images sharpened, and then the Dorset-dominated continents of Fith and Tregor came into view. Colored lights then were overlaid, and Picard was astonished to realize each one represented a recorded instance of the madness that was gripping the people.

Only it wasn't madness. It was their true nature, and they didn't know it yet. He was hoping to explain Crusher's news to the complete Council and dreaded having to do it twice.

As Picard idly watched Troi work her magic, Ensign George Carmona approached him. Picard was quite pleased with the man's dedication and performance during the mission. *Vale chose well,* he considered. The burly, olive-skinned man's curly hair was unkempt, but that could be forgiven under the circumstances.

"Captain, I tried to talk them out of it, tried to explain this was adding to the hazards . . ."

"Slow down," Picard suggested. "What do you mean, Ensign?"

"The Bader set up their base on the opposite side of the building. To get there, you cross an exposed courtyard. Any of the councillors or staff become targets when they go from one setup to the other."

Picard shook his head in disappointment. Ever since he had beamed down two days ago, his impression had been that the government seemed ill-equipped to make a lunch selection let alone rule the people. He had hoped that with Jus Renks Jus replacing Chkarad as Speaker, things would improve. Clearly, they had not, since they were not taking their security seriously enough.

"I've got Williams posted at the Bader entrance, and I've been keeping watch here. I think that's about all Lieutenant Vale can spare, to be honest, and I worry every time the door opens."

"As you should," Picard said. "But you can't influence the Council. I should know—I've been trying for days." He gave the weary guard a smile of support, which seemed to brighten the man's spirits. "We'll try and get you some support. Carry on."

Carmona nodded. He walked back across the office and left, no doubt taking up his post on the opposite side of the door. Picard felt safe, knowing how much he could trust the man.

Troi finished her conversation and came back to the captain. She looked pleased with herself, and Picard gave her a quizzical look.

"There's an old saying: 'It's the clerks who run the government.' "

Picard nodded. "I've heard it."

"Well, here it is in practice," she said, sounding just a tad smug. "Even though the Bader and Dorset councillors feel the need to separate, the aides and staff disagree. They are keeping links open between the two rooms, sharing information. Generally, they have a better grasp on the reality of the situation than either room full of councillors."

"Indeed," Picard said, only mildly amused and impressed by the revelation.

"They share their leaders' concerns but are far more fatalistic. They've seen the damage reports and casualty counts. Sir, it's far worse than they are admitting to," Troi said.

"I can't step in and tell them how to do things. I'm limited by our rules and regulations, including the fact that they are the sovereign government."

The captain then took a moment to wander to a far corner of the large office and contact the *Enterprise.* He wanted to check in before he got too distracted by the problems before him.

"Status, Mr. Data?"

"We have received no word from Commander Riker, and he is overdue to check in."

"Have you tried to hail him?"

"Actually, sir, we cannot seem to locate him."

"The sensors aren't picking up his badge?"

"No, sir. He has vanished like his father."

"I'd like to take that as a sign he has found his father. They had headed north, if I recall. Please see what you can do to find them. Anything else?"

"Geordi has had to take the warp engines offline to try and resolve a plasma injector problem. Since we are not likely to need warp power while in orbit, now seemed like the best time to deal with that."

"Agreed. Picard out." He only hoped that La Forge would be able to handle the repairs on his own without having to summon assistance from Starfleet. The captain thought he had more than enough to occupy his attention.

Beverly Crusher felt that she had a purpose again. Over the last few days, she had studied the Delta Sigma IV problem to find out what had turned a cure for a genetic disorder into a poison. She had finally figured out the mystery and could go to work on a solution. She let her coffee go cold as she worked in the lab without interruption. Fortunately, the casualties from the planet had slowed to a trickle as her staff set up triage stations on all four continents. Dr. Tropp was supervising the planetside work while she remained aboard and concentrated on the long-term issues.

Crusher pushed a stray lock of hair behind her ear and ran a series of studies on the brain chemistry of the five test subjects. They had spent nearly a year in quarantine, waiting to see if the cure provided by Starfleet Medical would change their genetic codes back to normal. Everything seemed to check out until one, El Bison El, killed

Unoo of Huni and fled the building, breaking quarantine and unleashing the problem on an unsuspecting world.

When the native plant liscom's natural gases were filtered from the blood, the body chemistry began a return to normal. But normal also meant that both races' violent tendencies reasserted themselves. The liscom gas had actually worked like a narcotic, lulling the people into a peaceful frame of mind and allowing the two races to coexist in harmony and to gain Federation membership for their world, unlike their belligerent parent worlds.

Rather than study the blood work, she concentrated this time on the brain chemistry, watching how the buildup of gas altered the way the brain governed personality. All in all, it was both fascinating and chilling, something she wanted to study in greater detail. Time, as usual, was the enemy. In fact, it was this kind of research, as opposed to the emergency room atmosphere of the last few days, that got her to thinking once more about Yerbi Fandau's offer. The current surgeon general had let her know, several months back, that he was planning on retiring and that she had been approved as his first choice to replace him. Given all she had been through over the last few months—the sudden return and departure of her son, Wesley, the loss of face within the Starfleet community, and the growing notion that Picard would never entertain a romantic relationship—made the offer incredibly tempting. She needed to make a decision whether or not to accept, but she didn't want to do it without discussing the issue with her longtime friend. However, the crisis below would have to be settled first.

Once again, she leaned into the microscope and

watched the microbes. Her left hand fine-tuned readouts, one finger activating a color-coded field that helped identify the various elements on the slide. A greenish tinge was suddenly highlighted, something she hadn't seen before. With a contented sigh, she straightened up and began taking notes.

Troi was leaning against a wall, watching the scurrying back and forth, wondering if things could possibly get worse. Aboard the *Enterprise,* she was counseling several crewmembers, many of whom were ambivalent about remaining loyal to the captain and staying on the *Enterprise,* or looking after their own careers and seeking safer assignments. Was it really only days ago, she wondered, that she and Riker were reviewing the latest transfer requests?

But not everyone was looking to get out. Anh Hoang, an engineer, didn't want to leave and didn't seem to be all that concerned about the current political brouhaha regarding the crew, but had other problems that were of concern to the counselor. After losing husband and child in the Breen attack on San Francisco several years back, Hoang seemed to have closed in on herself, holding herself in a type of personal stasis. No friends, no romance, no off-duty hobbies. It appeared her life was just work and sleep. And that, Troi knew, was only a recipe for long-term trouble. They had begun speaking over the last few days, and Troi began to wonder if she was using Hoang as an excuse not to focus on the horrible problems plaguing Delta Sigma IV.

She had walked the streets, felt the people growing angry, felt their sense of loss and their insecurity as they came to grips with their natural tendencies for the first time in their lives. The two races could not solve their problems entirely through diplomatic means, nor could they achieve any form of peace as long as the people gave in to their new impulse to violence. None of them had grown up developing the moral codes and internal governors sentient beings require, so things had spiraled quickly out of control.

An aide went by, surreptitiously handing her a glass of water. His body language indicated that the presence of the Federation was barely tolerated by the Council. Picard had quickly determined that keeping the contagion away from the Council was of paramount importance, and so far there had been little evidence of the "madness" taking hold. She presumed, though, that it was possible that someone had gotten infected during the escape from their chambers. Currently, there was no way to scan for the disorder with tricorders, a further complication. If the Council members were infected, the government was done for.

"This is Protocol Officer Seer of Anann."

The voice drifted toward her from the status board that had recently been completed. Two aides and a councillor drifted over to the board, all looking surprised. Their representative had clearly been forgotten.

"Councillor El Rodak El speaking," the woman began, only to be interrupted by a second voice chiming in from the other room, "Cholan of Huni here."

There was a brief flash of consternation on Rodak's lined features, but she willed them away and awaited Seer's report.

"We're still on the island of Eowand. There was a fight, and we spotted Kyle Riker. Commander Riker went

after him, and both appear to have vanished. The local officers and I have scoured the area, but there's no trace of either human."

This confirmed Data's earlier report that Will had not checked in on schedule. Troi frowned at the message, listening carefully to the cadence of Seer's report. He was telling the truth, and this bothered him. Clearly, he and Will had formed a bond that had no doubt helped them get this far. The concern in his voice was genuine. Just then, a hand gently grasped her right shoulder.

"It's all right, Captain," she said before turning her head.

"Counselor, I knew the *Enterprise* lost Commander Riker's signal a little while before the protocol officer's report came through. I took that to mean Kyle Riker had been found, so I was not concerned."

His voice was calm and professional, his use of titles reminding her that this was an ongoing mission. She turned all the way to face him, and his hand fell to his side.

"I have every faith in Will, sir," she replied, using his first name to indicate she was not going to treat this entirely on a business basis, because there were also personal issues attached.

"Good. So do I."

"I will continue to look for a little while longer, then return to the capital."

"Fine, fine," Cholan barked from the other room.

Jus Renks Jus, Speaker for the now divided Council, had joined the growing crowd, and his look of distaste spoke volumes to Troi. Someone, if not all the Council members, must be infected. Controlling the government was going to become a serious problem over the next few hours.

As Picard looked at the updating monitor screen, Troi stepped back, forced herself to drink the last of her water, and concentrated all her skills on finding her link with Will. Although she had been born with only half the normal Betazoid's telepathic talents, her bond with Will Riker was strong enough always to be there, online in her mind. When she discovered almost immediately after they met that they shared this bond, the knowledge scared her. No one except her mother had ever been able to achieve that level of intimacy with her before. Since then, though, the bond had been a constant source of comfort. Now she found it with little effort: a golden thread, glowing amid the shadows of her mind. He was alive, and that was enough for her.

For now.

Chapter Two

KYLE RIKER GOT UP from the ground, wiping the dirt from his hands. He didn't move with the same sureness Will always remembered. His father wore a bulky gray coat, not the same sort of flexible microweave jacket Will was wearing. His hands were bare because gloves would have prevented him from doing the delicate work that was necessary to steal a flyer. They were chafed and red from the cold, and scarred. Definitely the worse for wear, Will mused, watching without once lowering his phaser.

"I said, I'm listening," Will ordered.

Kyle looked over at him, pain in his eyes, something Will had not seen in his father since the one woman whose love they had shared, Will's mother, Ann, had died.

"You can put the phaser down, son," Kyle said.

"Right now, I can't trust you."

"Your own father?"

"Especially him," Will replied.

Kyle looked hurt for a moment but let it pass. "I

thought we tore that wall down a decade ago. I thought this was all past us."

"Funny thing about walls," his son said. "You can build them, tear them down, and rebuild them all over again."

"Is that what this is all about? My not being in touch? I've never been good about that."

"No, this is all about you leaving the scene of a crime and allowing yourself to become a fugitive. You need to come in and explain yourself."

Kyle gestured with his hands, palms up. "Can I at least put some gloves on? It's colder than a Romulan's smile."

Will gestured with the phaser. His father gingerly reached into his coat pockets, pulled out black gloves, and put them on. He rubbed his hands, trying to generate some friction to warm them faster. Will just stood there, sorting through the feelings that were conflicting in his heart and his head, trying to remain focused on the mission. While they had this reunion, a planet was falling apart, and he had to learn what role his father had played. Mixed in with it all was the dreaded feeling of guilt by association, and it nagged at him, fueling the anger he barely kept under control.

"Much better, thanks, son."

"Let's keep this professional, sir," Will said.

"Like we did on the *Enterprise?* What did you call it . . . your best Academy manners? Is the wall really that high and thick?"

Will did not reply, deciding to wait his father out. Get him to talk. Vale had taught him this trick some time back, and he liked using it. In the past he would have threatened or intimidated his subject, using his large physique to good advantage.

Kyle, no slouch as a negotiator, tried to wait him out too. Both must have felt the pressure of time, but Kyle seemed to think they both needed to settle their personal issues first. Will shifted his feet, sensing the cold seeping through his boots. He glanced up and saw the coming twilight. When the sun set, it was going to be a lot more uncomfortable standing in between parked flyers.

Finally, Kyle broke the silence. "Can we at least do this inside somewhere?"

Will stood his ground and started to reach for his combadge.

Kyle looked concerned and shook his head, saying, "No."

"*Enterprise* is a whole lot warmer than down here."

"My work isn't done. I have to finish, and you can be a part of it."

"You still haven't explained yourself."

"I will, but let's get out of the cold."

"How'd you get to Eowand?"

Kyle looked at the ground, almost like a child caught with his hand on the cookies. "I came on a flyer."

"Something you stole."

There was a spark of defiance in Kyle's eyes. "I intend to make reparations when this is done. But a stolen vehicle or two is nothing compared with the suffering these people are enduring." Some steel had also crept back into his voice, and Will tried to figure out just how broken a man Kyle was. Without answers, everything was conjecture. At that moment, he flashed on Deanna's face and wished she were here. She'd know what was in his father's heart.

"Is the flyer here?"

"Yes."

"Rather than compound your crimes, let's take that one. Do you have a destination in mind?"

Kyle gestured with his left hand toward a battered, pale blue and gold vehicle, somewhat haphazardly parked compared with the other ships on the ground.

"I wanted to change flyers, avoid possible tracking," Kyle explained, his frozen breath drifting around his head. "I've been doing it for days."

Will nodded and walked on the older man's right side, keeping out of arm's reach, his phaser on the side away from his father. A locking light blinked twice, and he heard a click. The hatch was a little wider than on Seer's ship, but the inside was much the same. He had to admit he was impressed by how easily his father slipped into the pilot's chair and began running through the preflight sequence. The flyer hummed to life, the engine sounding rougher than Seer's craft but more powerful. Kyle looked at Will and then at the piloting controls. Will nodded his consent, and Kyle's large hands struggled their way inside the two contoured holes that housed the controls. Within seconds, the engine's vibration grew a little rougher, and with a small shudder, the flyer began to lift into the air.

"I've changed flyers four times," Kyle explained as they traveled. "They're all built so damned consistently, it's a snap to master each new model." Will didn't reply, figuring the warming air would make his father more talkative.

Banking to the right, they swooped away, the town of Eowand rapidly growing smaller. The sky was now almost a royal blue before them, a golden haze behind them. They flew for several minutes in silence. The presence of two large men made the forward section of the flyer feel cramped, but Will made sure his right arm, which held the phaser, remained free to move. He rested the weapon in plain sight, certain that Kyle could do nothing as long as his hands were encumbered by the ship's controls.

"How'd you know where to find me?" Kyle finally asked.

"Someone was defusing things around the planet when no one else seemed capable. It didn't take a computer to figure out it had to be you."

"And here?"

"You seemed to stop following Bison; you followed the main path of the contagion. As I saw it head north, it became apparent you were heading for familiar climates."

Kyle nodded, a smile of approval on his features. He then narrowed his blue eyes, concentrating on a course correction that would take them directly toward the northern pole of the planet. "I lost Bison. Bet you did, too."

"Letting the magnetic field hide us?"

"If anything, it'll confuse the scanning and we can then go any direction we want."

"And this ship is shielded from the magnetic field?"

Will received a withering look from his father and he cursed himself for asking so naive a question. Was he an adult, or was he twelve again?

"We were never looking for Bison, to be honest. You didn't say, where are we going?"

"Next nearest mass concentration of people is here, on the Osedah continent. We'll check that out, make sure things are under control, and keep moving."

"What's your objective? What do you want my help for?"

Kyle adjusted their course, his arms wriggling back and forth as he struggled to work in the confined space. Will thought he wouldn't get an answer and was again growing impatient.

"The outbreaks of violence continue in this direction. Bison must also be in this direction, spreading it. He's my target." Kyle exhaled heavily, then glanced at his son. "How much do you understand about what is happening to these people?"

Will frowned for a moment, then began to summarize their mission. "The Bader and Dorset achieved unprecedented cooperation while colonizing this world. In turn, something native to this planet changed their chromosomal structure and they found themselves dying at a younger age with each passing generation."

"Good," Kyle said, nodding in approval. "And you know I was sent here by Koll Azernal to study the scientists' reports."

"Why would the president's chief of staff send you?"

Kyle evaded the question and continued speaking. "The Bader and Dorset scientists did their work independently of one another, and the chief medic here missed something I caught when reviewing the data."

Will considered just how brilliant his father must be to

do all the things he had done over the years. His accomplishments bordered on the legendary, but, prideful as he could be, he rarely spoke of them to his son. In fact, although he had been the sole survivor of a Tholian attack on a space station, Kyle never told Will of the incident, nor of the months he spent recovering and the torturous hours of physical therapy. Will only found out about it more than a decade later from Dr. Katherine Pulaski, who was the physical therapist. Will was not at all surprised it was his father who figured out the source of the problem on Delta Sigma IV.

"You were the one who figured out it was the liscom gas that affected the genes?"

Kyle shook his head and kept flying into the night sky. Below them, the sea was dusted with whitecaps, making for an eerie sight.

"No, the people figured that out on their own. It was the other effect."

Will blinked in surprise. "What other effect?"

Now Kyle blinked and looked alarmed. "Hasn't your Dr. Crusher figured this out yet?"

"If she has, then I don't know about it. After all, I've been chasing you around this world."

Kyle nodded at that and continued. "OK, so maybe *you* don't know. I can only hope to God that she figured it out."

"Figured out *what?*"

"No need for that tone," Kyle said harshly, trying to reassert his role as the alpha male. Will bit his tongue, waiting to hear what was happening to these people. "Didn't you ever wonder how two incredibly belligerent races could possibly bury the hatchet in the ground and not in each other's skulls?"

"I read the reports. They both decided to use Delta Sigma IV as a new starting point."

"Nice words, but that came months after both races tried to claim the planet for themselves. They did such a great job selling themselves as enlightened; the Federation never really questioned it."

"Questioned what?"

"Not only did the gas shorten their lives, but it drugged them somehow. I'm guessing it affected their brain chemistry and effectively lobotomized them."

Will was stunned at the revelation. Never once did he guess anything close to this. A planet full of drugged people, suddenly without the drug. The withdrawal symptoms alone must be horrendous.

"And they never figured this out during the one-year quarantine?"

"All the doctors saw," Kyle explained, "was that these peaceful people were acting a little less docile. But they certainly weren't aggressive, let alone violent.

"As the serum we devised worked its way through their systems, it took time before we figured out the right dosage. We kept a close watch, but it wasn't until they were back home that problems manifested themselves." Kyle looked less smug, definitely uncomfortable with the notion of Federation fallacy.

"And Bison was the first to experience the withdrawal?"

"So it seems. Without the gas in their body, their natural tendencies reassert themselves. Both races are violent, aggressive people, absolutely no fun to deal with."

Will was following the natural progression and saw where this was going. He didn't need a counselor's training to understand what happened next. "And these are adults who have never had to deal with these emotions before."

"So Bison couldn't control himself, and struck out at Unoo."

"He broke the quarantine, and spread the 'cure' like a virus. And you've been following him."

"Of the five test subjects, El Bison El reacted first. When we find him, we can have Dr. Crusher look him over and figure out why. I'm betting she's already looked over the others so his scans should be useful. I hate loose ends."

Will winced at that, since he said much the same thing to Deanna just days ago on the ship. He disliked resembling his father in any way.

"You saw the trend and extrapolated there might be a problem. Didn't you say anything?"

"Of course I spoke up," his father snapped. "I made it clear to Starfleet Medical that I thought there was a problem, but the doctors and psychologists disagreed with me, so I was outvoted."

Kyle fell silent for a moment, brooding over the defeat. Had things gone differently, needless bloodshed would have been prevented.

Will waited him out, looking out at the sea and noting they were nearing the shores of Osedah.

Finally, Kyle spoke again. "When President Zife agreed with the plan to reintroduce the test subjects during the planet's centennial celebration, it wasn't all that difficult getting included in the delegation. In fact, Zife liked the idea that someone more experienced than that pup Morrow would be on hand."

Will watched the emotions play out in his father's eyes. Kyle's jaw was set, as he concentrated on flying, but his feelings of failure were evident in his bloodshot eyes.

"As soon as Bison killed Unoo, I knew in my gut that my suspicions were right. I'm a tactician; I always think four moves ahead. I knew if he got loose, there was a good chance all these people would be infected. I had to contain it and him."

"So you ran."

"I pursued him, but he had already infected some members of the media. He was faster and younger than me, so he got away."

Will considered all this, accepted it for the truth, and tried to think ahead. How do you stop a people from acting naturally?

"I began trying to outrace the virus and catch Bison. Along the way I tried to stop things from getting out of hand."

"You were the planet's guardian angel, weren't you?" Even Will winced at the bitterness in his voice.

"I failed to stop this on Earth, I had to stop it here," his father said in a harsh voice. "This is *my* mess. *I'm* responsible. I suspected something was going to happen but never insisted on the proper security. Some tactician."

Will laughed coldly. "Then you'll be happy to know that you're not being blamed. The whole Federation is on the hook for this."

Kyle didn't laugh back. He was neither relieved nor pleased by the notion.

"Of course they are, and they should be. The studies were flawed, the research incomplete. They never should have come back here. I should have found a way to stop it. That's my job, after all, to stop things from getting worse. But this time, I couldn't do it."

The flyer was beginning to descend. Will watched as tiny points of light appeared in the distance: small towns with their night lights on to protect them. He was pleased to see nothing in flames, although that could change in a heartbeat. How on earth could Vale and her team contain this before Crusher could do her part?

"Don't you see, Will? I have to fix this. And with you at my side, we can be even more effective. We can complete this together and save the people from themselves."

Will wasn't sure if his father was cracking under the strain, but he had never heard Kyle pleading before. He wasn't surprised the request came, and had even anticipated it a bit.

"I'm responsible for so much that has gone wrong, and it is my job to fix it. Look, there're only so many undercover things I can do. If I'm at all under suspicion, you can get me into places. We can make a difference."

There it was. In a nutshell, the very essence of a Starfleet officer's job. Making a difference either through discovery or protection, but making the universe a better place to be. Will could certainly help his father, and he was surprised to discover that deep down there was a part of him that actually wanted to help.

"What do you say, son?"

* * *

"What island are we on now?"

"Told you before, it's Kagor," Studdard said, wiping sweat from his brow. His team had been among the first on the planet and they had just finished a rest rotation and were immediately beamed back to the surface with Taurik from engineering to handle some emergency repairs.

"Nothing like getting the grand tour," Clemons commented, taking up the rear position. The security detail was accompanying the Vulcan on the last stretch before their destination, a power relay station located on the island's highest peak. Something had taken it offline, and a string of islands and the western coast of Huni were without power.

"What is this?" he continued, puffing from the exertion of the climb. "Our fourth or fifth stop?"

"Third, you knucklehead," Studdard said with a grin. "You're complaining so much you're missing the sights."

"There are sights?" Weathers asked. He was broad and sported a small paunch. His hair was close-cropped, and his gray-flecked mustache betrayed his age. A fifteen-year veteran, he'd served with Picard since the early days of the *Enterprise*-D.

"C'mon, can't you see the beautiful horizon?" Studdard said, making a sweeping gesture toward the placid ocean surrounding the island. It was the calmest of the three places they had visited. The sun was rising high in the sky, there were no clouds, and other islands dotted the sea in a vaguely straight line toward the south. "Just about as pretty as Olivarez."

"Did you see what she did with her hair?" Weathers asked.

"Nah, man, she beamed down earlier with Gracin's unit," Clemons said.

"Looks like she stood too close to the warp reactor. Hair going every which way and all standing up," Weathers said, adding a guffaw.

"Don't think I'd like it too much," Clemons answered. "Now me, I like hair that's softer, with some body to it. Styled nice, you know what I'm saying?"

Reyes caught up to the much larger Clemons and shook his head. "Like who?"

"Well, we could always start with the lieutenant herself. Nice hair. Real nice."

"Don't know if we should be talking about Vale like that," Studdard commented. "You want to talk about hair, saw a real nice top to a yeoman near sickbay yesterday."

"Who was it?"

"Didn't catch her name, Reyes, but I hope to when this is over," the squad leader answered.

Taurik was walking directly behind Studdard, who preferred taking point whenever possible. The security guard was a little weary from battling people who seemed committed to mayhem, but his orders from Vale were firm: the people were to be either ignored or subdued with as little harm to them as possible. Studdard's gregarious nature and ready smile made him a popular squad leader, and despite the tensions created by the mission, his squad's visits to Delta Sigma IV had been successful. This one should be as well, since the people who had caused the damage appeared to have fled.

"Okay, I'll give you that it's pretty. No Risa, but nice enough," Weathers replied.

"This world has enough islands, you should find something you'll like," the leader replied.

"Not if they destroy them all," Reyes said grimly.

"Smell that sea air," Weathers said. "Nice."

"Nothing like a worrywart to spoil the sightseeing."

"I'm not a worrywart," Reyes answered. "Just a realist. The damage to this world is beginning to add up to some serious hours of repair work."

"Not to mention loss of life," Clemons added.

"You need a good breeze to really get a lungful of the stuff," Weathers continued, not noticing he was being ignored.

"Think we're making a difference?" Reyes asked.

"You're the realist," Studdard said. "You tell me."

"I'd say we're doing little more than putting a few dozen fingers in too few dikes. Sure, we're saving lives and even some vital utilities, but then we come here and it's already too late."

"Way I understand it, they can't help themselves, which, to me, makes this a tragedy," their leader said. And it was. Studdard had heard about the cooperation the two races on this world had achieved and admired them for that.

"Actually," Weathers added, "get up a good enough wind, you might even have yourself a real first-class surf. Enough islands here, surprised we don't see any action."

To Studdard the vista before him was pretty, and certainly a change of pace from most planetary assignments. With luck, they would stand guard, Taurik would effect repairs, and they would all beam out without a shot being fired. He pitied the people, and from what he understood of their problem, it was likely to get worse before it got better, so a simple in-and-out mission like this would be good for morale.

Taurik hadn't said a word since they beamed down, and Studdard had given up trying to engage him in conversation. They had served together aboard the ship for some time now but had never worked alongside each other before this assignment. He chalked it up to their differing positions as well as to the Vulcan's naturally reticent personality. A shame, really, since Studdard was always interested in learning more about the Federation worlds he had yet to visit. He even heard Taurik displayed a sense of humor, rare for a Vulcan. Someday, Studdard hoped to hear a joke.

Before them the gray and orange building appeared, the usual squat construction with little in the way of signage or decoration. Antennae covered the roof, angled in a variety of directions, relaying microwave energy that was desperately needed for homes, hospitals, and security workers. The double doors to the facility had been ripped off their hinges and were now lying at an angle against an outcropping of moss-covered rocks. Studdard waved an arm and signaled to the others to slow down. Crouching low, he examined damage to the wild flora near the entrance. He made out a variety of footprints, indicating that an unknown number of people had not been trying to be stealthy about their work.

Reyes, behind Taurik, was taking readings on his tricorder. He shook his head to indicate there were no other life-forms around, which confirmed their initial beam-down readings.

"Couldn't help themselves, huh?" said the shortest

and youngest member of the team as he pocketed the tricorder. "Just had to climb up here and wreck the place."

Studdard had no reply to that. He too thought that this out-of-the-way location was an odd choice for vandalism. In fact, it made him downright suspicious. Taurik was ready to enter the building when a meaty hand grabbed his arm and stopped him. The squad leader used a hand gesture to ask Reyes to take a different set of scans. Quickly, the guard made a sweep of the building, starting from the antennae and working down to the ground.

"No anomalous energy signatures," he finally said.

"Now you may enter, Taurik," Studdard said, a wide smile on his face.

The Vulcan nodded in appreciation and stepped inside, immediately snapping open his tool case. As he began surveying the damage, Studdard positioned Weathers by the door and gestured for Clemons to stay on the path, just in case. With a shooing movement of his hands, he sent Reyes on a perimeter check. Nodding to himself in satisfaction, he headed inside to keep watch.

Taurik had already placed the tool kit on an abandoned worktable and was walking from station to station to assess the damage. Wires and isolinear chips littered the floor. Cabinetry was broken, and monitor screens were cracked. One had a spanner sticking out of it like some form of absurd art.

"Kid asks a good question," Studdard said after a minute. "Why would they destroy a substation like this?"

Finally, he received an answer from the Vulcan engineer. "This was an act of rage. Unchecked emotions."

"How do you figure?"

Taurik propped up his own tricorder and called up schematics of how the station should function. He then knelt down and collected some isolinear chips, examining them between his tapered fingers. As he worked, he said, "I am reminded of the way temples on Vulcan were desecrated in the days before Surak. This was a target of that rage."

"But they had to hold that rage awhile to climb up here and do all this," the guard said, leaning against the doorjamb.

"You saw how many footprints there were. A mob can create a sustaining energy to feed its rage."

"Seen that too many times myself," Studdard agreed, then realized his companion wasn't in his line of sight. He continued to study the destruction, trying to figure how many people could effectively fit in the relatively small energy station and how the damage was caused. His eye followed a trail of debris to a panel of controls and noticed that the corner of one was askew. While there was nothing in particular to make him cautious about the panel, his instinct made him look again.

He walked over, ignoring the sound of chips clattering together, and looked at the panel. Its dark green edges were chipped, as if it had been pried off with purpose. Little else around it was damaged, and that also made him wary.

"Taurik, step this way."

Within moments, the Vulcan stood over him, one eyebrow cocked. Then he understood and lowered himself, the tricorder already humming with a steady whine.

He shut it off and placed it on a counter. Then he reached for a tool from the kit, clamped the corner of the panel, and gave it a firm tug. To Studdard's lack of surprise, it came off easily. Inside was a large, circular object, its bright yellow packaging in sharp contrast to the dull purples and greens of the wiring within.

"If I were to activate the substation, this would begin a countdown," Taurik said, gazing intently at the device. It was welded to the housing and had four distinct wires leading to the power connections within.

"Do you recognize it?"

"Not specifically, but I studied terrorism as an Academy elective."

"For my elective, I took history of exploration," Studdard said, but then realized Taurik probably didn't care. "Can you cut it out?"

"I cannot. The damage to this station is too severe for me to repair it in an effective manner. The bomb further complicates the situation. I'd need a complete damage control team and three hours minimum to ready this station for use."

"Why a bomb? Wasn't the damage enough?"

"Neither of us knows enough about the people and what has happened to them to formulate a proper theory," Taurik replied dryly.

"Well, then, let's call the ship and get Mr. Data to authorize the manpower."

On the engineering deck, La Forge had reconfigured one of the workstations to keep track of the myriad deals he had established over the last two days. One small screen monitored the path of the Ferengi Dex's small craft. He considered himself pretty clever to have "convinced" the trader to act as courier in exchange for an *Enterprise* crew's performing maintenance and upgrades on his battered old ship.

With all the rebuilding going on throughout the Federation in the years following the Dominion War, the farther from the Federation's core a ship was assigned, the more problematic it was to stay properly outfitted. The regional quartermaster was unable to fulfill all the starships' requisitions, so La Forge, at Data's suggestion, had created a trading network for the ships in the nearby sectors. The other ships had all responded positively to the idea.

He had been coordinating the incoming supply data and had started matching it against the needs of other ships. Kell Perim, the Trill conn officer, volunteered to help plot the optimal course for the Ferengi. After all, with the ship in orbit and not needed elsewhere, she had spare time, and this was as productive a use of that time as anything else.

One added benefit to the trading network was that the *Enterprise* was at the center. La Forge figured he could do some damage control by getting the word out about what really happened between Picard and Command and curtail some of the gossip. The tongue-wagging had besmirched the crew worse than anything officially reported through Starfleet channels or the news media.

But La Forge still had engineering to worry about. One of the plasma injectors on the starboard nacelle had acted up, and he had had to take the warp engines offline to handle the repairs. Anh Hoang, his alpha shift specialist, had already suited up to climb through the maintenance shafts from the pylon to the nacelle and visibly inspect the injectors. Without all thirty-six injectors working in perfect unity, a stable warp field could not be safely generated.

He looked up to see the white-suited engineer being checked over by Chintok. La Forge liked the notion of one of his Vulcan engineers doing the inspection, since they wouldn't overlook a thing.

"Ready?" he asked Anh.

"Yes, sir," she replied through the microphone. *"I estimate it will take me thirty minutes or so to get to the injectors and give them a good look."*

"You get thirty-two minutes," Geordi warned her good-naturedly. "If you don't have a report by then, we're coming after you."

"Not to worry, sir," she replied in a quiet voice.

"Good luck. Chintok, go down with her and see her off."

"Acknowledged." The Vulcan accompanied the petite woman off the deck and into the turbolift. La Forge saw the door close and then turned his attention to the diagnostic tabletop display of the ship. He activated the transponder that would follow Anh, and her red blip popped into view. Satisfied, he thought he had some time before he needed to check in with her, so he returned his attention to his new trading board.

He'd already arranged the swap for a new quad, sending a chambliss coil to another ship, and just got in a request for a new set of phase transmission coils for a ship that had gotten messed up pretty badly while surveying an ion storm. A quick check of Dex's ship's course against the various manifests showed that the *U.S.S. Jefferies,* a mere two sectors over, had a surplus. He made a notation to add the *Galaxy*-class ship to the itinerary.

Geordi chuckled to himself as he imagined the complaints from the Ferengi, knowing all the while the goodwill—and profit—he was earning with each new ship was as good as latinum.

As the two flew, the night giving way to day, Will realized his father was done talking for now. Kyle had his personal demons to wrestle with, and there wasn't much else to discuss.

Without looking at the pilot, Will reached inside his jacket and activated his combadge.

"Riker to Picard."

"Will! We were growing concerned." At the captain's voice, Kyle looked over at his son, a mixture of surprise and anger crossing his craggy features. Will ignored him.

"I am currently flying with my father, tracking El Bison El. My father is convinced that Bison holds a key to unlocking the cause for this problem."

"We'll take his word for it, for the moment. Is everything all right?"

There was a lot to be read into that question, and a lot Will wanted to say, but he was hesitant with his father hearing. Observations and conjecture he would have happily shared remained tucked away, waiting for a chance to be recorded in a personal log entry.

Will took a long look at his father, who refused to meet the gaze, keeping his eyes forward. They continued to fly in silence for several long moments.

"Everything seems fine," Will finally said, making an effort to keep his voice neutral. "With luck, our next stop will be where Bison is currently on the run. What's happening there?"

Picard rapidly filled in his first officer, and Will grew despondent, a sense of guilt building up in his own mind. Clearly, these people deserved better, and he could only imagine how something like this grew out of control. He hoped Kyle and Beverly would have time later to compare notes, match up bits of information and complete the puzzle. Starfleet Medical was never this sloppy, he knew, and that made him wonder about the Federation president's chief of staff. And once more he wondered how a tactician got involved in a medical issue.

When they signed off, Will settled back, lost in his own thoughts.

"See, we're better off solving this on our own, Willy," Kyle said. Will inwardly winced at the childhood name, but it passed quickly.

"Actually, I would think a starship's resources would be useful," Will countered.

"Sure, for the fires, the breakdown of society, and bolstering their joke of a government," Kyle said. "But we're on a manhunt and even your wondrous sensors can't pick out one native from among millions."

Will had to grant him that point. Changing the topic, he asked, "Dad, tell me again how you got involved?"

Kyle looked at his son for a long while before speaking. The look on his face was one Will had seen countless times before. He was calculating the odds, which told Will the answer would be crafted to Kyle's desires, not his own need for the truth.

"Let me save you the interrogation. This problem

came to light during the beginning of the war. Everything affecting a member world was suspected of Dominion involvement. I was screening hundreds of reports with Starfleet Intelligence and the president's office, looking for their crafty hand. Delta Sigma IV was ruled out but still, they had a legitimate problem. I got involved because of their homeworlds. We didn't need their belligerence right then so I had to make sure it wasn't going to be a problem."

Will absorbed the story, listening to the tone of the voice, watching the body language. He knew his father; his training completed the task. This was part of the story. But his father hadn't offered the Bader and Dorset angle previously, so this was tossed out like bait, with Kyle waiting to see what might happen. Rather than take the misdirection, Will ignored it.

As they flew, he knew he'd have to keep a closer eye on his father. Doing good was just part of the story but there had to be more.

Anh felt confined in the environmental suit, but recognized it was going to protect her from severe radiation exposure. She disliked the feeling of such close confinement, and it made her sweat. It was a rare instance that anyone climbed into the nacelles when the ship was anywhere but in spacedock. Still, balky plasma injectors meant the ship couldn't go faster than impulse, and that meant the nearest starbase was months away. And that wouldn't do at all.

Chintok, a Vulcan colleague who had been with the ship for some time, walked beside her, saying nothing. She didn't mind the silence and was thankful La Forge hadn't sent someone chattier, such as Beloq, the recently assigned Bolian. As they walked through the maintenance corridor that connected the secondary hull to the nacelle support struts, she reflected on her role. She had done her assigned work on the *Enterprise* and been commended for her efforts, but she had never really had much opportunity to show what she had learned while on Earth. She had made fixing the plasma injector sound like routine repair work, something she could do with ease. However, the last time she had touched a plasma injector was three years ago, in a lab, after it had been removed from a nacelle. She hoped it really would be easy to inspect and repair.

This *Enterprise* had endured many more critical problems in its short life; that was part of its allure for her. That, and the fact that it was rarely back at Earth.

When they reached the access point, Chintok placed his palm against a sensor that checked his DNA and recognized him as an authorized member of the engineering staff. A series of loud clicks reverberated through the deck as massive magnetic locks opened, granting access from the strut to the nacelle itself. There were ladder rungs built into the hull, constructed to fit the boots of environmental suits.

Anh looked at Chintok, but his features hid his thoughts completely, and she idly imagined being able to do that. It might keep well-meaning people like the counselor from thinking there was anything wrong. Feeling she needed to do something, she gave him the traditional thumbs-up gesture, turned her back to him, and placed one foot within the nacelle.

As she climbed, it wasn't long before she heard the access panel close and the locks being reenergized. In an emergency, a locked access panel would slow down a rescue effort, but it was necessary to prevent any radiation from seeping anywhere near the crew. Now it was just her, alone in the nacelle, with the various humming sounds of the systems doing their work. Since there was no crew nearby to be disturbed, starship designers didn't feel the need for sound baffling. Anh tested herself, trying to match the high-pitched squeals to systems she knew. *Those are the power transfer conduits.*

She had not been alone like this in a long time, not since the Breen attack. After the attack, her family and friends looked after her so diligently that she began to feel constricted. She couldn't yell at them to leave her alone; they were too well meaning, and she was too polite. She couldn't walk away from her position at Starfleet; it was all she had left. But when it all got to be too much, and the memories wouldn't leave her dreams, she knew it was time to leave. Not Starfleet, but Earth. Not once did she feel as if she were abandoning the rebuilding efforts. No, she convinced herself that the starships protecting the Federation from even worse damage needed qualified help. The casualties among experienced crew were quite high, and she told everyone she was needed.

And now she was, finally, needed.

She looked at the power transfer conduit that paralleled her path to the top of the nacelle. It was thick, with magnetic forces pushing the plasma to the nacelles where it would be used for propulsion. Her job began where the conduit ended, at the injectors. The injectors fired the plasma into each of the corresponding warp field coils, the sequence depending upon the needs of the warp field. Each injector was constructed from arkenium duranide and single-crystal ferrocarbonite, some of the most durable materials found in the Federation.

Her first stop was to visibly inspect the eighteen injectors in this nacelle and try to see if there was a physical defect that was causing the problem. If not, it was more likely a programming glitch, but diagnostics had ruled that out. As she neared the first injector, set smack in the middle of the nacelle, she debated with herself as to which problem she wanted. A physical one was more serious, allowing her to prove her worthiness to La Forge. But it also represented more dangers, and Anh wasn't sure how much more danger she wanted in her life right now.

The injectors were set below the warp coils, and she had to maneuver herself carefully to avoid disturbing the coils and their careful alignment. She decided her best approach was on her belly, snaking forward and ducking her head inside access points to begin her visual inspection. Each plasma injector was set apart, making the inspection fairly easy. "Diagnostic tricorder on," she commanded, activating a helmet display system that acted as a tricorder, keeping her hands free for work.

The first several injectors seemed absolutely fine. At most, there might have been a buildup of dust around the fourth one, but nothing that would prevent it from firing at low frequencies for slower warp speeds or higher frequencies for greater speed.

As she made her way along the row, the engineer concentrated on the inspection, but a part of her mind was aware of the isolation. It was just like when the Breen attacked Earth by surprise. They had first taken over an orbital platform, creating interference that garbled communications. Three ships, small ones actually, then managed to enter Earth's atmosphere and strike with precision. They first struck the Golden Gate Bridge park and museum, but then switched immediately to Starfleet Command targets. They hit several major buildings, but not the one she worked in. Not that she escaped unscathed; there was enough debris and damage to trap her in the building, cut off from all outside contact, for hours.

The Breen ships slowly crisscrossed San Francisco, laying down sustained fire, causing fear, consuming life and destroying property. Among the buildings struck was the one containing her apartment, where her husband had just brought their son home from school. It was toward the end of the school year, and they had planned a wonderful vacation to Yosemite Park. The weather had been warm and sunny, and all had seemed idyllic.

But the Breen changed all that. After the *Columbia* and the *Enterprise* stopped them, there was so much to do. It was nine hours before a rescue team could clear a path for the trapped Starfleet personnel to leave. With communications commandeered for emergency use, she remained to help with the injured and to restore the remaining Command buildings to operational status. It wasn't until nearly twenty-four hours after the attack that she managed to make it home.

The first thing she noted was that her building was scorched. Immediately she feared the worst. Local police and fire rescue teams were still going from apartment to apartment, looking for survivors and carrying out the dead.

Before an official could reach her, a neighbor came running up, tears streaming down her face. All she could do was sob and hug Anh. Since the neighbor lived alone, her actions said what her mouth could not.

All she could think of then was the silence during the time her team had been trapped. After they had given up trying to get out, they had sat in the dark, wrapped in their own thoughts. Anh had thought of her family and the planned vacation.

She again wanted that isolation after the attack, after the funerals. Anh would never tell the counselor, but the notion of staying curled up in a ball, away from the rest of the world, was a very appealing notion and every so often still tugged at her. Her home had been obliterated by fire, so she had no mementos of her wedding or her son's birth and early development. All she had were memories, and when alone, she could concentrate on preserving them. They gave her strength to get out of bed in the morning, even here, many light-years from Earth.

Anh shook her head, her hair making a brushing noise inside the helmet, and forced herself to focus. She didn't dare miss a thing.

The ninth injector looked fine, at first, but then she saw a hairline crack at the base. "Magnify times five," she commanded. The image on her viewplate wavered a moment and then reappeared, greatly enlarged. She could see that the crack was maybe seven to ten millimeters long, placing the injector out of alignment and causing the frequencies to fall off. The crack had to be recent; otherwise, the ship wouldn't have been able to arrive at Delta Sigma IV. But what could have caused the crack? That would be her problem to solve once the injector was replaced.

"Hoang to La Forge."

There was some static on the com channel, which was not surprising given the amount of energy flowing around her.

"La Forge. What did you find?"

"Starboard injector nine is cracked."

"How could that happen?"

"I can't say right now, but it's enough to cause trouble. It should be replaced and studied. Transmitting my visual."

"Ah, right, that looks odd. Now that's going to be an interesting problem."

There was a beat of silence, then Anh said, "We don't have a spare."

"Do you think you can repair it?"

"I can't answer that, sir, without studying it in the workshop. But I have to try, don't I?"

"I'll see if I can rustle up a replacement, but for now, pull it and bring it with you."

"I'll be more than thirty minutes."

"We're not going anywhere. I'll inform Data of our status. La Forge out."

Anh Hoang let out a deep breath, one she didn't realize she had been holding, and then reached for the emergency tools that were packed into a case on her right thigh. This was certainly not something she had expected to do when she had gotten out of bed that morning.

* * *

Crusher was tired, and she wasn't sure if it was sheer physical exhaustion or the result of having spent too many tense hours in front of the microscope. She decided to grant herself a break and breezily told Nurse Susan Weinstein she was going for a brief walk.

The walk, which qualified as brief—taking under four minutes—led her to the nearest rec room. It held only six people, several playing a board game, one reading something on a display screen, and Geordi just turning from the replicator slot, a plate in his hand.

"Can I join you, Geordi?"

"Sure thing, I'll be over here," he said, tilting his head toward an empty table in the rear corner.

Crusher ordered a cup of coffee, her fourth of the day, and brought it to La Forge's table. La Forge hadn't waited to tuck into his jambalaya.

"Hungry?"

"Sort of. I have a busy few hours ahead of me, so this is my last chance for a real meal."

"What brings you up here to this particular rec room?"

"I'll let you in on a little secret. I have absolutely no idea why, but if you want something spicy, these replicators do the best job."

Crusher let out a small laugh. She then asked what was happening in his domain. He explained the problem with the injector and the supply issues he had been wrestling with.

"I had no idea," she said, amazed at the notion that something so big was happening without her knowledge.

"Well, you are busy with your own problems," La Forge said helpfully.

"Still, we're department heads; we have to be aware of things going on with this ship." She shook her head, staring at her cup. "I don't even think I wanted this, but I ordered it out of habit. Been living on caffeine the last two days."

"Still going crazy with casualties?"

"That's slowed to a trickle. Tropp has been down below, helping them work with emergencies. While their police seem inefficient, their medical resources are top-notch."

"Guess that happens when you have a peaceful society."

"Some peace." She laughed bitterly. "They claim to have put their aggression aside, but they have no idea they were doped by the plant life. Telling them isn't going to be easy for the captain."

"Is there something you can do?"

"That's what I'm working on now. I stepped out to clear my head a bit. Actually, I'm glad I ran into you, since I could use some advice."

La Forge's eyes widened and he grinned. "The doctor asking the engineer for advice? This is new."

"Very funny. Seriously, Geordi, something's come up, and I need some perspective. You and I have served on both *Enterprise*s with Jean-Luc since Farpoint. How much longer do you give it before it's down to just one or two of us with him?"

La Forge put a spoonful of food into his mouth as his brows knit in concentration. "Hunh. I hadn't given that one some thought in a while," he admitted, clearly surprised by the topic.

"Come on, I'm sure it's crossed all our minds since he

wrangled with Command over the demon ship." She sipped from her mug, waiting for a comment.

"Well, I guess it crossed my mind then, but things changed so rapidly, it wasn't a deep thought. Except for Worf, our command staff has been pretty stable. Sooner or later, one of us will get an offer they can't refuse."

She smiled at him. "That might be me. The surgeon general is retiring soon, and he asked me to consider replacing him. If I want it, he'll support me. He already has the Federation council's thumbs-up."

"That's very impressive. Will it hurt that you held the position once and gave it up after just a year?"

"Maybe, but not damaging enough to prevent it," she replied. "But I don't know if I'm ready to walk away from the ship. Then again, I don't know if I want to be the last officer remaining."

Geordi took another mouthful of the colorful Creole food, chewed, and thought. Beverly looked at her coffee, considered taking another sip, and then pushed it aside.

"We're all getting older, and sooner or later, yeah, either we'll get ambitious or Starfleet will need some of us elsewhere. So I guess I'd say go for it before they give you an assignment you *don't* want. We'll still be around the galaxy to visit."

Crusher considered his advice and the wisdom of taking charge of her destiny.

Then he asked, "What does the captain think?"

She shook her head, then tucked a lock of hair behind her ear. "I haven't had a chance to bring it up. We have been a little busy, you know." It was natural for La Forge to ask; it would if their roles were reversed, the first thing she'd bring up was whether or not he'd discussed it with Data.

"Of course," he agreed.

He was keeping the conversation professional, and not referring to her and Picard's personal relationship. He knew he could mention it without offending—they had known each other long enough—but he was being a gentleman.

"And what if Wesley drops by again and I'm back on Earth?"

"He's a Traveler these days, Doc. He'll always find you."

Crusher took comfort in those words and held on to them as she returned to her office and the monumental task Picard asked of her.

Testani's flames had long since been extinguished thanks to the combined efforts of firefighting teams from neighboring towns. Still, as Vale materialized, the odor of charred building materials hung thickly in the air. Whatever was used to construct homes on any world, the smell of destruction seemed pretty much the same.

She looked around, saw a heavy-duty blue-and-white flyer take off to return to its base, the job complete. People, despite the late hour and the chill in the air, were cordoned off behind barricades, and the local peace officers were assessing the damage. From early reports she had scanned aboard the *Enterprise,* about twenty-five percent of the city had been destroyed. The rebuilding would take months.

Seo, the field leader for the team assigned to Testani, came running up to her. He skidded to a stop and waited at attention. Vale thought he was taking his first field post way too seriously. There was a time and place for behavior conforming to the rulebook, but this wasn't one of them.

"What's the status?"

"Fires are out throughout the city, ma'am," he reported in a clipped tone.

"Relax, Jae. Take a deep breath. What's *really* going on?"

He took a deep breath and willed himself to release the tension in his body. "People are blaming each other, blaming us, blaming everyone except maybe the Klingons. They're upset; no one can even remember anything this monumental happening in the city."

"Do all the locals have someplace to sleep tonight?" Vale wanted to yawn, breathed in deeply instead. She needed to keep pushing herself until things were more under control.

"We're working on that right now. T'Sona's coordinating with the local relief people."

"Good. Now, what about the water pumping station? That got trashed pretty good, from the reports."

"Yes, ma'am. It's a mess, but Commander La Forge's team is almost done."

At that she cocked an eyebrow in surprise. She knew La Forge's people were good, but this was even faster than she had expected. With a gesture, she indicated she wanted to see for herself. Seo—lithe but muscular—hurried to keep ahead of her to both guide and protect. He was more nervous than he should be, but that wasn't entirely unexpected given his recent posting.

As they passed a barricade, she was heckled by those

who rightly assumed she was a leader from the starship. Vale ignored the taunts and continued moving.

A few minutes later, the noise began to abate as they moved farther into an industrial portion of the town, one the fire had not touched. Vandals, though, had paid a visit earlier, and that was when the water station was wrecked. En route, Vale took note of the dropped weapons, debris, and various dark fluids that stained the area. Whenever the healing began, the people were certainly going to be kept busy.

Finally, Seo slowed down as a very wide, obsidian-black building appeared around a corner. At least a dozen fat, dark gray pipes connected the building to the street and to other buildings. Graffiti marred some of the pipes, and one was damaged. Water leaked out of it at a steady rate, reminding her of a fountain she had seen on her last shore leave. Atop the pipe, working with a welding tool, was one of the engineers. Below, DeMato, looking alert, kept a watch.

She strode over to the other woman, who was several inches shorter, and they greeted one another. DeMato, with a nasal twang to her voice, reported, "It's almost done. That's the last pipe to be fixed."

"Great news," Vale said. "What's happening inside?"

"Caldwell's there with two more damage control specialists. They're making certain that the pumps still work."

"Have there been more protesters?"

"None, and I gotta say that's a good thing. I've been at this for hours, and I want my lunch."

Vale stopped, looked at the night sky, which remained

obstinately black, and smiled. "Well, you'll be off duty in time for breakfast. Best I can do."

The other woman nodded, her full head of hair moving freely around her face. "What's happening?" A natural enough question, although, for some reason, its lack of specificity annoyed Vale. She guessed she was letting the hours catch up to her, too.

"More of the same around the world. The captain's with the Council; the doctor is trying to find a miracle. The usual."

The three security officers continued chatting for several minutes, all appreciating the respite. However, their rest ended abruptly when the engineer, Beloq, cried out a warning.

Vale whipped around, her hand already going for her phaser, when she heard the sound. People—lots of angry people. Another mob was on its way, having somehow broken through the barricade. She practically bellowed into her badge for Caldwell to join them outside. Going silent then, she began scanning the immediate area and started pointing. Seo was dispatched to a corner position, behind supply canisters, where he could flank the mob. DeMato was sent to the opposite side, setting up a possible crossfire.

Caldwell, her blond hair flying behind her, came charging out of the building, leaving the doorway wide open. Vale signaled to her, indicating she should join her right below Beloq.

"Are you done?" she yelled up to the Bolian engineer.

"Done enough for the water to flow. If you ask me—"

"Then get back to the ship!" Vale interrupted. The

last thing she needed was to be distracted by a chatty mechanic. She tightened her grip on her phaser and listened carefully. She heard the approaching people and then the telltale whine of the transporter effect. *Good, one less person to worry about.* She presumed the other engineers inside would have the smarts to get out of the way.

The people emerged from around the corner, and Vale saw they were armed. In fact, they were fairly well equipped, almost as if someone had organized them into a fighting force. Several brandished knives, a few seemed to have pistols of some sort, and others had sharpened pikes made from, it seemed, tree limbs. They were not here to protest the Federation's presence; they were here only for violence.

"Stun setting only," she called out. It was a needless reminder, but she wanted her people to focus.

She then walked toward the mob.

Several in the front pointed and shouted as they spotted her in the dim light. Vale intentionally made herself the target, walking at a steady pace until she reached a spot less than ten meters from the people in front.

"Can I convince you to go home and let us finish repairs?"

"Sabotage is more like it! You've poisoned the people! You killed El Bison El, and now you want to take the rest of us!"

"Federation bitch!"

"Really," Vale said, keeping her tone light even as her body tensed. "Name-calling will not get you your water any faster. If you don't disperse, I *will* have to open fire."

"You can take down a few of us, but we outnumber you!"

"Have it your way," Vale said. She raised her weapon in full sight of the other security team and fired a wide dispersal stun beam.

As expected, several staggered and fell, others scattered. Those on the periphery saw this as their chance and rushed her. They got close, closer than Vale would have liked, but then came powerful amber beams from DeMato and Seo's positions. The security chief herself kept firing directly into the mob. Finally, people got the idea that scattering and retreating might be the best thing to do.

Some, though, clearly wanted a fight. They charged toward the flanking guards, but Vale's people were able to take clean shots, bringing down one Delta Sigma IV inhabitant after another. Still, one woman reared back and hurled her sharpened branch at DeMato, who was concentrating on a man in closer range.

The wet sound the spike made as it pierced DeMato's abdomen could be heard across the tarmac, followed less than a second later by her scream. Vale broke from her point position and fired at anyone near the fallen woman. She saw blood flowing freely from the entry wound, darkening DeMato's uniform. It looked bad.

Seo and Caldwell were behind her, providing protective fire. Most of the mob had either fallen or dispersed, so the din had lessened dramatically, which only emphasized the gasping sounds from DeMato as she struggled for breath.

"Emergency transport to sickbay," Vale said as she slapped DeMato's badge. As the beam took hold of the woman, Vale felt the sticky blood on her fingertips and wiped them on her pants.

She then turned and spotted Seo and Caldwell within meters of her, their backs turned, keeping her covered. At that moment, she also saw that two members of the mob were entering the plant. "Get them!" she commanded.

As Caldwell ran back into the building, Seo took up a position by the entrance to make sure no one else made it inside. He picked off three more people as Vale surveyed the area, looking for anyone trying to be sneaky. She saw no movement, but she crept around the perimeter to be safe.

Finally returning to the entrance, she and Seo stood by, assuming Caldwell could manage two crazed people. That assumption proved false. Hearing the sounds of a struggle, Vale pointed for Seo to remain in place and dashed inside, expecting the worst.

What she saw sickened her. One of the engineers had not returned to the ship, but was lying on the ground with a head injury. Caldwell was on her back, wrestling with one of the Dorset attackers, a burly male who was fighting in a frenzied way. Vale quickly scanned for the other native and nodded to herself when she spotted him. He had gone up the catwalk to one of the control stations that managed the pumps on this side of the building. With a metal rod, he was trying unsuccessfully to pry open the casing.

Vale returned her attention to Caldwell. She grunted, took three steps, and lashed out with her right boot, smacking the attacker off balance and giving Caldwell the edge she needed to break free. Without pausing to see the rest of the bout, Vale found a good angle, took aim, and fired at the man above her.

The phaser blast rang out with a satisfying sound, and her aim was true as it hit the man. It also hit the machinery, edges of which were finally wearing away from the constant battering. Some of the ambient energy seeped inside, overloading the fragile circuits. The man slumped, hitting the ground about the same time the cascading energy surge knocked out the pumps.

Vale holstered her phaser, put her hands on her knees, and bent low, catching her breath. With a glance, she saw that Caldwell had lived up to expectations and subdued her opponent. The downed engineer was starting to come around.

"Vale to *Enterprise*."

"Data here, Lieutenant."

"I need Beloq back. The pumps are damaged once more. Also, status on DeMato, please."

"I am relaying your request to Mr. La Forge," Data said. *"Sickbay reports Ensign DeMato is not expected to survive."* It sounded worse coming from an android, without any inflection. Vale took several deep breaths, fighting back emotion. Caldwell, having also heard the announcement, bent her head down.

"Damn," they both whispered.

Chapter Three

PICARD STRODE DOWN the corridor, his boots making clacking sounds against the tile. His swift, steady pace gave no hint of the anger that was smoldering deep within. He had been crossing the same space, back and forth, since beaming down hours ago. The day was waning, and he needed to get the feeling that some form of progress was being made. First, he had visited with the Dorset and then had gone to the Bader's makeshift operation across the courtyard.

The captain couldn't argue with their belligerence, since, after all, it was only their true nature seeping through. What made his task more difficult was that he had yet to reveal the true source of their problem, because he wanted to explain it only after a solution was available. While he waited for a medical solution, the situation on Delta Sigma IV continued to worsen. With each flare-up, he was sure the planet would be plunged into a bloody civil war.

After listening to a litany of concerns from Cholan of Huni, the designated spokesman for the Bader side, he was now heading back to hear more from Jus Renks Jus, the Speaker for the now divided Council. An aide, having heard Picard's approach, opened the door with a weary smile. If anything had improved, it was the morale among the Bader and Dorset clerical staff, since Troi had been talking to them almost exclusively. They had offered up opinions and observations that demonstrated in-depth knowledge about the workings of the world, giving her and Picard a better understanding.

Not that any of that information was proving useful right this minute. With cities in flames or out of power and water, the infrastructure under attack, and racial battles growing by the hour, Picard needed to find a plan of action that would stem the violence and buy Dr. Crusher the time she needed. The captain knew he asked a lot of his chief medical officer, but there was little choice.

Renks was sitting behind a desk and looking out a window, his back to the door and one foot up against the windowsill. The other three councillors were studying monitors and talking among themselves.

As Picard approached, his footsteps now muffled by a light violet carpet, Renks began to speak.

"When does the fun part begin?"

"I beg your pardon?" Picard was genuinely confused by the question.

"I grew up watching the Council," he continued, oblivious to Picard's presence. The man could have been speaking to anyone. "I wanted to serve since I was of age. Getting elected locally was such a thrill. And my mother was still alive to see it. Then the opportunity to be on the Council came up and I grabbed it. All along, I secretly hoped to be Speaker."

"Why?"

"The Speaker got to travel the world, speaking at important events, opening local government meetings, being out among the people. And everyone applauded, laughed at his jokes. He got the best travel, the best food. It looked . . . like fun. Even that stiff Chkarad reveled in it. Now look at the poor bastard."

"Wasn't the Speaker the first one called upon to maintain the peace?"

Renks shook his head, still not turning to look at Picard. "You still don't get it. We always were peaceful. We considered ourselves above war. Above petty racial issues. Everyone on Delta Sigma IV rejected the ways of our ancestors."

Picard once again held his tongue, not wishing to reveal the truth. Not yet. He heard the sense of loss and the disillusionment in the other man's voice, and he couldn't be certain if the feelings were genuine or triggered by the stripping away of the liscom's effects.

"You calm the people down, and you can enjoy your office," was all the captain managed to say.

"Tell me what to do, Picard," Renks said. "Tell me how to stop the people on four continents."

"I have never governed a world. You grew up desiring public service; I grew up looking at the stars."

Renks nodded in understanding, still looking out his window.

Picard hated hiding behind the regulations, especially

when he *could* be doing something. There was often a thin line between aiding a planet and controlling it. Some starship captains had tripped over the line through the years, and Picard was very conscious of that. Especially now, with Starfleet watching his every move.

He doubted even Admiral Upton understood what a thorough mess the *Enterprise* had been handed.

"I have offered you my security team and my engineers and my doctors. But you have to create the plan and lead the people," Picard continued.

Renks looked over his shoulder at the captain. "You kept urging Chkarad to act. And when he didn't, I did. Look what's happened."

Picard wasn't sure what else to say. Instead, he decided to take the man at his word and go check the monitors. One screen showed the four continents with Starfleet emblems indicating where his people were. They were scattered farther than he liked. Other insignia denoted peace officers and medical personnel. And there were the brown lights showing scenes of violence, which were now in just about every city and town with a population over five.

Troi wandered over and stood by his elbow as he studied the screen.

"So many of our people . . ." she muttered.

"I've lost track of them," Picard said softly, and cursed himself for letting everything get out of his control. He needed to start asserting himself. First, he wanted some answers. He tapped his combadge and summoned Vale to the Council office. Within moments, his security chief materialized. She looked exhausted. There were dark smudges beneath her large brown eyes, and her usually well-groomed hair was askew. He couldn't help but notice the bloodstains on her pants and the scratches on her hands. Picard almost envied her being out in the field, making more of a difference. He wanted to will Ambassador Morrow back to health so he could be freed from this thankless chore.

"Lieutenant, status please, and you can skip the formality."

"Aye, sir. We're rotating everyone twelve on, twelve off, as we discussed. But those twelve on are tough. It's messy and unpredictable, and we're severely outnumbered."

"Casualties?"

"We've lost two, at least seven injured," she said softly, real pain in her voice.

Picard was alarmed that he hadn't known a second member of his crew had died for these people. Vale explained the situation in Testani. She managed to maintain her poise, but the captain knew she was hiding pain.

"How bad is it out there? Do we have any hope of stopping them?"

She paused for several moments before speaking. Picard gave her time to collect her thoughts. He needed honesty, but, more importantly, he needed a rational answer. "Honestly, sir, at best it's going to be a holding action until the doctor devises a solution."

"And if she doesn't?"

"Well, I don't suppose you want the phaser banks to stun these people into submission."

"I'm tempted, to tell you the truth, but it would only be a temporary answer."

"I thought as much," Vale agreed. "Sir, can the doctor really find something soon? It seems like an awfully huge task."

Picard smiled at her, yet his eyes were hard. "It is. And she's our best hope. If she fails, I am not at all sure what we would do next. But I do know we have to give her the time she needs. Can your people keep up the holding action?"

"Of course, sir. I told you the other night: you have the entire complement ready to give their lives if that's what it takes. I remain proud of them." There was a look of defiance in her tired eyes, showing she meant every word.

"When was the last time you ate?" Troi asked in a soft tone.

Vale gave Picard a grin. "If I know the captain, about the last time he did."

"Well, if it's been that long, you both should return to the ship for something. I doubt much will change while you're away."

Picard looked at her and saw the same determination that made her mother, Lwaxana, one of the most powerful forces of nature found in the galaxy. Getting some food and getting away from the sense of despair radiating from Renks might be the best action for the moment. It solved nothing, though, and that rankled.

The captain was about to speak when Troi cut him off. "I'll be fine, sir. You can be bring me a salad. Thank you for asking." And that sealed it. He had no choice.

Was it only yesterday, Riker mused, he was telling Picard how nice it was to actually see the planet rather than just a series of rooms? Now, he was tired of the world, tired of the fighting, tired of the seemingly endless strife. Unchecked, things would get worse long before a large enough body of the people could rein in their emotions long enough to restore order.

They had kept at a low altitude since they were over land, and were now descending near a city. The buildings were boxy and fairly uniform in construction, like so much else on this world. Will was beginning to think one architectural firm had designed the entire world, and to his way of thinking, botched the assignment. Such thoughts, he knew Troi would say, were good; they meant he was observing. Troi was with Picard, and he wished it were otherwise. She would provide insights he could only guess at. They had worked so well together for so many years that he could no longer imagine working apart from her. Their complementary skills and temperaments made them an effective combination of officers that any starship captain would want. What was it Picard said when he first learned Troi was to be ship's counselor? "I consider it important that my key officers know each other's abilities." Well, Deanna and Will made quite a duo after all these years.

And he missed her. Missed her more than he imagined possible, and the depth of that feeling was no surprise to him. That too came from their years together. Happy as he was that the romance was back in their lives, he suspected it was time to make some decisions about their future. Both their future as a couple and, honestly, the future of his career. This time, he wasn't about to let career aspirations cloud his judgment.

Now, though, was not the time for those decisions.

This mission required unusual amounts of concentration, and despite his fatigue, he needed to stay sharp and keep his father in line.

"Why here?" he asked. "Have you tracked Bison?"

Ignoring his son, Kyle said, "The communications channels indicate a portion of the city is being evacuated. There has to be a reason, and we can help."

"So that's it," Will said, some anger unwillingly creeping into his voice—again. "We just fly around and around this world, stopping off to fight the good fight? What does that accomplish?"

"It keeps them alive until a cure is found!" Kyle said loudly.

"I thought your goal was to find Bison and study him," Will snapped.

"It is, but I'll be damned if we let people suffer when we can help!" his father retorted.

"Don't you think we'd be more effective working with Picard?"

"No."

"No?"

"He's Starfleet," Kyle continued, "a by-the-book man who will slap me in irons the minute I'm in sight. How can I fix things, how can I find Bison, if I'm in orbit?"

"Then you don't know him at all," Will said. "He'd hear you out before putting you in the brig. And I'd pick up the hunt."

Kyle shook his head. "And I'd still be out of the picture, my experience wasted."

"Your experience? What does that have to do with finding Bison? You're a tactician."

"Son, I've saved countless lives over the last twenty-four hours. What have you done? You've hunted me down. Well congratulations, you've found me. Has that saved anyone?"

Will fumed, trying to avoid getting caught up in age-old arguments, the same ones that had never been resolved in his youth. He didn't want to try and finish them now—it wasn't the time.

"Why are *you* here?"

His father's question was blunt and direct. Will considered several ways to answer it.

"Delta Sigma IV is a powderkeg," he replied.

"No, that's why Starfleet sent you here. You. Here. Right now."

"Because I was assigned to find you."

"No, that's why Picard sent you here. But you're in this flyer with me. Why?"

Riker felt the anger bubble up, and he was shouting before he knew it. "Because you're my father, dammit! If I was anything first, I was a dutiful son. And I'm back to playing that role again."

"And you hate it." It wasn't a question.

"Duty is supposed to go both ways," Will said, some pain unexpectedly creeping into his voice. "I was the good son. Making good grades in school, the right circle of friends, taking care of the house. Visiting her grave. But you never reciprocated."

The silence hung heavily over the two men. Neither looked at the other; instead they watched the city's white lights twinkle as they circled the outskirts.

"How were the doctors on Earth to know about this

result? Nothing in the simulations or tests indicated the gas was at work on the brain. Removed from their natural environment, maybe it would have worn off," Kyle finally said, clearly not wanting the argument to escalate.

"Answer me," Will said through clenched teeth.

"No," Kyle said. "You're too tired and angry. You want to get into it, want to hear why I left Earth? Why I don't go and tend her grave? Fine. When this is done and we're on the ship. I'll buy you a drink and we can hash it out man to man. But not here and not now. We have a man below that's spreading this thing, and sooner or later, he's going to go past the point of no return."

"Meaning?" The anger remained in his voice, but Will was forcing himself to agree with his father and stick to the mission. Any discussion of abandonment could wait.

"Without a cure, too much of the planet will be infected, with no hope of maintaining order, let alone vital services. Your ship is huge, but even you don't have the manpower to settle every fight, fix every optical net, and protect the weak. I've been giving this thought and will bet that you get to the fifty-eight to sixty-two percent infected rate and this planet's ready for permanent quarantine."

The death sentence hung in the air. Will was impressed by his father's reasoning and couldn't argue with the conclusion.

"It's in their blood, their genes. This wasn't going to vanish even in a year." Will was content to play the game and avoid ripping old wounds any wider.

"The doctors said they knew what to do," Kyle said again. "They were wrong. And now I have to fix it."

"Why you? You're not a doctor."

"Because that's what I do," Kyle said with an edge to his voice. "Every time Starfleet gets into trouble, I'm called in to strategize and get them out of it."

"And how do you propose to strategize two races out of their very nature? Quarantine them like you mentioned?"

Kyle fumed, but had no answer.

"You *can't* fix it with quarantine," Will said with equal bluntness. "They'll just kill each other. You can't fix it, but you certainly helped create the mess. You helped it along, you nurtured it, and then you were here to unleash it on an unprepared people."

"*I* didn't declare them fit," Kyle said, his voice suddenly weak. The sudden change in tone startled his son.

"No, but you suspected something was up and let those five come back home, didn't you?"

Kyle blinked once. "Yes."

There was silence, and Will hoped his father was finally going to listen to reason. He agreed that his father had indeed saved lives, but he felt the tug of duty, the need to be with Picard and Troi. Will truly believed that only through a united effort, could a solution be found and implemented.

His father continued to bank the craft, coming in lower toward what was clearly a port for vehicles. There were green lights marking spaces and indicating directions, and his father proved to be a fast study.

As they were lowering themselves into position for a vertical landing, Kyle's right hand pulled out from the controls and smashed into his son's throat. The same hand then grabbed a hank of hair and used it to yank Will's head into the dashboard. Stunned, Will fought back weakly, constrained by the chair's safety belts. His head was pounded a second time against the dash and his vision started to go black. Just as he lost consciousness, Will felt his father's hand now work its way inside his coat. Then there was nothing.

Kyle removed his son's combadge, dropped it to the floor, and destroyed it with his boot heel. Looking over at his son, slumped against the side of the vehicle, Kyle felt nothing. The emptiness gnawed at him, but he ignored it. He expertly landed the craft and then shut down the engines. He would sit and wait a few minutes for his son to wake up and then, with no one to call for help, father and son would go out and continue to make things right.

Fire rained down from the rooftop to the street below, splattering for several meters and igniting nearby buildings. Some people screamed and fled, but others stood and watched, transfixed by the conflagration. Dozens more hurled obscenities at the Starfleet personnel who were fighting the blaze.

"This just got worse," Van Zandt said to no one in particular.

The team he led had been on the ground for two hours, working to evacuate the hospital, which had become the center of a protest rally. As far as he knew, no one had explained why the hospital should draw protesters. What the veteran officer did know was that there were Bader and Dorset inside the building and they were not receiving much help. He had summoned medical help from the *Enterprise* to identify the most serious cases and get them out first. He was pleased Dr. Tropp, who liked to talk as much as Van Zandt, kept it short and sweet.

Van Zandt had escorted the last of the critical care patients out minutes before the first firebomb struck the building. That told him one thing: someone had been watching and recognized it was now a safe time to demonstrate their displeasure. Although Van Zandt had wanted to show the attackers his personal displeasure—with his phaser—he'd directed his team to continue evacuating. Fortunately, several of the hospital staff remained to help, concerned that the Starfleet personnel would be unfamiliar with the medical equipment still hooked up to many patients.

Rasmussen and McEwing were coordinating with the local fire teams, which had arrived minutes after the first of several bombs went off. Van Zandt was thankful the fire teams had arrived, since that was one less problem to worry about. Liryn and Tyrell were checking nearby rooftops to track the bomb throwers.

"What a mess," Van Zandt said out loud. Shaking his head, he walked around the building, shooing gawkers away from the perimeter, ignoring the heckling of the protesters. Fortunately, the local peace officers had set up an effective barricade that was keeping the troublemakers out of the way. But more were arriving to either watch or shout, none to help. And he knew that soon a critical mass would be achieved, and then his team would be vulnerable.

He had to help put out the fires. And quickly.

A sound made Van Zandt look up and he jumped back, an epithet escaping from his lips as a piece of the roof came tumbling down. It fell heavily, cracking the concrete walkway where he had stood a moment earlier.

Enough was enough. He turned around, brandishing

his phaser, and shouted, "The next person I catch doing anything—anything!—to slow us down, I will shoot!"

The bystanders were undeterred, and the protesters were now chanting about Federation aggression.

So much for being a diplomat, he thought with a shrug. Back to business, he decided, and checked in with his people.

"I think they're done firebombing," Tyrell reported, her voice sounding strained. *"We found the launch equipment, but no more bombs and no people."*

"Got it. Break the equipment and get back down." Van Zandt looked around and saw a fire chief shouting orders. He jogged over to the woman's position and asked for an update.

"I've got more help coming, some big rigs that will drop a chemical retardant," the Dorset woman said. Van Zandt nodded in understanding. "But I need that building emptied before I can authorize the dump. The retardant is very toxic."

"McEwing, Liryn, get back to my position, on the double," he shouted at his combadge. Looking at the fire chief, he asked for handheld equipment, portable oxygen masks, and someone trained in medicine.

"What do you plan?"

"Cleaning out the building, like you said. What did you think I was going to do with extinguishers?" His flippancy earned him an angry look, but the woman directed the materials to be brought. There were no trained medical personnel available—or willing—to go back inside.

Van Zandt slipped into a backpack that housed extinguishing chemicals, then tossed a similar rig to McEwing, who skidded to a stop in order to catch it. Liryn returned from the rooftops moments later and hefted the oxygen rebreathers. By the time the trio was ready to work, the chief had returned with smaller masks to help them breathe.

"All right, we work from the bottom up. Chief, have people ready to take the patients we bring out. We're fighting the fire's progress, and that roof won't hold much longer. It's already started coming apart. I think the design means this will pancake down, so we need to get out before we're the hidden surprise underneath the stack."

Without waiting for acknowledgment, he shouted for Rasmussen to secure the area and then jogged ahead, straight into the building, past a burning window.

Inside the hospital there were four corridors that snaked back in different directions. He wished he had more people—volunteers from the populace would have been nice—but he'd have to make do. He steeled himself for the possibility that some people would die before this was over, and he was powerless to do more to help.

As they worked their way down the far left corridor, Liryn, a Bajoran woman in her mid-thirties who had transferred aboard immediately before their previous mission, asked about using the transporters.

"Can't do that safely for those hooked up to medical equipment," Van Zandt replied, his voice muffled by his mask. The stench of smoke was already getting to him, and there was purplish haze ahead. Not enough to indicate fire, but it meant the flames were generating enough heat to send smoke not just up but everywhere.

The first five rooms they checked were already empty.

Liryn kicked open doors to closets and supply rooms, stuck her head in, and then moved down the hall, taking up the rear position each time.

McEwing, shorter and older than Liryn, was a perfect complement to Van Zandt, and the leader appreciated having him at his back. They pushed aside curtains in a large examination area, McEwing dropping low to check for huddled patients, and then moved on. As they completed one corridor, they worked their way through a curtain of smoke and began the second corridor. Here, they heard faint squeals.

"Oh no," Van Zandt muttered and broke into a run, ignoring several doorways. He skidded to a stop, his hand reaching out to steady himself.

"What is it?" McEwing asked, only a step behind him. The leader shouldered the door open, and the source of the sounds became painfully obvious.

It was the nursery, and no one had bothered to remove the dozen or so infants still in warming containers. At a glance, all appeared healthy, wrapped in identical dull green blankets, but none too happy with the stench from the flames above.

"Liryn, get in here and let's grab 'em up," Van Zandt yelled.

Liryn arrived quickly and didn't hesitate before grabbing babies. With one arm holding two, she reached for another and noticed a bright white light blinking on the baby's container.

"Hey, Loo," she called. Van Zandt, already holding four screaming babies in his arms, gave her a look. All

Liryn could do was shrug, but the expression on her face communicated enough to the squad leader.

Van Zandt moved toward the container and saw the light. Clearly there was a problem, and he muttered a curse at people who couldn't label things in easy to comprehend terms.

"Call up to the ship, get us a nurse with a kit," he ordered.

Seconds later, Nurse Susan Weinstein materialized in their midst, tricorder at the ready, medical kit strapped to her hip. Van Zandt nodded toward the container with blinking light and then headed out with the babies in his arms.

Weinstein waved Liryn away and within a brief time, all the babies were collected except for the one she needed to work on. Leading the way out, Van Zandt continued to mutter curses, which were ignored by his subordinates. They broke into a cautious but steady jog. The group went straight down the second corridor until they saw the doorway. Once Van Zandt spotted Rasmussen, her back to the team, he screamed her name. It took a moment for her to register what was needed, and then she came at a run to help with the babies. Several hospital staff, identifiable by their uniforms, were among the bystanders. Van Zandt didn't pause to ask for volunteers. He simply handed over the babies and hoped that they had some sort of equivalent of the Hippocratic oath.

"You check the rest of the floor," Van Zandt ordered his people. "I'll be with the nurse."

"Lucky you," McEwing cracked with a smoke-smudged smile. "Hear she's got a great bedside manner."

"You know," Van Zandt said, "she's probably been

hearing that since school. Say it to her and you're likely to wind up in traction. Now go on, get outta here."

The trio ran back into the building, where they split up, with Van Zandt making a direct line for the nursery. There, Weinstein was leaning over the infant, his chubby little fingers wrapped around her left index finger while her free right hand waved a medical scanner over him. Van Zandt kept his distance, letting the nurse work, biting his tongue to keep from rushing her.

"We've got kind of a situation," he finally said.

"Worse than the building being on fire?" She finally pocketed the handheld scanner and withdrew a small device he didn't recognize. Deftly, she placed it up against one of the boy's nostrils and gave a squeeze.

"Much worse," Van Zandt admitted. He explained about the roof and the lack of time.

"The baby'll be fine. He's just congested from the smoke. If the corridor is clear, I can get him out. Don't worry about us."

Without hesitation, Van Zandt turned and ran, hoping he'd see the nurse and baby soon. Knowing the others were almost done with the first floor, he hurried up a winding staircase to the second floor. As he ran, he could hear the roar of the flames and feel vibrations in the floor. He didn't know if the vibrations were caused by the pounding of his own feet, or if the building was giving warning that it was going to crumble.

On the second floor he broke right and ran flat out, calling out for anyone to respond. At the end of the corridor he doubled back, slowing down just enough to kick open doors and check the floors. Nothing.

The vibrations under his feet grew worse, and he now knew for certain that it was the building trembling. He hoped, as he began checking the other side, there was enough time to complete a sweep of the floor and get out. The first room was empty, so was the first closet. A supply room looked ransacked but devoid of life, so he kept moving.

As he pushed against the next door, he felt resistance. He called out but didn't receive an answer, so he pushed again with more force. As he slowly pried the door open, he saw a slumped figure. Given its height, he knew it was a Bader man, who must have collapsed as he tried to escape.

Finally inside the room, Van Zandt leaned close to the man's face and felt a faint exhalation. A quick check indicated he was free from any medical devices and that nothing external seemed to be wrong. From the wrinkles around the man's eyes and ears, the security officer figured he'd been hospitalized for geriatric problems. He then reminded himself there were nurses just outside who were more qualified than he to help. He managed to heft the man into the traditional firefighter's carry and had taken a step toward the door when a shuddering roar erupted. He lost his footing and fell to the ground, dropping the Bader patient. The sounds of utter destruction grew in volume as concrete and metal collapsed. Quickly he shoved the man under the bed and crawled in after him, getting most of his body under the bed just before the ceiling gave way and tons of equipment, medicines, beams, lighting fixtures, and other debris rained down in torrents.

Before the billowing dust obscured his vision, Van Zandt saw an arm swing by, and then he felt rubble strike the bed and the floor. For no reason at all he flashed on Weinstein and wondered if she would have fallen for McEwing's sad joke. Then total darkness gripped him and he lost all feeling.

Picard threw himself over a metallic planter, landing behind it and waiting for the next volley. Sure enough, a hail of stones rained down around him, but none came close to hitting him. He risked looking over the top of the planter and saw that Carmona was standing up, hiding behind a tall, thick tree. They made eye contact, reassuring each other they were fine.

Since Picard had begun shuttling back and forth between the Council rooms, he had heard angry chants and shouts from people in the streets. They were blaming the Federation, Starfleet, the Council, and someone called Mordran for their lot in life. There were scuffles and occasionally rocks were tossed.

By this time, though, they had figured out Picard was making regular trips between portions of the building, and they were ready. No sooner had he exposed himself in the courtyard than rocks began flying over the low iron fence. The first struck his shoulder, and the captain dove for cover.

And now he felt stupid and angry, hiding from a rock-throwing crowd.

Carmona gestured to catch the captain's attention and then made a show of using his phaser to cut down the mob. Picard gave the idea serious consideration, hoping it might scare them off. He was afraid it could just as easily incite them to further violence. Before he could make a decision, a phaser beam rang out, cutting down the first row of people. As expected, some scattered, but a few threw more rocks. A second beam cut down more people and created a gap in the center of the mob.

"Go home!"

Picard glanced over his shoulder and saw Christine Vale standing in the doorway. Her phaser remained aimed at the crowd, and her fearless stance made them hesitate. Carmona emerged from his hiding spot and took up a position at her right, his own weapon raised. Finally, Williams emerged and completed the triangle. People finally began to back away, drifting off in small clusters.

Now the captain was feeling a bit foolish, crouching on the grass. As he rose, Vale lost her composure for a second, and he was certain he saw a smirk.

"Excellent timing, Lieutenant," he admitted.

The smirk vanished, replaced by her professional expression. "Came looking for you and then heard the ruckus. Didn't hear an SOS, but figured you could use some help."

"Yes, thank you," Picard said, dusting off his pants. He tugged his jacket into place and walked over, an expectant look on his face.

"Came to check up on the situation," Vale continued. "Make sure George here was right and he and Williams were all the help you needed."

"I appreciate it. You left me in very good hands, but clearly getting from here to the next setup is becoming a problem. I would hate to waste more personnel just standing guard."

"Might I suggest having yourself beamed from point

to point? It's the only way I can make sure my teams are in good shape."

"It's the most efficient way to traverse the globe," Picard admitted. "But it seems a waste of energy to go from one end of the building to another."

"What about a barricade, something to keep them out?"

Picard nodded in agreement. He looked at Carmona, who was a step behind his superior, keeping a watchful eye on the area. "Have the ship send down portable shielding and we'll use that. This way we don't waste more people."

"Aye, sir," Carmona responded. He stepped away, his hand already reaching for his badge.

"Now then, what is happening around the planet? I dislike feeling so isolated from my crew."

"They're tired, to be honest. Every team has seen some sort of action. We're seeing damage to the infrastructure so Geordi's people have been helping out."

"Very good." Picard paused. "Any more injuries?"

"Just before I arrived, I got word from Dr. Crusher that a hospital caught fire and caved in. We lost Van Zandt." She stopped a moment. Picard's brows knit with concern, both for the fallen officer and for the toll it was taking on Vale. "He was inside rescuing patients. Just finished . . . there were babies and they got them out . . . I'm sorry, Captain." Vale paused and took several deep breaths.

Picard grimaced at the images Vale had evoked, but he gave her time to compose herself. After a few moments, she shook her head, letting her brown hair fall into place, and then met his gaze. "Thank you, sir," was all she said.

He nodded in appreciation.

"Sir, any further sign of Commander Riker?"

"Not since his initial check-in," the captain said.

She nodded. "I'm getting back to it, if you don't need me."

"I'd say I'm in very good hands, Lieutenant. You have a good man there."

They both watched as Carmona silently set up the portable field generator, which neither had heard materialize.

"That he is, sir. So was Van Zandt. I'll be in touch."

"Do that." And he meant it. He had been reminded all over again how much he valued his command staff—indeed, his entire crew—after all they'd endured together the last few months. Even when he had been relieved of duty and spent weeks away from them as Riker sought the truth from the demon ship, they had remained loyal and had proven once more how lucky he was to be their commander. Sometimes lessons needed to be relearned, but he was determined not to forget this one anytime soon.

As Vale vanished in a flicker of light, Picard removed the last bit of grass from his sleeve and headed once more for his initial destination, the Bader's base of operations. As he opened the door, he could hear Carmona's footsteps approaching. Feeling well protected, he entered the building.

Inside the Bader base Picard watched as Cholan of Huni, the man speaking for this delegation, gave out some instructions and waved away an aide carrying a steaming pot.

"Ah, Picard," he said in a mild voice. Whatever strain

he felt certainly did not show on his features. If anything, he seemed particularly pleased.

"Cholan, how go things here?"

"Well enough, I suppose. Got everything wired up, getting identical reports from the field offices. I'd say we're ready to start handling the problem."

"And how do you propose to do that?"

"First, we must protect the general populace. Your people have been most kind in helping us repair vital systems. They almost have the water on again in Testani."

"That's something. But how can you keep people from fighting?"

"Well, that's a very good question. We don't have an immediate answer."

Picard saw that behind the confidence was uncertainty. It was all there in the man's eyes. And he was too proud to ask for help. At least Renks had the sense to admit he was in over his head.

As Picard bit back a comment, Cholan said, "One thing we can do is lodge the appropriate diplomatic complaints with the Federation. Clearly, they were at fault for what has befallen this planet. They will need to send in more support until the problem is resolved."

"You do realize that what you're asking for is most likely weeks away from arriving. The postwar rebuilding efforts have taxed resources throughout the Federation. Humanitarian aid is possible, but be realistic. What will happen in the weeks between now and then?"

"Won't you help keep the peace?"

"We can't stay here indefinitely," Picard said flatly.

"Your government is at fault, Picard—" Cholan began.

"It's your government, too. Delta Sigma IV is a member of the Federation. I am tired of the Council's pointing a finger at the very body it asked to join and is now trying to repudiate."

"Trust me; our ambassador to the Federation Council is filing formal complaints concerning the medical malfeasance that has taken place." Picard saw that Cholan was using bluster to hide his fear, and wanted to rid himself of the man's company. Duty, however, demanded he stay.

"Accidents happen, Cholan. You're starting to sound like one of the protesters, not a leader of this world."

"Does that mean I cannot protest actions taken against this world? I don't recall my office being denied that privilege."

Picard grew concerned, wondering if the disease had finally found its way to the Council. Morrow had been here longer and would be able to tell if this was a natural tendency or a part of the problem. The last time he checked, Morrow had been upgraded to stable, but he was certainly not in any shape to come back to the surface.

"Of course you can protest. It's a basic right. But, Cholan, as a leader of the people you need to set priorities. What is the Council doing now to help?"

The councillor fell silent at the question.

Colton Morrow finally opened his eyes, then immediately shut them. The pain was dull now, but it affected his entire torso. Then his mind began to spit out questions, and the only way to find answers to them was to open his eyes once more and face the situation head-on. During his time in the Diplomatic Corps, he had been spit on, slapped, and insulted any number of times. But this was the first time he had ever been physically assaulted, and he didn't like it.

He reopened his eyes and slowly swiveled his head, taking in his surroundings. Sickbay, as he expected. The steady beep of the monitor over his head gave him reason to believe he wasn't a critical case. He flexed his feet and felt no pain there. He tried to bend his knees and was rewarded with free movement. All right, then, it was his torso that had taken the brunt of the attack. Morrow recalled the mob in front of the Council building and Picard trying to shout them down. Morrow had made the mistake of ignoring Picard's admonishment to stay inside and opened the door. Within moments he became the target, and now he was paying for it.

"You're awake," a woman's voice said. Looking up, he was greeted with a smile from one of the nurses, one he had not seen before. "How do you feel?"

"Thirsty."

"We can fix that," she said, still smiling, and handed him a sealed cup with a straw. He took several swallows, enjoying the coolness as it entered his body.

The nurse checked the bio-bed's readouts and made notes on a padd. Her expression remained neutral, so he couldn't tell if his wounds were serious or not. He sipped some more and watched her saunter off.

Moments later, Dr. Crusher was in his sight, also wearing a smile.

"How do you feel, Ambassador?"

"Colt, please," he said. "Pretty sore, to be honest."

"No surprise. You got banged up pretty badly," she

said, reaching for a small stool and wheeling it over. Sitting, she looked at the padd and then at him. "What do you remember?"

"The mob. Things being thrown. Falling."

"Right. You cracked three ribs, one in the fall. Your right kidney is badly bruised but will heal. You have some lacerations on your right shoulder as well. And I hate to say this, but that suit you wore is now good for rags."

He chuckled at that, wincing at the pain. "When can I get back to work?"

"I've done all I can, and your body has to heal. It will be a few days before I can certify you fit."

"Do we have a few days? What's going on?"

She briefly filled him in on the current situation, and he nodded once. It was getting worse, and a few days might be too long. He also knew doctors, especially those in the field, and knew he was going to be confined to the ship. So he took a different tack.

"Can I be transferred to my quarters and then be provided with an uplink to the captain? Maybe I can still help."

Crusher looked surprised and then thoughtful at the notion. She looked once more at the padd, glanced at the current readouts above his body, and then smiled. "I suppose something can be worked out. I'll be in touch with Data and see what can be done."

Well, if that was the best he could hope for, he just hoped it was going to be good enough. He didn't necessarily feel guilty about the problems besetting the planet's inhabitants; after all, he had known nothing of the disease before it spread. He had had no knowledge of

Kyle Riker's involvement or the escalating problem. He did feel angry at not knowing the tactician's deep involvement from the outset and regretted ignoring Picard's direct order. Now he just wanted to make amends and do something positive to help.

Morrow just prayed there was still time for Crusher to find a cure and for Picard to get the people to listen to reason.

As Picard struggled with Cholan, Deanna Troi was in the other building, talking to an older woman, a Dorset named An Revell An. The two were in a corner of the bustling room and were trying to stay away from the din. And, Troi had to admit, avoid being seen.

"What have you learned?"

"Cainam has managed to hook their systems up with ours for real-time feeds from the world link," she replied. Her voice was rough with age, cracking at times. Troi estimated her to be fifty, which meant old age for this short-lived race. She admired the woman's dedication to duty and her refusal to hide in the safety of her home.

"He also says the power grid has shorted out on Eowand, and the world link lines were shattered on the coast of Huni. Five of the larger islands are also offline. That's only helping to spread the panic."

"I understand. What can be done?"

"Cainam didn't wait for directions; he's already summoned help for Huni from the nearest island. They can use microwave relays until things are repaired."

"Well, then," Troi said, "that doesn't sound too bad."

"It's not, really. But things are only going to get

worse, aren't they? And it's coming here, too. I heard the fighting outside."

Deanna put a comforting hand on the smaller woman's arm. "We're doing what we can. Our doctor is very good, and so is your Dr. Wasdin and the others working on the problem. I expect this to be solved."

"But when?"

"Now that's a question I can't answer. I can be here, and I can help if you need me."

Revell took some comfort in that, Deanna sensed. But it wasn't nearly enough, and she was feeling time slip by. Things were getting worse. Cainam had told her earlier that the death toll was now in the thousands, and the number of injured at least four times that.

Troi looked around the room and saw that each councillor was being attended to by assistants, a mix of Dorset and Bader, belying the notion that they would work better if the races were separated. The government never seemed to notice those that did the legwork and actually kept the government running. Off on the opposite side of the room, she watched as two aides entered and immediately began sharing information with their peers. And only afterward were the councillors informed. If she had to guess, she would suspect Revell was the longest tenured member of the government and therefore the best informed person on the planet.

And somewhere out there, amid the growing chaos, Will was still alone. Or rather with his father, which might even be worse. Kyle Riker had made a strong impression on her the one time they spoke. He was a dominating, if not domineering, personality, and she could tell he was strong. She also detected the pain he still carried over his wife's death from illness when Will was but two.

Will rarely spoke to her of his mother, keeping much of his childhood to himself. She understood that, after all; Lwaxana had suppressed her memories of Deanna's sister Kestra until Deanna was an adult. A sibling who died at age seven was a tragedy, but one she never knew about. It explained so much about the way her flamboyant mother acted as Deanna grew. It was a shame death had to overshadow the lives of the young, but there was no changing what had happened or who they were. For a moment, she flashed on her half brother, Barin, who was seven years old already. She hadn't seen him in ages, since the last time she'd been to her homeworld, which was still recovering from Dominion control. Family certainly meant more to her than it did to Will, despite his deep pride in the Riker lineage. While she had never met Barin's father, Jeyal, and had only met Odo—who had married Lwaxana so she could gain custody of the boy—a few times, Deanna was still close to her mother. Exasperating as she could be, there was never any doubt that Lwaxana loved her daughter fiercely and truly wanted what was best for her.

Would she and Will ever marry? Would they have children? Their romance had started again three years ago, and she was beginning to wonder where they were heading. Just days ago, Will had said he hated unfinished business, and she gathered he meant more than his father. And if they married, then what? They never seemed to talk about the future, taking things a day and a mission at a time.

Thinking about Will must have focused her senses. Her eyes went wide and her breath caught in her chest. She steadied herself against the wall with one hand and ignored concerned queries from Revell.

Will had been hurt. She didn't know where or how, but she sensed his pain. A part of her grew very cold and very tight.

Chapter Four

"SO, IF YOU CHECK the rate of cellular degradation, you can begin to see the effectiveness of the antibody," Dr. Tropp said. Nurse Weinstein nodded as he continued to explain the particular treatment he was performing on Chief Tognetti, a Bandi.

Crusher was working at a nearby station, looking over the results of an experiment. The computer analysis blinked to indicate it was complete and she awaited the results, too tired to build up much enthusiasm for the process. She needed to keep moving or she would give in to weariness. She also did not want Tropp to recognize her stress and nag her to rest.

His voice droned on, so she knew he wasn't paying much attention to her work. That was fine with her, because she was beginning to think this particular treatment was going to be failure number eleven. Sure enough, a red light presaged the computer's voice. *"Test number eleven has failed."*

"Something I can help with?" Tropp asked. He had completed his work on the crewman, and Weinstein was finishing up, singing to the Bandi as she worked.

"Just another failure," Crusher said irritably. He meant well, she knew, but there were times his attitude was grating, and now was one of them.

"Let's work through it," he said encouragingly. "Maybe there's something you missed."

"We know the liscom gas affected not only their blood and chromosomes, but also the brain chemistry . . ." she began.

"How has it affected the serotonin levels?"

"Good question. They have elevated levels of serotonin compared with baseline readings for both races."

Tropp studied the large screen's readout over his colleague's head and nodded. "Three times higher, at least, from this study."

"The elevated levels also seem to have worked with the liscom to alter the pineal hormones. Their version of melatonin has changed, and that accelerated not only their body clocks but their entire life cycle."

"Fascinating," he said, studying a new readout. She had previously dispatched him to deal with the wounded, letting her concentrate on the liscom gas problem, so he was just now coming up to speed on her research. "So, these people have normally very low levels of serotonin and the liscom forced their bodies to produce higher amounts, effectively drugging them."

"Right. And I've been trying to find something to regulate the levels without harming the rest of their brain chemistry. It's all very complex and still not entirely understood."

"Where would our quest for knowledge be if we had mastered everything, hmm?"

She ignored that and reviewed the results of tests ten and eleven, looking to see what changes to make for the next round.

"The uptake inhibitors seem to be withered," he noted, pointing to a close-up of the Bader neurons.

"I saw that, too," she said. "That helps explain why the serotonin levels grew over time."

"May I see an image of the baseline Bader brain as well as the test subjects'?"

Crusher hit several tabs on the panel, and the two requested images flashed side by side on-screen. Tropp murmured to himself as she studied the fluoxetines of the Bader brain. If she could decrease their production, she mused, it might lower the serotonin. It was all such delicate work, given the balances required for a healthy mind and body.

Once more Crusher thought about performing such research back on Earth, with state-of-the-art equipment at her disposal and the cream of the crop of medical students to draw upon for support. And then, she thought about her morning breakfasts in Picard's quarters.

A shake of her head refocused her thoughts, and she was once again looking at receptors, inhibitors, and levels of neuropeptides.

"The Dorset test subjects show below-normal amounts of serotonin," Tropp offered.

"I saw that once I knew where to look," Crusher said.

"In humans, it's as likely to cause depression and suicidal thoughts, but for them, it seems to amplify their aggressive tendencies."

"So the liscom increased serotonin output, dampened the aggression, and also threw the melatonin levels off the charts, and now you're trying to rebalance the brain," he said, more to himself than to her.

Crusher just nodded and began looking at ways to filter the liscom gas from the brain by using fluoxetines, a naturally produced chemical. She had abandoned that line of research after the fifth try but thought it might be worth another look.

"Sulfur," Tropp said out loud.

Crusher looked at him in mild confusion. "What about it?"

"The Bader and Dorset barely produce any," he said. "If we can naturally stimulate its production, it would clog the receptors."

"And the serotonin levels wouldn't spike, which in turn would leave the melatonin unaffected," said Crusher in a rush.

"The people would stop aging prematurely, but they would regain their normal levels of serotonin."

Crusher nodded in agreement. "But that would return them to their natural behavior, right?"

She looked at Tropp, thankful for his insight. She now had new avenues to explore, but new problems to consider. "Don't you see, if we leave them aggressive, the fighting below won't stop. They'll just live longer, with more opportunities to hurt their neighbors."

Tropp nodded slowly, the implications now settling in

his mind. His posture changed, reflecting the gravity of the situation.

"Let me work on this some more, and if we're right, I'll tell the captain we have something. Thank you, Tropp."

"I'll be checking on the patients if you need me further," he said, and left her alone. She was grateful, because she really didn't like the direction her research was taking her.

"The injector is cracked, sure enough," La Forge said, looking at the scans Hoang had taken.

She and the chief engineer were standing in a small workroom where repairs were made or new equipment fabricated. The scans were on a large screen with readouts on both sides giving almost microscopic details about the injector, which lay atop the table, and the damage.

"I can try to patch it," she offered.

"If this is off kilter by so much as three microns, it won't fire in sequence at the higher frequencies. We'd lose warp integrity around five-point-five," he said.

"Actually, I think it's closer to five-point-nine," she said in a quiet voice.

"Well, you're the expert, so five-point-nine it is," La Forge said. "Still, we need a replacement, and of course we have none. Starships don't usually need to replace their injectors."

"Have you checked the inventories on your trading list?"

La Forge shook his head and grabbed a padd from the tabletop. Quickly he thumbed it active and then scrolled through lists indexed by ship. He shook his head slowly as the lists floated by and Anh craned her neck to watch.

"Sir, we just need pieces, not an entire injector. If we

have even a spare bottom half, I can do the weld to within one micron."

"Have you done this kind of thing much?" he asked, barely keeping the sarcasm out of his voice. He was feeling the stress of keeping the starship functioning while playing quartermaster to ships in the nearby sectors. It was heady work and he was taking pride in the wheeling and dealing, but now that his own ship was endangered, he grew angry at the situation. There was no one person at fault, unless he wanted to blame the Founders for starting the war that left the Federation still in rebuilding mode years after the war's end.

"I'm not even sure if we can find components. Let me think about this," La Forge said, his voice drifting off.

He walked out of the workshop, leaving Hoang to fuss with the damaged piece. He'd already informed Data of the problem and said he'd have a solution soon. Now he had to make good on that promise.

He went to an alcove, pulled out the seat, and called up a companel. Seconds later, he was talking with his old friend, Whis, chief engineer on the *Nautilus*. Quickly, he sketched the problem and asked for suggestions.

"That's a tough one," the Andorian said. *"None of us have needed spare injectors before. What about replicating one until you get to a starbase?"*

"I've already run simulations, and a replicated injector couldn't withstand the tolerances required at high warp. We'd be vulnerable if anything came up."

"And something always comes up with your ship, doesn't it? Sounds like quite a mess beneath you."

"Haven't been down there myself, but yeah, it's gotten pretty complicated."

The other engineer seemed lost in thought and then looked up, his eyes intent. *"The* Bartlet *just collected a lot of debris from where we lost the* Lakota *during the war. They wouldn't have inventoried the materials the same way. If I remember it right, the secondary hull and at least one nacelle were left intact."*

"All I need is one," Geordi said with a slow grin.

"Give them a call. The engineer there is named Ranzz."

"I owe you one," La Forge said.

Minutes later, Ranzz, a blunt-featured Rigelian, was on-screen. La Forge briefly filled him in on the problem and his needs.

"Heard about your project. Do you really trust a Ferengi to play courier with that much valuable property?"

"He's my best option, and I really think his desire for profit will keep him honest. For now, at least."

"I don't trust them at all. Even with the new reforms. Just don't see them changing fast at all."

"So far it's working out, and I'll trust him for the moment. Besides, if you have what I need, then he's my only option."

"Turns out, we do have what you need. In sight, anyway. We left the nacelle alone, scavenged for other stuff we needed. Never thought we'd have to recover supplies from salvage like . . ."

"Like a Ferengi, huh?"

"Guess so. Anyway, I figure we're about three hours away from the site. I can ask our captain if we can return and pick up what you need. Hell, I'll grab up all

seven from the nacelle, send you one and keep the rest since, well, you never know."

"That's great! I'll contact Dex and reroute him, making this a priority."

"Okay, so now that I'm helping save the mighty Enterprise, *tell me, what really happened with Picard at Rashanar?"*

With a deep sigh, La Forge launched into another retelling of Picard's confrontation with Starfleet Command, recognizing the need to get the word out.

She had waited long enough.

Troi approached Picard, who was once more speaking with Cholan. They were figuring out the best way to help put out a fire in a remote village. He seemed tense and agitated, clearly in need of rest but refusing to allow himself the luxury.

Waiting patiently as he finished the most immediate work, she strained her senses once more, seeking out her *Imzadi.* He was alive but in some pain—maybe physical, maybe emotional. It was hard to tell, and not for the first time did she wish for a full-blooded Betazoid's mastery and telepathic skill. However, she also knew she'd never want to give up the short time she'd had with her father before duty claimed his life.

Finally, Picard noticed her and excused himself from the councillor. He first looked relieved at seeing her, but her expression telegraphed her concern.

"I know that look," he said. "Something's happened to Will."

"Yes, sir," she said, trying to maintain her professional

demeanor, although she was warmed by his reaction. "He was in a great deal of pain a little while ago. I could tell that much. He's alive and the pain seems to have lessened, but something's wrong."

Picard tapped his combadge. "Picard to Riker."

Silence. Troi started to lose control of her professional demeanor.

"Picard to Riker, respond." After more silence, he tapped his combadge again.

"Picard to *Enterprise.*"

"Data here."

"Mr. Data, check the sensor logs and let me know the last time we had a fix on Commander Riker's combadge."

Seconds passed as Picard and Troi exchanged looks, waiting for their friend to give them news. Any news would be better than speculation.

"Captain, there was a microburst of a signal twelve minutes ago at a location north of your position. We have tried to reestablish contact but have not been successful."

"I assume you've searched for human bio-signs?"

"Yes, sir. We have screened out our personnel, and no other humans register on the planet."

He gave Troi a look that said he was not at all surprised. Picard then asked for a general update, frowned at news of the plasma injector, but nodded to himself as he heard how Geordi had located a replacement. Troi was pleased the ship was not troubling him, because he needed to focus on Delta Sigma IV.

Picard reached out and placed a hand on her arm. His expression softened and he radiated reassurance. She soaked it up, feeling the need for every bit of friendly emotion. "I'm sure the commander is fine, and right now we need to trust that he is capable. I can't spare anyone to track him down with so little to go on."

"Our link confirms he's still alive, but I'll certainly feel better when I see him for myself."

"Why, Counselor, aren't you the one who tells us to trust our feelings?"

"That might work for most people and their problems, but this is Will we're talking about. We've all been through enough for me to harbor some doubt until I see him."

He nodded, his expression grave once more.

"We'll find him."

"Yes, sir."

"He'll be fine."

"Yes, sir."

Now she just had to believe the captain's words and ignore her own feeling of dread.

Chapter Five

VALE MATERIALIZED in the courtyard between the Bader and Dorset factions of the Council. The sounds of protests reached her ears even as the transporter effect faded. The protesters were begging the Federation to leave them alone, or for the Starfleet personnel to die in a bloodbath. She nodded gravely to Carmona, who remained on duty with Williams. The portable shielding was holding just fine from the looks of it. There was something slick on one side of it, sunlight reflecting off it. She then spotted Picard emerging from the building to her left. He looked worn and troubled.

Picard gestured for her to enter the building. Once inside the dim hallway, they stopped, needing some relative privacy. He looked at her, eyes intent and all business.

"Report."

"The problems have been growing worse. Huni's power will be restored within the hour, we think, and they finally got water back on line at Testani. Eowand's power grid is a total loss. And, sir, it's only going to escalate. I could empty the ship of security and it won't be enough."

Picard crossed his arms over his chest, tucked his chin down, and thought for a moment. "What do you need to do differently?"

"All hands."

He gave her a look that made her doubt her own sanity. Taking a deep breath, she forged ahead, "Sir, we have too many crises for my teams to be handling damage control. We have hundreds of people on board with little to do while we remain in orbit. But down here they can fight fires, handle triage, keep watch as engineers repair vital systems. If you want this planet left intact, then I need more people."

The captain nodded, giving the request serious consideration. Seconds passed as she intently watched his face, trying to read the emotions in his eyes. The rest of his features were set and unreadable.

"It would have to be voluntary," he began. "Some people will feel totally out of their element. And no team is formed without your people in the mix. Coordinate with Dr. Crusher and Mr. La Forge. Form medical and engineering task forces; keep them moving with site-to-site transports. See if any of our pilots will take the shuttles down to help with the fires. Stay alert and keep yourself free to move about. I may need you here, or Mr. Data may require you on the ship."

"Aye, sir. Thank you, Captain. If it's not asking too much, I would suggest the initial request for volunteers come from you. If you can spare the time."

Picard let out a weary sigh, and Vale saw his shoulders sag. She had rarely seen him look so tired. "Time, Lieutenant, is something of which the planet has far too little, and I have far too much. Beam up and start coordinating with the department heads."

"Sir, is there something I can do to help you?"

There was a grateful look in his eyes, but she knew her offer was futile. Unless she could pull off a medical miracle, Vale doubted there was much more she could do in the way of help. He didn't say anything as he stepped back to allow her clearance to request transport.

After making the request, she arranged her features to give him the most promising, upbeat look possible. She knew, though, it was nothing but a sorry masquerade.

"All hands, this is the captain," Picard began as he paced the hallway outside the Bader headquarters. "The situation on Delta Sigma IV has grown worse and will continue to remain this way until a cure for the disease afflicting the people is found. Until that time, we need to maintain vital services and help keep what order there is. The peace officers native to this world have been outnumbered from the beginning because their society had always been a peaceful one. Lieutenant Vale and her team have done valiant work despite growing casualties, but the situation has grown even beyond their abilities.

"Therefore, I am asking for volunteers from the entire crew. We'll be assembling damage control and security parties. Obviously, engineering support and medical help are the top priorities, but people in other departments can also volunteer. No pair of hands will be turned away. Those who choose to volunteer should make their wishes known to their department heads. Everything will be co-ordinated through Lieutenant Vale and Commander Data.

"The people of Delta Sigma IV are dealing with feelings they've never encountered before, and they are letting fear take hold. Their medical problems occurred entirely by accident, despite what you may hear when you arrive. While the Council tries to work together, we need to demonstrate through word, and more importantly, through deed, that the United Federation of Planets and Starfleet will stand by a member world in need.

"For those who volunteer to come down, you have my personal thanks.

"Picard out."

He knew his crew. They had stood behind him when things seemed hopeless only months earlier. There was little doubt that the crew would live up to his faith and expectations.

Although comforted by that thought, Picard was chilled at the notion that a holding action was the best they could do, and they could keep it up for only a few days. After that, they would be overmatched.

Silently, he urged Crusher to hurry but refused to call and distract her when he knew full well she was pressing herself harder than anyone else possibly could.

Finally, the dark question rose in his mind. What would happen if she failed to find something to regulate the behavior of the inhabitants?

* * *

"Commander La Forge?"

Geordi turned, and Anh gave him a small smile in recognition.

"How long before the plasma injector arrives?"

"We've given it top priority with Dex, but even at his top speed, we're looking at another two days."

Anh absorbed the information and made a decision, one she had been wrestling with for some time.

"Sir, if I may, I'd like to join the volunteers below."

She didn't know his eyebrows could rise so high and was somewhat bothered that her volunteering was such a shock. Hoang thought she and La Forge knew each other well enough to know that of course she'd volunteer to help out.

"Of course you can," La Forge said.

"But you're surprised," she challenged.

Caught, he smiled and shrugged. "I guess I am, a bit. You've kept to yourself a lot."

"I'm still Starfleet and go where I'm needed."

La Forge didn't know what to say, and she felt good about making it clear that she was ready to put her personal problems away as the need arose. And if ever there was a need . . .

As they made arrangements to cover her shift, she paused to ask herself if she was running away from a stable environment into something dangerous for a reason. It wasn't all about duty, she admitted to herself, but what other reason did she have for putting herself in a threatening situation? She could imagine having a conversation with the counselor about this and being asked "Do you have a death wish because of your catastrophic losses?" It was a question she hadn't yet asked herself.

As Dr. Tropp took point in coordinating the reduced medical staff still on duty, Crusher refined her research, fighting the excitement she felt welling up within her. She may have done it, may have actually found the cause of the problem and a useful solution. Her exultations were tempered, though, by serious questions and doubts.

As she wrestled with her thoughts and emotions, Crusher completed downloading her research onto a padd and decided she needed to discuss her findings privately with the captain. Would he be willing to leave the fractious Council, or would she have to head down for the conversation? Well, she decided, she'd leave the decision to him.

"Crusher to Picard."

When he answered, she knew from his voice that he needed a break. Changing her mind, she insisted he come aboard because she had news for him. It was enough to bring renewed vigor to his voice.

They had agreed to meet in his ready room and she headed there immediately. Passing Data on the bridge, she noted how busy things were now that the entire crew had something to do, something they could all contribute to the mission. All too often, certain sections of the ship were asked to be idle, even during the tensest missions. Here was an infrequent opportunity for every crewmember to make a difference.

Without pausing to distract Data, she slipped quietly into the ready room, and ordered a mug of hot vegetable soup for herself and a cup of Earl Grey for the captain.

Placing the steaming cup near one end of the couch, she waited. For a moment, she imagined doing this in his quarters and under less trying circumstances. She paused to ask herself why she kept thinking of him in romantic terms now that she had an option to actually leave the ship and go off on her own. Was the hope of romance all that was keeping her tied to the *Enterprise?*

Before she could ruminate further, the door slid open and Picard walked in, breaking into a smile at the sight of both Crusher and the tea.

He sank heavily onto the couch and breathed in the steam for a moment.

"That bad?"

"Worse, perhaps," he admitted, and then helped himself to a sip.

"Tell me."

"Not if you have news, or was that a pretext to get me to rest?" Picard eyed her warily, disturbing her relaxed mood.

"No, I have news. I understand what happened to the people and how to undo it."

He raised his eyebrows in surprise and looked inquiringly at her. In response, she activated her padd and handed it to him.

"I'll give you a crash course in brain chemistry to help explain," she said. "The liscom gas not only got into their bloodstream, but into their brains, forcing them to pump out excessive amounts of serotonin, which depressed their aggressive tendencies. The excess serotonin in turn affected the production of melatonin, which for both races meant their life cycles were shortened.

"Starfleet Medical determined how to screen out the gas from their bloodstream, putting these people back on track for a normal life span. The catch is you also return these people to a natural state of aggression.

"I've synthesized something that we can introduce into the atmosphere through plant life, just like the liscom. If it works, I can suppress some of the serotonin production without changing the melatonin levels. I'd effectively be allowing them to live their normal lives but drugging them at lower dosages."

Picard studied the graphics on the padd, thumbing ahead to check readings. He'd ignored his tea, and Crusher turned her attention to the soup in her hands as something to do while he absorbed it all.

He finally paused to finish his cup in several deep mouthfuls and pondered the padd some more. There was a gravity settling over him, one she appreciated given the subject. "How certain are you that this new breed of plant will do the job?"

"Lieutenant Moq in botany is completing a simulation now. He thinks it's promising."

"Beverly, you may have saved a planet today."

"Have I?" She tucked a stray lock of hair behind her right ear and refused to meet his eyes.

"What's wrong?"

She looked up sharply, feeling the intensity of her feelings on her face, in her eyes. "It's the Dokaalan all over again," she began, putting her mug down. The captain gazed at her and she couldn't read the expression. "Jean-Luc, these people are finally in their natural, undrugged state. This is the way nature meant them to be.

What I'm doing is effectively exchanging one drug for another. No doctor would want an entire world permanently on medication. I've been looking into this from a sociological viewpoint as well. Do you know why every building down there is drab? The liscom gas not only robbed them of their aggression but also dulled their creativity. Compare the Bader and Dorset capitals to the city you've been in. Trust me, there's no comparison.

"What I don't know right now is how much of that creativity I'd be keeping from them even at lower dosages."

Picard rose. He was filled once more with tension, and she felt a flash of guilt for making him feel that way again.

"And how is this like the Dokaalan?"

Crusher frowned at the question. Since it seemed so obvious to her, she was frustrated he didn't see it. Or was he simply using the time to order his own thoughts?

He continued before she could formulate an answer. "We're looking at the line once more. And once again we need to decide if it's time to cross the line and interfere with the people." He chose his words carefully. "Unchecked, they're likely to kill each other before they can get a grip on their feelings. They don't have time to wait for a Surak to rise up and get through to them. If you can give them their lost years and make them see some reason, then that is for the best."

"Is it? Or is it just convenient for the people? Stay drugged, you'll live longer."

"I see the moral dilemma here, Doctor," Picard said, standing by his beloved ancient tome of Shakespeare.

"But what you don't see are the lost lives and destroyed property. If we have something that can help them, then we should use it."

"Jean-Luc, this isn't a temporary cure that we can remove later when we have time to prepare them. Once we seed this around the world, there's going to be little chance of eradicating it. Same with the liscom."

They both fell silent, each with their own thoughts. For a moment, Beverly imagined getting such a report while running Starfleet Medical and wondered if she'd reward or damn the doctor filing the information. Did she really want a position with that much authority over countless lives? For a moment she wondered how Yerbi Fandau managed it. Her year was uneventful, but he oversaw Starfleet Medical during several sector-wide outbreaks and an entire war. It wasn't all research: there were certain elements of galactic politics involved; some of the same reasons that had driven her from Earth back to the *Enterprise* over a decade ago.

"And are we two wise enough to decide the fate of a world?" she asked quietly.

"No, and it will not fall to just you and me. It hasn't in the past nor will it today."

"The line keeps appearing and every time we skirt it, it brings us closer to the time we trip on it and really foul things up for someone." She tucked her hair behind her ears with both hands, steadying herself and ordering her thoughts. Then she adjusted her position and gave him a wan smile. "It's not getting any easier, is it?"

Picard gave her a tight smile in return and nodded once. "I know what you mean. We're taught that with experience should come wisdom and you think the solutions will more easily present themselves."

"And they don't, do they?"

"Not always."

"Is it me or is the galaxy growing more complex?"

"With every new race we meet," Picard told his longtime friend, "the odds for confrontation grow and the neighborhood gets a little more crowded, a little more complex. That's why it's not getting any easier."

"And we face the unexpected time and again," Crusher added glumly.

He gave a kinder smile than before, saying, "Well, I for one wouldn't want to get bored." Picard sat down once again, planting his feet on the carpet. "If we were to introduce this new drug, how long before things calm down?"

"I'd guess the first effects would be noticeable within hours as the body absorbs and processes the new element. The plants would take longer to take hold in some locations. And we're still modeling how the liscom and the new plants would interact. It's a fragile ecosystem we're monkeying with."

"All right, and it will take you some time to synthesize enough to spread among the people. When will the simulations be complete?"

"Another hour at least."

"You're right, this is too large an issue for us to decide over a cup of tea. I'll convene everyone in three hours. That should give you time to analyze everything and be prepared to give us the facts."

She looked into his eyes. "Will you be open to a debate?"

"Within reason," he responded steadily. "I need my senior officers to give me their unvarnished opinion. But trust me, the final decision and responsibility will remain with me."

Standing up, she asked, "What if we don't find Will by then?"

"We can only wait so long. I have to trust that the commander is alive and dealing with his father. I would like his counsel but we need decisions sooner rather than later. Should this fail, Starfleet will have my head."

"Think they're still going after you?"

"I honestly haven't thought about it of late, Beverly. Some members of the admiralty would probably prefer my head on their wall instead of on my shoulders, but probably no more than before the demon ship."

"Fine with me, I think it looks just right where it is."

"Why, thank you," he said, his tone losing some of its severity.

"Three hours," she said, seriousness creeping back into her voice. Walking out of the ready room, she thought about the consequences of her research and grew concerned all over again.

Chapter Six

WAVES BROKE OVER the barrier that kept people from tumbling off the large platform and into the roiling sea. Rain lashed down in torrents, rocking the platform and making it hard to stay upright. Between the surf and the wind, it was difficult to hear anything, so shouts were lost. What Tropp knew was that he had at best fifteen minutes to complete his task or he would lose his patient. He hadn't lost a patient since the *Enterprise* arrived in this solar system, and he wasn't about to lose one now.

His team had beamed down only minutes earlier, summoned by an automated distress call. From what Data told them as they assembled in the transporter room, the platform was a marine research facility that everyone assumed had been abandoned when the "madness" broke out. Yet, the signal had been received by both the emergency services people on Delta Sigma IV and the *Enterprise,* so someone had to be there. Scanners indicated there were two bodies, but weak life signs from only one.

There were no nurses available to beam down with Tropp, so the Denobulan accepted offers of help from a stellar cartographer and a security ensign he had never met before. As soon as the three of them arrived in the small structure that housed the research equipment, the doctor kneeled beside a body slumped over a fallen chair. It belonged to a Bader woman whose skull had been caved in by a heavy object.

"They had some fight," the ensign, a young man named La Rock, observed, letting out a low whistle.

"She's dead," Tropp said. "Where's the other one?"

"No one else is in here, Doctor," said the cartographer, a tall woman named Neumark.

"Ensign, check outside, please," Tropp said. La Rock's only reply was an expression that clearly questioned Tropp's sanity. The doctor and the ensign locked gazes. Finally the nervous young man looked once more over his shoulder at the rain beating against the window.

"Lieutenant, please see if you can find a recording of what happened," Tropp said, pleased with himself for finding something for the cartographer to do. As the woman busied herself without comment, he gazed out the window to watch the ensign.

La Rock, thin and wiry with dark black hair that was now a wet mop on his head, was edging carefully along the exterior of the structure. Tropp watched as he rounded a corner and was lost from sight. The doctor began to relax, thinking the other victim must be outside, so all the ensign had to do was find him and drag him back in. He mentally began listing the first steps required for his research into the other plant life on the planet. If the liscom could affect people this severely, he began to wonder what other toxic substances were part of the ecosystem. While he generally preferred to work alone, he suspected he'd need Moq for the research. Normally people considered Tropp talkative, but compared with the Bolian, he was as mute as a Minaran.

He was so lost in thought he missed the slam of the metal door and the ensign's yells. Tropp was about to admonish the young man for not bringing the wounded native back with him, but then the words started to register.

". . . impaled . . ."

Tropp uttered a short prayer and then told Neumark to stay where she was. He took a deep breath and stepped out into the driving rain. Almost immediately, his left foot slipped and he fell hard on one knee. He yelped in pain but ignored it as La Rock helped him up and they inched around the corner. There was another Bader woman, this one covered in blood but still alive. Tropp began to wonder how she could be as he shielded his eyes with one hand and studied her condition.

Somehow she had been skewered to a series of metallic rods that were affixed to the exterior. They might have been atmosphere gauges or antennas. He couldn't tell because the ends were still inside the struggling woman. Blood trickled from cuts on her face, and her coppery hair had been either cut away or burned. Her eyes were alert, so Tropp assumed she knew what her situation was.

"Madam, you have to be cut away from the building before I can properly treat you. Do you understand me?"

She nodded once, too weak to speak.

He pulled out his medical tricorder, waved the hand

scanner over her entire form, and then focused on the rods. There were four in all. Three had punctured organs, and the fourth was just below a lung. The woman would need major surgery once she was free, surgery he could easily do back aboard the *Enterprise.*

"Doctor, what can we do?"

"Be quiet, Ensign," he said sharply. He needed to focus and didn't want any distractions. Bad enough having to deal with a frightened kid, but the deck kept moving in reaction to the buffeting from the waves. While he would have preferred a stable environment, he mentally shrugged, knowing one cannot always have what one wants.

Finished with his examination, he reached one damp hand to the rods to see how they were connected to the building. They were almost certainly welded to the structure in order to withstand the worst the sea had to offer. Cutting her loose was not going to be easy. Instead of a cartographer, he wished he had a spare engineer with the proper tools, but he determined there was no time to seek out additional help.

"Listen carefully, Ensign La Rock," Tropp began, then raised his voice, shouting to be heard above the roar. "She needs to be cut free. The only tool we have for that is your phaser. You will need to melt each of these rods until she is loose. Then we can beam up and I can operate. Your phaser must be set on a narrow beam and at a high intensity. She doesn't have much time."

The ensign grabbed his phaser and began making modifications, swaying with the ever-shifting deck. "Doctor, won't we burn her in the process?"

"Well, the good news is that the rain will help cut

down on the heat you generate. I can only hope the instruments inside the rods are not good conductors. Please begin."

Tropp looked at the woman, saw the understanding and fear that clouded her face. He patted her left arm and then was banged against the building.

La Rock hesitated, rechecking his setting, and then moved around, looking for the best possible angle. Tropp grew impatient, but realized he needed the ensign to be comfortable in performing his task. Finally, La Rock took aim and depressed the trigger. A thin amber beam lanced through the rain. Tropp could hear the sizzle as water was instantly turned to steam. He watched as the base of the first rod grew red. The steam grew thicker, obscuring some of the target. After nearly thirty seconds, the rod was cut free and Tropp saw the woman's right side sag a bit. She let out a cry of pain, the first real sound she had made since they found her.

"Very good," Tropp said encouragingly. He blinked away rain that fell freely into his eyes. "Now the second one, please."

La Rock nodded and took aim once more. The beam went to work and Tropp paused to study his tricorder. The woman's breathing had grown shallower, her entire body in shock. He estimated they had ten minutes, maybe eleven before her vital functions shut down entirely. At nearly half a minute per rod, that was two minutes to free her, plenty of time left to beam up and get to work.

"Tropp to sickbay."

"Sickbay. Please state the nature of the medical emergency." The voice belonged to the Emergency Medical

Hologram, which told Tropp that things had gotten busier. If Crusher was letting the hologram answer hails from the planet, she and her staff must have their hands full.

"I need to perform surgery on a Bader female, approximately thirty years old. She's been impaled in four places and we're cutting her free. I need a bed ready and as much A-3 blood as we can spare."

"ETA?"

"Five minutes tops," Tropp replied. "I'll need at least one nurse."

"In a pinch I have the requisite programming to act as a nurse."

"We'll talk later. Tropp out." Rather than chat with the hologram, Tropp needed to hold on to a railing with both hands as a wave crashed right over them. La Rock fell flat on his front, still gripping the phaser, but the water made the woman, now half free, thrash about, and her moans told him things were getting worse.

The ensign hesitated at the sounds of her anguish.

"She needs to be freed now!" Tropp yelled.

La Rock nodded and got to his knees, took aim, and fired once more. Before the woman was freed, Tropp heard a sound and saw the cartographer on the deck. She had quickly sized up the situation and had brought some cable. Without a word, she inched forward and tied a loop around the doctor's leg. She then connected the patient to the doctor, ducking low enough to avoid the phaser beam. He watched her wince as a molten piece of the rod struck her damp shoulder. He had to admire her for both her courage and her good thinking.

"One more time and we can get out of here," Tropp shouted encouragingly.

"Aye, sir," La Rock called back, pausing long enough to be added to the human chain. As soon as the doctor had firmly wrapped the cable around his waist, La Rock rose on one knee and took aim.

"Did you find anything?" Tropp shouted to Neumark.

"No logs of any kind. I can only begin to guess what happened here."

"It really doesn't matter at this point," he replied.

Another wave crashed over them, but no one stirred. La Rock fired his phaser and Tropp willed the heat to work faster. His tricorder indicated that the woman's kidneys had failed, so he mentally rearranged the order of surgery. Then he shoved the device into his pocket, ready to catch the limp, now unconscious woman.

She was falling, her weight finishing the job of breaking the melting rod free. Neumark reached out and grabbed her. Holding the woman in her arms, she nodded to Tropp, who ordered emergency transport direct to sickbay. The woman wasn't out of danger yet.

Will's head throbbed and he seethed with the knowledge that his father deliberately hurt him. When he regained consciousness, he fought back the urge to vomit and recognized he was still strapped within the stolen flyer. His father had gotten out and was doing something nearby. Freeing himself, he quickly checked the communications system and wasn't at all surprised to find it disabled, key components missing. A check for weaponry also turned up nothing immediately useful.

He did find some water and took several swallows, which felt wonderful. There was also a first-aid kit and he found some tablets to help with the pain. When he thought of a souvenir from the planet a day—or was it two?—ago, he never imagined it would be a lump on his head, a gift from his father.

It was chilly, but nowhere near as cold as the place where he had found Kyle. Pleased he at least had the clothes for the environment, Riker decided it was time to hunt down his father one more time. He recalled Kyle said this city had a problem, but he struggled to remember the nature of it. Finally it came to him: there was an evacuation going on, and Kyle decided they needed to help.

Stepping out of the flyer, Will saw that the sun was just rising. They had landed in a clearing, not far from where a large number of flyers had been parked earlier. Now the field was empty, and he could hear sirens and broadcast announcements in the distance. People were leaving the city on foot or on the local version of a motorized bicycle. They moved without panic, so he assumed there was no immediate threat. Most carried cases, and some carried children on their backs. He had seen this sort of evacuation before, when people had little time to prepare and grabbed whatever they could. Old and young huddled around the sturdiest, so the line was actually a series of clusters.

Finally, he spotted his father's gray hair. Kyle was on the opposite side of the evacuees, and he seemed to be directing the traffic.

Will allowed the painkiller he had taken to do its job as he watched his father. He also studied the people, a mix of Bader and Dorset, of course, but what was remarkable was the lack of fighting and yelling. Had they been spared the disease? Or did something happen in the city that was bad enough to convince them to put aside their differences and escape together? Will turned his attention back to his father, watching him at work. As ever, Kyle seemed in command of the situation, taking time to make comforting comments to the occasional passerby. He even pulled a family out of line and rearranged their belongings, making them easier to carry.

After all this time, Will wasn't sure what to make of his father. Kyle Riker always seemed to know what to do, what he wanted, and how to get it. His accomplishments were never in question, his manner was above reproach. Even when he was implicated in the Tholian attack on the space station, he had enough supporters within Starfleet Command to buy him time to prove his innocence. So, Will asked himself for the thousandth time, why couldn't he communicate effectively with his son? And of course, there was never an answer that satisfied the first officer.

He longed to talk to Troi, and receive not only competent guidance, but emotional comfort. It had taken him a long time to understand women and be comfortable around them, and as a result he knew he had let promising relationships slip by him, starting with Felicia at the Academy. His time with Deanna, starting when he was an inexperienced lieutenant on Betazed, had been wonderful but, even so, distanced. He had placed duty over love at the time and had come to regret it. Still, five years later when he found himself working alongside her on the *Enterprise*-D, he wasn't sure of himself around her. Awkwardness had finally given way to a deep, abiding friendship, and despite their mutually exclusive romantic entanglements, there was always something in the air between them. Will was certain he had lost her forever when Worf entered the picture, but he hadn't begrudged his friends their happiness. He had had his chance and let it pass by. It was Worf who ended the relationship, transferring to Deep Space 9 and, like the younger Riker, put duty before romance. If there was anyone who was always putting duty first, it was his Klingon friend.

Now, here they were, finally reunited after twelve years. And it felt right. Will was thrilled the effects of the Son'a planet helped reignite the romance once and for all, but that was over three years ago. They were happy, but at this stage in his life, Will was asking himself if there should be more. At forty-two, Riker figured that he would have been married by now if it was going to happen at all. He and Troi were as close to being a real married couple as possible. But, as he said to her before leaving the ship three days ago, he disliked unfinished business.

The Delta Sigma IV problem was the immediate unfinished business that gnawed at him, and he hated being out of touch with Picard and the ship and therefore out of the flow of knowledge. For all he knew, Crusher was administering a vaccine and the problem would be over by lunchtime. Not bloody likely, he knew, but still, he craved contact with Troi. And the captain.

During his musing, Will had lost track of his father. He narrowed his eyes and scanned the crowd, hoping to spot his all-too-human form amid the tall and thin Dorset and stocky Bader. A sound caught his attention, and he whirled about to spot his father standing by the entrance to the flyer. He was breathing hard, but damn, he was still good enough to avoid detection.

"We've got to fly, Willy," Kyle said, a look of determination on his face.

"Where?"

"Follow me," he said and clambered aboard. Refusing to be left behind, Will followed. Within seconds the hatch was sealed shut and the engines hummed to life.

"How much longer do we do this?" Will asked.

Without taking time for the usual preflight check, they were lifting into the air. His father was a machine, taking control of the vessel and giving it his total concentration. It was a look Will had seen many, many times before. His father had a goal and was going to accomplish it successfully, damn what lay ahead.

"This pointless running around, flitting from problem to problem. You can't solve them all, I told you that. You told me this was getting too big even for the *Enterprise.*"

"But I also said I was going to find El Bison El," Kyle reminded him, sounding more confident than he had before.

"Where?" Will repeated, more forcefully this time.

"Into the city, about half a kilometer up," Kyle replied.

"How'd you find him in a city emptying out?"

"Used a padd with his picture, asked people as they filed by. Took a while since it was just me, but I got it done."

"Did you ask the peace officers for help?"

"They're busy with the evacuation. That's why I need you, son. We have to go get him and bring him to the doctors."

This was all making sense to Will, and he was finally feeling like things were falling into place. Something remained nagging in the back of his mind but he wasn't sure if it was a lingering headache or an unrecognized problem.

"Rather than explain what was happening, you cold-cocked me, so fill me in," Will insisted. "And don't leave anything out." Will saw to it his voice was officious and all-business, indicating to his father there would be total honesty on this point.

"A wild rumor got out that the power plant in the center of the city was going super-critical, leaking toxic fumes. We got the blame for it, of course, and people took it upon themselves to leave the path of the gases." Kyle concentrated on banking the vessel and then it accelerated. Before Will could say anything, Kyle continued. "No, it's not going super-critical. Like I said, a wild rumor."

"How do you propose we actually find this guy?"

"The people who spotted him last saw him by a bar. They described it to me. We'll fly by and survey the scene and then make a plan. But I figure time is of the essence."

"Hasn't it been that way since Bison broke containment?"

Kyle, typically, said nothing.

Minutes later, the flyer was snaking between tall and wide buildings, Will using his station to do a detailed scan of each exterior. The family that told Kyle about Bison was less than exact in their description of the bar. It was going to be guesswork, Will assumed, and some luck. Most of the buildings had no exterior walkways; few were even connected by any sort of bridge, making it easier to eliminate targets at a glance. For the first three buildings that might match the description, Kyle flew around the structure at varying heights while Will looked. No building resembled any bar Will had ever seen. The two men worked in silence, each performing their tasks and knowing the other would not shirk from saving a life.

The fourth building had light movement and Will focused the scanner, magnifying the image. Sure enough, it was a bar, with optics blinking in an ever-changing swirl of logos, promising a wide variety of drinks from Omega IV to Andor. Will watched for another few moments and pointed it out to his father.

"No people around, no other flyers in sight. He's not going to outrun us. We can land on the roof and come downstairs and grab him." Kyle was quickly assessing the situation, reaching conclusions as fast as Data would under the same circumstances.

"And we have no way of calling for any help should he walk out while we land. We're going to make some noise that'll alert him," Will said.

"I'll just have to land quietly," Kyle said with his first genuine smile in the last few hours. And there was the face of his father, the one Will remembered when they were hiking or camping. For a brief moment, Will felt like he was ten again and the world offered him hope.

Sure enough, Kyle cut back on the engines, dimming their roar as the flyer neared the roof. With minute adjustments, the craft tipped left then right and finally settled into a perfect landing that barely jarred its passengers. Kyle actually winked at Will, much the way he did those long years back, and smiled.

Will began to smile in return, but his head throbbed and he was reminded that his father recently knocked him cold. He dropped the smile and frowned, which seemed to confuse Kyle. *Let it,* Will decided.

They found an access hatch and entered the building. Neither man carried a weapon, Kyle having assured his son that Bison posed no threat. From the surveillance video he saw at the quarantine center, Will had to agree.

It took less than three minutes for them to make their way down the stairs and to the rear of the bar. They emerged into a large storeroom with case upon case of liquors from around the quadrant stacked haphazardly. As Will admired some of the more exotic labels, Kyle was checking the possible exits, looking for booby traps, weapons, or anything amiss. Will had to admire his father for falling into smart habits that no doubt saved his life time and again.

Kyle gestured to Will, signaling everything seemed clear. Will nodded in return and they headed for the door that would bring them into the public portion of the establishment.

For a bar, it was exceedingly quiet. On the other hand, the city was in the process of being evacuated. Still, Will expected some people to fortify themselves with some liquid protection so he expected something, even if it was tinny music from a bad speaker.

Will took point, accustomed to leading what was essentially an away mission. He placed his left hand flat against the swinging door and tested it. There was no resistance so he took one deep breath and pushed it open, quickly stepping into the bar proper.

There were identical highly polished, angular bars, each with attached stools. Glasses and mugs littered the tabletops and floor, lights continued to flash around what appeared to be the daily special, a bottle in the shape of a fat and happy Ferengi. A hologram danced at either end of the bar, a scantily clad Dorset woman, her hands moving in a complex pattern.

But no sound.

No movement.

Will's eyes scanned the room and saw that past the twin bars was an adjacent room with tables, chairs, and a slumped figure. He pointed to the doorway and silently waved his father to follow.

El Bison El, test subject for the greater good of Delta Sigma IV, was in a drunken stupor, half leaning atop a short round table. Four bottles of something red were stacked by his arms. A loud snore signaled he was asleep and Will let out his breath and grimaced at the sight. He didn't have to be a trained tactician to understand that this was a man who drank out of guilt, to wash away sorrow for something that was not at all his fault.

"What do we do with him?" Kyle asked in a whisper.

"We start by not whispering," Will replied. "Then we haul him up those stairs to the flyer. On our way out, we can see if they have something to help wake him up, maybe some coffee."

"Do you have a destination in mind?"

"The capital, of course. The chief medic is based there. She can begin a workup and then consult with Dr. Crusher."

"Bit of a flight," Kyle said, mentally making calculations.

"Well, you saw to it I couldn't signal the ship."

"Point taken," Kyle admitted. He clapped his hands together. "You want the arms or legs?"

"I was thinking left and right, should make it easier on the stairs," Will said. And without waiting for a reply, he bent over and grabbed a limp arm. With a tug, Bison moved like a rag doll, half falling out of his chair and interrupting the pattern of his snoring.

Together they struggled with Bison, especially as they took to the stairs, which were a little too narrow for them to handle Bison three abreast. Fortunately, he seemed totally oblivious to being manhandled so the men were perhaps rougher than necessary in moving him, but they finally got him to the top of the stairs.

As the hatch opened to the roof, Will was met with a rush of cold air and he blinked a few times to fight the sting. Once Kyle joined him on the roof, they were able to move more freely and got Bison into the flyer without delay. The two men strapped Bison into the one chair in the rear and then Kyle looked him over. There was stubble around his chin and he looked as if he hadn't bathed in days. His clothes were torn in spots, mud on one leg and something that may have been blood on the other.

"I'll power her up and you can look for that coffee," Kyle said, reaching for an overhead panel. His right hand was stopped by Will's own hand wrapping around Kyle's wrist.

"And let you fly out by yourself? I'm not a kid anymore. We'll go down together."

With a shrug, Kyle pulled his right arm free and rose from his seat. They left the flyer in silence and quickly returned to the bar. Will flipped on the computer mixmaster and checked its menu for non-alcoholic drinks. He didn't find coffee but did locate *raktajino,* which served the purpose just fine. Kyle had already turned up a thermos so they filled it to the brim with the Klingon brew. Grabbing three mugs, Kyle turned to leave. Will cleared his throat.

"What?"

"We have to pay for this," Will said. "Otherwise it's stealing."

Kyle fumed for a moment and then turned toward the door once more. "Sorry, son, I don't carry any native chits. I doubt they'll notice, and you can always send them something when this is over."

Will didn't like the notion nor did he see much in the way of alternatives. He mentally added it to the list of things his father needed to atone for.

Kyle took the flyer back into the sky minutes later. The sun had risen higher, the air getting warmer. It looked to be a sunny, cloudless day over the emptying city.

"Good work, son," Kyle said as the city receded.

Ignoring the compliment, Will poured some of the Klingon drink into a mug. He started to pour a second cup but realized his father couldn't take his hands out of the control sleeves. Shrugging, he capped the thermos and said, his voice cold, "Chalk up another success for Kyle Riker. You're still looking to balance the books, aren't you? What do we do when the flyer needs more power? Steal another? You'll just keep justifying to yourself that stealing in this case is the appropriate action. But guess what, Dad, you can't stop this."

Kyle looked straight ahead, jaw muscles tightening, clearly biting back a response. Will thought it interesting his father didn't want to renew the argument. Changing tactics, he said, "By the way, thanks for hitting me. Can you explain that one?"

Seconds passed and Will watched as Kyle adjusted their course, heading southeast now. The jaw muscles stopped marching across his face and he was going to wait the man out.

"If you called Picard, we wouldn't have found Bison."

"Bull. You want to stay out here, free. I want to know why. I think I deserve an answer."

Kyle remained silent, staring ahead and flying.

Will continued: "And without contact with the *Enterprise,* we have no way of knowing what else is happening. For all you know, there's a cure or civil war has broken out. So, where do you want to go if not the capital?"

"Old Iron Boots knew all about that war," his father said randomly.

His father was talking about Thaddeus Riker, a colonel for the northern forces during the American Civil War. Still, it wasn't like his father to bring up something that odd.

"He marched with Sherman, knew exactly where to go and what to do. Followed his orders and survived. We have to do the same. Save the people, repair the damage I caused. And we're going to do this together."

"This has grown beyond any one man's ability to solve."

"No, son, have you forgotten one of Starfleet's most important lessons: one man can make a difference."

"But that man, in this case, may not be you."

"I'm the man who fixes things," Kyle said defensively. Will heard the strain creep into his voice with increasing regularity. "The doctors got it wrong, did something to exacerbate the problem. I should have foreseen being ignored and done something differently when they were returned to the planet. Since I didn't . . . I . . . we . . . have to keep things in check."

"And you don't know how to fix this one, do you?"

There was a long silence. Neither looked at the other.

"No." Kyle's voice was rock hard.

Will struggled to modulate his tone, swallowing the bitterness he felt. In a softer tone he said, "Then let's go back to the capital. Let's work with Beverly and the doctors. Let's solve this together."

Over the years Will had heard his father angry, happy, determined and all the usual emotions one would expect of a father. But right now he heard something for the first time.

Guilt.

He was taken aback by the intensity of the feeling and desperately wished Troi was beside him to help understand the situation better. This was something she was more accustomed to dealing with, something he didn't necessarily feel anywhere near as qualified to handle.

Will grew worried about his father, hearing the mental stress in his voice and the message contained in the words. What had he missed, what signals did Will not see in his father's behavior the hours they'd spent together for this to seem so revelatory?

"You can't solve this alone, and we can't make that much of a difference by ourselves. This is a time for a team effort. If I know the captain, he has the doctor working on finding a cure and Lieutenant Vale coordinating emergency security efforts. We can join them and make our difference *there.*"

Kyle flew them in silence and Will began debating his chances at taking control of the ship, returning the favor and knocking out his own father. He'd been watching first Seer and now Kyle use the flyer and he was fairly certain he could master it without effort. But the conditions were cramped and given the strain his father placed on himself, there was no knowing how he'd react to being attacked.

Rather than risk crashing, Will decided he would next act when they were on land. Instead, he concentrated on getting through to his father, trying to make him see the reality of the situation.

"You said the chief of staff had you look into this. Where was the tactical advantage in a peaceful planet?"

"Ever hear the phrase 'If you could bottle the air, you'd make a fortune'?"

"I don't think so."

"It's archaic, I suppose," Kyle said, his voice sounding distant. "Once we figured out the people we drugged, the question was could the drug be used elsewhere."

"The Federation wanted to use it—for what?"

"Think about it, Willy. We were fighting the Dominion, and losing. We had to examine any and every option for fighting. Imagine being able to reduce the aggression in the Jem'Hadar."

And there it was. The Federation was ready to use drug warfare, as unethical as it sounded now; it probably sounded a whole lot less objectionable during those desperate days.

"But your studies . . . ?"

"Abandoned when they surrendered. We never figured out if the natural gases here could be synthesized. A dead end. Or so I thought until this disaster."

"Dad, can you see the futility in doing this alone? We won the war because of joint efforts. No mavericks, no Garths to do it single-handedly. Those days, I think, are gone. We've become too complex, too large a galaxy. Now, tell me, where are we going?"

"Back to the capital, I guess," Kyle said. There had been no course change, and Will studied the displays to gain some idea of their heading. He was surprised to realize his father had them aimed at the capital the whole time.

"All I ask is that I save one world," Kyle replied. "Is that so much?"

Will looked at the man, broken but determined, ready to risk everything to fix the unfixable. "No, Dad, not so much."

And the ship flew on.

It felt good to get off the bridge. That was the first thing on Kell Perim's mind as she worked with a detail to sort out a problem at a marketplace on Osedah. After watching the world spin on the main viewscreen for two straight shifts, she was bored. A part of her wondered if she was the fastest officer to volunteer when Captain Picard's announcement was made. Certainly, she was the first one to receive Commander Data's permission.

"I can understand your desire to do something proactive," he had told her. "I have frequently seen conn officers chafe in their seats during such missions. Do be careful."

She thought his final warning was sweet. Although he had turned over his emotion chip to Starfleet Command some months back, he was still caring and even compassionate. Commander La Forge had told her about what Data was like in the days before she signed on board, when his positronic matrix had not yet developed enough to properly handle the complex sensory input the chip would provide.

She hurried to transporter room two. While she enjoyed flying the starship and thought herself more than competent at the job, she envied those who frequently went on away missions. She imagined what it must be like to accompany Commander Riker or Data to the surface of a planet, either to explore or to handle a problem. Either would have been fine with her. Being the patient officer that she was, Perim had decided a few weeks earlier, after the *Enterprise* had completed its mission with the Dokaalan, that she would ask for some away duty during her next performance evaluation. After all those years as alpha shift helm officer, Perim thought she at least deserved consideration.

Nafir stood behind the controls as Jim Peart, security's second-in-command, issued instructions. Perim had worked alongside Peart. She considered him a handsome fellow and had more than once considered inviting him for a drink. He spotted her coming in and gave her a friendly smile.

"Kell, I'm placing you with Gracin's team. We have a marketplace that needs taming," he said, handing her a phaser. She hefted the device, trying to remember the last time she had used one. It was probably during the mandatory weapons proficiency evaluations six months earlier. Her test results were in the average range, which, considering she had rarely touched the weapon since the war, was good enough. She holstered it and looked at her comrades. Gracin was stocky, with short curly hair and a dimpled smile.

"Bring you back anything?" she asked Peart.

"No souvenirs on this trip," he said, all serious.

"You're taking all the fun out of my first away team mission," she said, and gave him an exaggerated pout.

"Come back alive and we can talk about . . . souvenirs," Peart said.

Gracin spoke up, cutting off her next comment. "We just know there's a problem, but nothing specific. It could be a shoplifter, or the entire place could be one free-for-all. Phasers remain holstered until we get the gist of the problem. We're spread thin, so if there's trouble, we're likely to be on our own. Perim, Goodnough, you follow my lead. Davila, you bring up the rear. Everyone, stay close."

Perim took a step toward the platform, then turned and flashed Peart her most dazzling smile. He almost did a double-take as he looked right into her eyes. There was a curiosity there; she could practically see him reevaluating her. *Damn, he's good-looking,* she thought.

"You bet I will," she replied, and quickly stepped on

to the transporter platform. Beside her was a female engineer, Goodnough, and then there was Gracin, looking grim and determined. Behind him stood another security officer, Davila. *Four against how many?* she wondered as they readied themselves.

Osedah was experiencing fall, Perim thought as she materialized. There was a familiar sting to the air, and sure enough, trees in the distance were dropping multihued leaves that fluttered on the soft breeze. Before them was a huge entranceway coated with signage, practically begging people to enter the bazaar. Food, spices, perfume, crafts, everything was promised, prices were reasonable, and no one would walk away unhappy.

No one was at the entrance. There was no one anywhere in sight. The bazaar—broad, one story tall, made out of canvas coverings affixed to metal posts—was located at the intersection of three roads, with plenty of space for local vehicles as well as a station nearby with what appeared to be a monorail track. Local time was late morning, so the Trill expected the place to be bustling. Of course, there was supposed to be a problem, so something must have scared the people away. She remembered her training and surveyed the scene using all of her senses. She couldn't hear any screams. The air smelled of cooking meats and something else, but nothing was burning. It was downright odd.

With a glance, she saw that Gracin was scanning the area with a tricorder, a frown etched across his face. It made her feel somewhat better to know that this situation baffled a more seasoned officer. Goodnough seemed confused, too, turning in slow circles, trying to figure out where the problem was.

"All life signs are clustered deep within the bazaar," Gracin finally said. "From what I can make out, the entire layout is designed to force shoppers all the way through the bazaar before they can leave. One pathway, blocked emergency exits."

"How many life signs?" Davila asked.

"Forty-two. A mix of Bader and Dorset, strong and vital. Okay, here's what we do: we work our way deep inside, slowly, and survey. Davila, you take the rear and keep your phaser at the ready. Everyone else, stay holstered."

Everyone acknowledged the order, and then Gracin spun on his left heel and strode forward with an air of confidence that Perim didn't share. Within seconds he was past the arch and inside the artificially lit structure. As Perim walked behind Gracin, she saw that to each side were low tables piled high with items for sale. On each metal post were prices, specials of the day, manager recommendations, every trick she had ever seen to get people to buy goods. There wasn't anything like this on her native world of Trill, but she had seen many such places while at the Academy on Earth and then on other worlds, from Farius Prime to Sherman's Planet. She missed the sounds of haggling, of people shouting with pride about their wares, of old friends reunited. The silence was more than disturbing, it was alarming.

As they hit the first bend, they went right, then a quick left. Whoever had been staffing these booths had left them in a hurry. Candles burned, a cash box lay atop a stack of garments. At one table she saw small carvings of

Bader children at play and idly thought that one might be nice for Peart, but knew there was no time for shopping. Along the way, the deeper they got, the more disheveled the tables were. Then they saw one overturned. Another left and they found one broken in half, the pottery once displayed on it broken into countless shards.

Gracin stopped so suddenly, the distracted Kell smacked into his broad shoulders. She immediately stepped back, biting her tongue from uttering an apology. With a quick hand signal, he communicated something to Davila and remained still. Finally, Kell heard the sobbing sound that must have alerted her squad leader. It sounded like a child. Kell knew that whole families usually worked these sorts of places, and it made her angry that children should be victimized by violence as well as adults.

Gracin began moving forward more slowly, his right hand just inches from the phaser still at his hip. He paused at a right-hand bend and peered around it, jerking back after only an instant. He waved the others close so he could speak in a whisper.

"The Dorset have all the Bader in a group. They're brandishing knives. I'd say an almost even split."

They all exchanged alarmed glances. That meant twenty or so weapon-bearing Dorset against just four Starfleet officers. Kell didn't like the odds at all and was wondering why she ever talked herself into beaming down, let alone volunteering. She flexed her knee, the one that had been troubling her for months now. Crusher kept pushing a mechanical replacement, but Perim had remained hesitant. It felt fine, but she feared it would give out on her while in action. With a violent shake of her head, she banished her fear, knowing full well she was trained for this sort of problem. She was in Starfleet for a reason, and saving lives was part of that. She would do her job and make Gracin and Data proud. Oh, and Peart too.

"Goodnough, Davila, you backtrack and come around to their position on the opposite side of the canvas," Gracin instructed in clipped tones as he handed the tricorder to his partner. "When you're in position, I'll startle them. We need to attack front and rear if we have any hope of saving these people."

Davila nodded once and tapped the tip of the phaser against his temple in a salute.

"Okay, Perim, ready to make a stand?"

"Give me the word," she replied.

"Good," he said, and turned his back, straining to listen as the other two retreated. Perim watched them hurry along, careful to step over broken items. She couldn't hear more than a scratch in the dirt, not loud enough to alert the Dorset.

"What are we going to do?" she whispered into Gracin's ear.

"I'll count down with my fingers. On my mark, we will emerge in their line of sight and immediately stun those closest to the Bader. You fire to your right. The phaser fire will be all the signal Davila needs. He will either fire on those trying to escape, or cut through the canvas and herd the Bader out."

"Wait, do you mean it's you and me against twenty?"

"Odds too small?" he asked with a tight smile.

"Odds too great," she countered. "You've never seen my scores." She hated the notion that her first mission would involve shooting a phaser. She would have preferred a rescue mission that didn't put people in harm's way. Once phasers were fired, people could panic and wind up in the path of a shot. Or be shot by frightened Dorset. But without backup, Gracin had little choice but to plan an offensive approach, and to be honest, she couldn't think of a better plan.

The seconds passed slowly. Perim saw that Gracin was not only concentrating on the sounds before him, but also mentally tracing Davila and Goodnough's path back out and around until they were in position. There was no way to signal one another without alerting the terrorists, so silence was their only option. Perim didn't doubt that Vale had trained her troops well during the days en route to Delta Sigma IV; she'd overheard enough reports to know the score results had pleased Captain Picard. If he trusted Vale and she trusted her people, then she was going to trust Gracin.

Finally Gracin was satisfied that the others were in position. He held up his left hand, fingers spread wide. Five. His other hand gripped his phaser, and it practically nodded toward her. She got the signal and withdrew her own weapon. The phaser felt heavy in her hand, and nervous sweat was already forming on her palm.

Four.

She checked the setting, satisfied it wouldn't slip from stun to disintegrate.

Three.

She ran her free hand through her hair, making sure it wouldn't fall into her eyes.

Two.

She took a deep breath and exhaled it slowly.

One.

She muttered a very short prayer.

Mark.

In a burst of motion, they rounded the corner and were firing before she had fully cleared the space. Some Dorset fell; others screamed. At least one attacked back, a knife flying close to her but missing.

Gracin fired at one, then another, with sure, true shots. Perim barely let go of her trigger, so the crimson beam was continuous, striking Dorset, pillars, a table. Things and people went flying, but fortunately, the Bader knew enough to stay down.

Sure enough, several Dorset used their knives to cut the canvas and try to escape. No sooner did a hole appear than a phaser beam cut through the air and knocked the would-be escaper backward over the shoulders of hunched-over Bader. Once the Dorset was in their midst, the former prisoners pummeled the man.

Davila was through the ragged space and firing as well. Goodnough scrambled through the sliced fabric right behind him, firing with much the same continuous motion Perim used. That made her feel better, but she suspected it wasn't by-the-book.

One Dorset, screaming something about Bader treachery, grabbed a woman by the hair and tried to slit her throat. Gracin threw himself over huddled Bader and grabbed for the man's knife hand. The two men grappled, and Perim took the opportunity to yank the woman out of the way. Then, when the Dorset man presented his back to Perim, she fired.

"Thanks. Duck!" he shouted.

Without hesitation, she bent her knees and dropped low, and he fired where she had been standing a moment before. Only then did she turn and watch a Dorset woman pinwheel backward into a table.

It wasn't long before the Dorset were rounded up, the Bader using whatever they could find to tie them up. The cacophony of voices gave Perim a headache. People were accusing one another of fomenting a rebellion, while others were hurling epithets at Starfleet and still more were crying over their destroyed belongings.

Davila gave her a smile and patted her shoulder, indicating he was pleased with her work. Goodnough sidled up to Perim and said, "Are all away missions like this?"

"No, from what I hear, they're an awful lot more dangerous."

And she couldn't wait until the next opportunity.

Picard was fuming. When he told his senior staff they were to convene in three hours, he didn't mean three hours and five minutes. Still, Crusher was missing, and she was the most important member of the staff, given the topic for discussion. Everyone was busy, and he hated pulling La Forge away from the engines—he really needed to ask about the plasma injector problem, but it wasn't immediately vital. Data was clearly running the ship effectively, but Picard hadn't taken the time to inquire as to the crew's mood. In fact, the captain had been falling more and more out of touch with everything but the Council, and they were moving with less than deliberate speed. He'd much prefer to handle things aboard the ship, but he had time for only the most important matters. He had hastily drunk a cup of soup while going through the last communiqués from Starfleet before checking in with the recovering Ambassador Morrow and then called down to verify that the Council halves had, as expected, done nothing while he was away.

Once that was clear, he asked Troi to come back aboard and do a fast analysis of Crusher's issues concerning her plant seeding scheme. The last thing he wanted was to approve a solution and then discover it would violate some cultural taboo. The concerned look in her eyes when she grasped the issue didn't tell him which side she favored, and maybe that was for the best.

Still, a part of him wanted to postpone the meeting until Riker had been found. The captain had become so used to having the first officer's insight that it felt wrong not to have him seated by his side. The hours had ticked by and any hope he had of a miraculous rescue evaporated, especially when Lieutenant Vale was the first to enter the observation lounge. She gave him a wan smile and a shrug of her shoulders.

Everyone who had been planetside looked exhausted, and Picard hoped that when this mission ended, Command would allow them some shore leave.

Finally, a whoosh of the doors and Crusher entered the room, hair flying, hands thrust deep into her lab coat pockets. She muttered apologies as she passed Picard and took her seat to his right.

"Everything okay, Doc?" La Forge asked.

"Fine," she said a bit breathlessly. "I was helping Tropp finish with a patient he rescued."

"The impaled one," La Forge added. "Nice work on that, I hear."

"She was a mess, but she'll live," Crusher finished.

"That's certainly good to hear," Picard said, regaining control of the room. All eyes turned his way, expectant. "After I present the facts, I will need everyone's considered opinion on what we do next. Either choice will have long-lasting consequences to both races.

"The liscom gas Dr. Crusher discovered in the bloodstream has acted like a narcotic. It has effectively drugged these people into peacefulness. They grew up believing their history, which says it was an enlightened view of the universe that led to the peaceful colonization of Delta Sigma IV. They were wrong. The gas also altered their life cycles, accelerating them so they are now dying off at a faster than normal rate.

"What Starfleet Medical discovered was a cure for the aging but totally missed the tranquilizing effects of the gas in the natives' systems. Their cure neutralized the gas's soporific effects, and the natives reverted to their true natures. As you know, those natures are anything but peaceful and cooperative. And the cure has spread like a virus, igniting the violence that has become our preoccupation.

"From what the doctor has determined, these people have never experienced such feelings before and are completely untrained in handling the emotions coursing through them."

"There's more to it than that," Troi interrupted. Picard nodded for her to continue. "All the more extreme emotions were suppressed, which not only led them to peaceful cohabitation but also stunted their emotional growth. I took a quick look at their native music, art, and literature. It's all very basic and bland. As some of us have noted, their buildings are not very interesting to look at. It's because they lacked the passion for creativity. The inability of the government to act during this crisis also seems to be a by-product of the liscom gas. On their original homeworlds, those natural aggressive tendencies had been channeled into governance and creativity. Once those abilities were removed by the liscom gas, the spark was essentially snuffed out."

"I didn't think two races could be so boring," Morrow chimed in from the rear of the room. Picard shot him a look, and the ambassador slumped a little lower in the seat. The captain noted that the man looked healthier than before, which was good since he would need his help before this mission ended.

Picard continued after another moment. "What Dr. Crusher has determined is that we could let things remain as is, let the people belatedly come to grips with their natural tendencies, learning through experience and living out their normal lives, or she can introduce something that would neutralize the liscom gas's effects on the chromosomes, letting them live peacefully but keeping them drugged.

"Neither the doctor nor I want to make this decision ourselves. We certainly can't expect the divided Council to make an informed choice. Therefore, I now open the floor to debate. While I'd like to give this a proper airing, time is definitely against us."

Picard stopped and let his words sink in. As expected, Data, without an emotional filter, was the first to speak.

"Captain, if these people formed a peace that led to membership in the Federation under altered circumstances, does it not follow that the Bader and Dorset governments should be consulted?"

Picard looked at Morrow, glad to have immediate input from the Diplomatic Corps, especially from one who had spent some time with the people involved. Morrow sat up straighter, wincing as his left hand gently rubbed one of the almost-healed ribs.

"That is one course of action, certainly, but not a required one. The gas is a natural phenomenon, so the situation is much different than if they all ingested something illegal, like Red Ice. In fact, both governments might see this as a way to press their claim to the planet, which in turn might ignite a new conflict, and the citizens below would be caught in the middle."

"So you would not suggest that approach?"

"No, Mr. Data." Picard inwardly winced at the simplicity of expression on Data's face. He missed having his second officer complete with emotions, and he suffered on his friend's behalf since, after all, Data couldn't fully comprehend his loss.

"My chief concern," Crusher observed, "is that by administering yet another element into the ecosystem I'm treating people who are not technically sick. I'm changing them permanently because of my own moral system."

"But don't we recognize the need to change the status quo because it's killing them?" La Forge said. "Left as they are, either they'll kill each other or the survivors will die prematurely. Let the liscom gas take hold once more, they'll just die more slowly."

"Death either way is no solution," Troi said.

"Starfleet Medical's code of ethics isn't clear on this sort of subject," Crusher said. "I spent some time checking on it, while Moq finished the simulation. Still, I cannot in good conscience risk changing these people again, possibly for the worse. They tested five subjects for almost a year, and you'd have me introduce my 'cure' immediately, with no test subjects at all."

"So noted, Doctor," Picard said, wondering what Riker would think about all this.

"Sir," Vale spoke up. "I have people down there giving their lives to preserve a peace that maybe never should have existed at all. Maybe the best course of action is to abandon the world entirely. It's toxic to both races."

"I'm not sure either of the original homeworlds would welcome back the descendants of those who left," Morrow said. "Checking would take time, which I'm told we do not have."

"Besides, this ship isn't big enough for the population. Even with the other ships in nearby sectors, it still wouldn't be enough," La Forge said.

"We can't introduce this without at least telling the Council about it," Troi said. "And I have no real sense that they will accept what they consider further meddling on our part. A central theme of the protests has been an objection to the Federation's role."

"I think it's safe to say that few are left who might be considered to be in their right minds," Morrow said.

"On the contrary," Data interjected. "By now the majority of the planet has had their minds restored to what would be considered proper by any medical authority."

"Quite right, Data," Picard said solemnly. "But in so doing, we've unleashed a firestorm of unrest that will certainly claim countless more lives before we have any hope of restoring order."

"Captain, what would it take to do just that?" Troi asked.

Picard looked at Vale. "Lieutenant?"

"Well, let's see," Vale began, her brow furrowing. "We'd need thousands of peace-keeping troops to keep everyone from arguing and fighting. That would mean using troops, who are more used to ground actions than police work. Then, the Diplomatic Corps, I suppose, would need to send hundreds of teachers or psychologists to give them the kind of moral training that most people receive as they grow up. And, given that both races naturally tend to be aggressive, there would probably be resistance to being taught how to behave. The majority are adults, after all, so they would resist training."

"Following that scenario, sir," Data said, "I would estimate it would take seventeen months three weeks and five days before enough personnel were on this planet to make an effective difference."

"Thank you, Mr. Data," Picard said.

"What you're missing," Morrow said, "is that we don't have hundreds of people available today. With the rebuilding going on throughout the Federation, plus the aid we've been giving the Cardassians and to the Genesis sector, we're stretched beyond thin."

"And I gather there are other hot spots brewing, as always, where our forces might be required," Vale added.

"It seems there's a chance for peace to properly take root," Morrow muttered.

"Too true, Ambassador," Picard said. "Our corner of the universe has so many intelligent races that there will probably always be some form of trouble. However, history has shown us that things do change, usually for the better. The Klingons became our allies after decades of carnage, and recently even the Romulans proved helpful in our war with the Dominion. One can only hope the Praetor has learned some lessons and one day they too may be called our friends."

"I hope you're right," Vale said.

"We clearly do not have the manpower this world needs, so we're faced with our original choices," Crusher said.

"Any further opinion?" Picard paused and was met with expectant looks. "Very well, then. I will consider all that you have said and will issue my orders shortly. For those of you heading back to the planet, I suggest you take advantage of being here to eat and clean up before returning. Dismissed."

Everyone stood, and Picard let them all pass by as they headed either to the bridge or the corridor. In their faces he saw a mixture of concern and confidence. He and Beverly exchanged a long look that he had no trouble reading. He knew her heart, her reluctance to tamper with an already afflicted people. She looked exhausted, in desperate need of sleep, but he found himself noting how attractive she was despite the strain. He shoved that stray thought aside and remained in the lounge as the doors closed. Taking his seat once more, he gazed out among the stars and let the arguments echo again in his mind.

A stray spark caused Anh Hoang to drop her tool. It fell ten meters to the ground and reverberated with a loud clang. People scattered, some automatically putting their hands over their heads while others scurried into doorways, seeking shelter.

"It's all right, I just dropped the spanner," she called out.

"You must be more careful with your tools," Taurik said. He appeared completely unruffled, which was to be expected. She envied that self-control, the ability to remain calm regardless of the madness surrounding them both. Her team had beamed down to the city—she'd already forgotten its name—an hour earlier. Taurik had requested additional engineering help to repair damage to the power generators. His team had consisted of himself, a sociologist, and a security officer who professed to being completely unskilled with tools. As a result, Taurik had tried to handle the repairs while the other two kept watch at the main entrance.

Hoang had beamed down with Cobbins, a tall, painfully thin black woman from security, and Chafin, a gamma-shift maintenance worker. Immediately, Cobbins had gone to plan with her colleague from security while Chafin had ambled over to the sociologist, whose name Hoang couldn't remember. It didn't matter, since she had to concentrate on helping Taurik with the mess that was the main control panels. A mob had managed to get past the local peace officers. Their rampage through the building had caused a cascade effect that robbed the city of light and power. Fortunately, the weather was warm, so heat wasn't an immediate issue.

While Taurik had set to work deep within the machinery, Hoang had clambered up a ladder and begun checking connections between the control panels and the generators. Things seemed fine; no one had bothered to climb this high just to cause trouble. However, several connections had been jarred loose, spoiling the alignment, and she was working with the spanner to set things aright.

"Do you require assistance?"

"No thanks, Taurik," she called out. "One of the lines sparked. I've got it tightened down."

"But your spanner is still on the ground."

"I improvised." She grinned and held up a different tool, similar in length to the spanner.

"It is not recommended," he said dryly.

"No, but it sure beat climbing back down and then back up just to tighten this up. Besides, I'm done up here. I was about to come down anyway."

"Acknowledged." Without another look up, he turned and resumed his work. By then, the others had realized they were in no danger and resumed their posts. Cobbins felt that all doorways should be manned until the sensitive work was done. Chafin took the doorway least likely to be used while Cobbins took the main entrance. While they watched the streets, the security team tidied up the place, collecting the debris into one area.

Hoang climbed down and put her hands on her hips, staring at the control panels. With many of the interfaces shattered, she could either create new temporary interfaces, just to give the controllers something to work with when they returned to maintain the facility, or simply jury-rig everything to run at a steady cycle until new panels could be properly fabricated. On the *Enterprise,* she knew La Forge would prefer interfaces that would enable him to control the flow. For a city, there was less of a varied need for power. She had charts that showed the peak use periods, so she could rig everything with a timer and the machinery would virtually run itself, allowing the staff to rebuild or help elsewhere. Neither solution was elegant, but to her mind, it didn't matter. Once they left, the building would be vulnerable again, and who was to say the mob wouldn't return and destroy things all over again?

No, better to get it up and running in a steady state, leaving the fine-tuning to the local engineers. That decided, she reached into her tool kit and withdrew a padd with a complete set of schematics of the station. There were wiring charts that enabled her to understand where she could reroute power, and she lost herself in thought as solutions presented themselves. A small part of her mind appreciated the work, the distraction from the more exacting problem of replacing the plasma injector and from her personal troubles.

Her brief conversations with Counselor Troi over the last few days had forced her to look at the life she was leading and to question her career choices. Having made the decision to leave Earth and serve on the *Enterprise*, she didn't wish to reevaluate it, but sure enough, she was doing just that. And by thinking of Earth, she was reminded that the bodies of her family were back there, the remains reduced to a few ounces of ash kept in ceramic urns kindly provided by Starfleet. Her apartment had been destroyed in the Breen attack, so she didn't even have a proper place to display them. They were carefully wrapped in silk cloth and locked away with her few other mementos in Starfleet storage until she found a new home. It never occurred to her to bring the urns with her aboard the *Enterprise.* They would only remind her of just how much she had lost during the war.

Carefully, she wrapped her index finger around a loose connection and pulled it, detaching it from the wrecked innards of the station. It was a dull green and frayed in spots. If there were time, it could be replaced, but Hoang suspected such niceties would have to wait. She reached in for the bright yellow wire that was its mate and heard Taurik working farther away. For not the first time, she idly wondered if she should ask him for some tips on keeping painful memories at bay, but once more rejected the idea. This was her life and she would have to deal with it in her own way.

With the two wires now exposed, she was able to reach in and carefully remove the damaged isolinear chips that controlled most of the power flow. These would have to be replaced, she realized, and carefully built a stack of them. So lost in the work was she that it only slowly dawned on her that there were new sounds in the facility. Angry sounds.

The mob was returning, she concluded, suppressing a shiver. She looked over her shoulder toward the main door and saw that Cobbins had taken charge, repositioning the few Starfleet personnel available.

"Keep working," she snapped at Hoang with a powerful voice that belied her small frame. "Finish and we can get out of here. How long do you and Taurik need?"

"I'm not sure," she said in a surprisingly small voice. It was a voice she didn't want to hear anymore.

"Well, keep at it!" Without waiting for a response, she jogged toward a supply closet, looking for something.

Hoang continued to work, forcing herself to focus on each chip as she removed it, inspecting it for flaws and adding the chip to the growing stack. There were far more damaged chips than she expected, which implied a deeper problem within the control station.

Despite the work at hand, she paused for several moments and listened to the noise outside, finally recognizing it as similar to the sounds of panic she heard in the streets of San Francisco, when the Breen ships came to rain fire and death. Her fingers twitched at the memory, losing their grip on a chip. It tumbled to the concrete floor, shattering on impact.

Beverly hated waiting. She had waited for Jack to come back from his mission, but he had never returned. She had waited for Wesley to come back from his journey with the Traveler, only to have him make a brief visit and vanish again. She was waiting for this damned mission to end so she could talk to Jean-Luc about her future. And right now, she was waiting for him to summon her to his ready room and make his decision known.

After leaving the captain's conference, she had checked with the nurses on the status of the few patients remaining in sickbay. With violence escalating on the planet, she was more than a little surprised to see so few serious injuries among the crew. Like the other department heads, she hadn't stopped a single crewmember from volunteering to go planetside and help out. But with so many inexperienced people below, she had naturally estimated a higher incidence of injuries.

That left her with little to do until the decision came. So, she sat at her desk and began completing patient reports and delved into the paperwork that was so vital to future needs but so deadly dull in the present. Whatever dent she could make, she knew, would be helpful in the days ahead.

And yet, she continued to feel uncertain. Rarely had she and Picard been on opposite sides of a debate, and this disagreement came at a time when she was thinking of moving away from him—no, away from the ship. She knew Starfleet Medical offered a lot of opportunities and would give her access to colleagues she rarely saw in the flesh. Still, the *Enterprise* remained in the forefront of exploration, encountering more new life-forms and more cosmic conundrums than could ever be experienced on a single planet. And the ship had become her home.

So lost in thought was she that it took the sound of a throat-clearing cough to make her look up. Picard stood there, a sympathetic look on his face. He took a seat opposite her and waited for her full attention.

She saw the answer in his eyes. The set of his firm jaw.

"You're ordering me to introduce my cure," she said quietly.

He nodded. "I've been through the arguments several times, Beverly. Clearly, this planet and its people do not have the luxury of time. You will give them that time and let them live."

"But live what kind of life? Emotionally and creatively stunted?"

"Until now, they were happy and proud. That should be the same when this is over," he said. "The Federation opened their eyes to one problem, and you are giving them the time to decide their fates for themselves."

"When the new plant life is introduced into the environment, it needs to be as pervasive as the liscom. We've already determined that eradicating that plant was impractical. The same will be true for this plant. What choice are we really giving them?"

Picard folded his hands on her desk, leaning forward. His voice was that of a captain making a hard choice, and she felt some sympathy for the position she helped put him in. "The choice to take a long-term approach to their planet. I keep coming back to that. It's not for you or me or even the Federation to decide. They can keep your solution or systematically eradicate it. But they will be choosing for themselves, as it should be."

"But they have tasted these emotions," she countered. "Who knows how this will affect their future?"

"Not us, certainly," he agreed in a sympathetic voice. "But you're offering them a future, which is more than they'll have if we do nothing. Have the simulations been double-checked?"

"Yes, of course," she replied, putting on her business voice. "Moq is certain we have it right."

"Begin synthesizing the compound. I'll recall our best pilots and prepare the shuttles to begin seeding the world. I need to inform the Council. Do you want to be there to help explain matters?"

Crusher considered, mentally delegating work to Tropp and Moq, imagining having to explain the problem and the cure to the two Councils. Then she imagined Picard or Troi trying to do that and she nodded her head slowly. "I found the answer, I should be the one to explain it."

"You sound like you're admitting to a crime, which this is not," he said with true sympathy in his voice.

"No matter how you explain this, Jean-Luc, I do not feel good about what we're about to do," she replied.

He gave her that sympathetic look again, which this time made her want to scream. Picard then got up, clearly done with his task. At least he had the courtesy to give her the bad news in her own office.

Chapter Seven

"WHAT'S THAT SMELL?"

Will was startled by the thick, husky voice. He turned his head and studied the waking form of El Bison El. The once-drunk man was stirring and studying his predicament.

"More importantly, I guess is: where am I?"

"You're with me," Kyle said. "Remember me?"

"Rugan. Ruken. Rucker."

"Riker."

"Yeah, that's it," the man said, his voice still slowed by drink. "You tied me up."

"Didn't want you to hurt yourself," Kyle said without looking back.

Bison looked once more at his bindings, shrugged and tried to get comfortable. He winced once or twice and then focused on Will.

"Who're you?"

"William Riker, first officer of the Starship *Enterprise.*"

"That's a long name. You guys related?"

"I've been asking myself that question for years," Will said, earning him a disapproving look from his father. "Why have you been running?"

"I murdered Unoo."

His voice implied remorse, which Will appreciated. Sympathetically, he nodded and said, "Yes, you did." He poured some of the *raktajino* into a mug and handed it over. Bison had just enough mobility to accept the drink and reach it to his lips. He smelled it, wrinkling his nose and started to lower it. One glare from Will and he picked up the mug and took a sip.

"She was a pain in the ass. And this drink tastes like dirt."

"And she deserved to die?"

"No, but she was still a pain." Another sip. "And this mud needs a kick."

"I can agree she was a pain," Kyle added, and Will returned the angry look.

"So why did you grab me? To take me back for more experiments? Maybe carve out a bit of my brain this time? Well, this time there'll be a fight. Count on it."

Will and Kyle exchanged glances, the younger man concerned with the rage he saw in Bison's eyes. He had expected remorse for the murder of Unoo, but there wasn't even a hint of that now.

"We've come to take you with us," Kyle said. "No more experiments. No more tests or drugs."

"And I can take your word for it, eh? You, my jailer?"

Kyle didn't let the barbs bother him and he remained steadfast in dealing with Bison.

"Take my word or not, you will come with us."

Bison pulled on his restraints, careful not to spill his drink. "And where might we three be traipsing off to?"

"Back to the capital. To the chief medic."

"Can't come up with a good enough lie, can you? So it is back for more tests. Federation cretin. I have a good mind to bring legal action against you and your president."

"He's your president, too." Kyle's tone indicated that he wasn't amused by Bison.

"Didn't vote for him," the Dorset commented.

"Doesn't matter," Will said, getting frustrated by the lack of control he had over the situation. "If we say you're to come with us, then that's what you'll do."

"And stand trial for what . . . for what I did to Unoo? No thank you!"

Will looked over at Kyle, who remained still, taking in the exchange, his face unreadable.

"Plenty of flyers in the capital," he said.

Before Will could ask him what he meant, the flyer violently shook. There was a loud sound as metal was punctured and they began to fall. The feeling in Will's stomach did nothing to help his mood.

"We're going down," Kyle yelled. He punched at controls as Will gripped the armrests and studied the monitors. Sensors were limited and he suddenly missed being on the *Enterprise* bridge. Something had fired on them but he couldn't tell what or from where.

He glanced back at Bison; he was finishing his drink and then dropped the mug, his hands also gripping the chair's arms.

"Can you stabilize it?" Will asked his father.

"Shut up and let me try," Kyle snapped. His arms jerked and twisted and Will couldn't see what he was doing. They wobbled for another few moments and then his father must have found a way to steady them. Still, they were descending so Will was thinking ahead. There were three of them, with no weapons and not a lot of experience on this world. He had no clue what Bison would do.

The former test subject chose that moment to get violently ill in the back of the flyer. If the *raktajino* smelled bad, this was far worse.

"One hundred meters," Kyle called out. "Brace yourselves. Fifty. Thirty-five. Twenty."

The flyer crushed the ground beneath it as it heavily met the earth. Will had seen from the windows that they were in a heavily wooded area, with no town in sight. They were isolated and, of course, unable to communicate. He'd survived worse landings and even before the ship settled into position, he was unstrapping himself. Free, he spared a look at the sick Bison and then his father. Kyle seemed to be staring at the dead controls. Will gritted his teeth.

"We need to get out of this ship," Kyle said.

"Yeah, it stinks back here," Bison said.

Will activated the door hatch and it slid open. He listened for a moment, hearing some form of insect life outside and a breeze through the trees.

As he cleared the doorway, Will was stopped short. Five men circled the flyer, several brandishing weapons more sophisticated than mere sticks. Kyle followed him out and stopped right behind his son. He then took a step, was suddenly beside him, ready for a fight, his feet firmly planted in the dirt, hands balled into fists. Bison, now free of his bindings, remained maybe half a step behind the elder Riker and didn't seem ready to run. In fact, he looked ready to fight.

"Looks like we shot ourselves some Federation folk," one man said in a slight twang.

"You here to pollute the lake? Or maybe take your new friend for some testing?"

They continued their jibes, and Will admired his father for not answering back and not making the first move. He was taking their measure, just as Will was doing. The men, a mix of Bader and Dorset, looked middle-aged and not top condition. Their weapons, though, gave them an edge, but with his own training, Will suspected he could disarm one or two to even the odds. His father and Bison, though, would be wild cards. There was no opportunity to even whisper instructions, so Will had to control the situation.

"You shot us down," Will said. "We intended to fly right by and ignore you."

That answer didn't please them at all. The men continued to hurl jibes but were now taking slow steps toward the trio. Kyle remained where he was, but Bison had taken a step to the left, either removing himself from the obvious targets or preparing to engage the men himself. Will couldn't move too quickly for fear of inciting a fight, but he needed to get closer. He too began taking small steps forward, but he kept his hands open, trying to convey that he wasn't looking for a confrontation.

"I know you won't believe me," he said as a way of distracting them from his movement. "But we're not here to cause trouble, pollute the lake, or any of the other things you've accused us of."

"Liar!" shouted one of the men. Another raised what looked to Will like it was a phase pistol, an ancient model nearly two hundred years old. There was no way to tell if it was an antique that would blow the man's hand off or if it was a perfectly maintained heirloom that was capable of hurting them all.

Will looked around for an advantage and saw none. The space between them was level, a mix of dirt and straggly brown grass. Nothing to grab for offense or defense, so it was going to be man versus weapon, Will concluded.

A Bader man also raised his weapon, taking aim squarely at Kyle. He was saying nothing, but hatred smoldered in his eyes.

Will judged there were maybe five meters separating them now. The Bader man kept his weapon aimed at Kyle, but Will noted that the other armed man seemed less certain of his target, wavering between Bison, who remained still, and Will. To contain the situation, Will would have to make the first move. He ran several scenarios in his mind. None of them were elegant, none of them would end in clean victories, but most would get the job done.

Sucking in the cooling air, Will let out a shallow breath and then strode forward, drawing attention to himself. Sure enough, the five men started toward him, all weapons now aimed his way. As soon as they had formed a semicircle before him, Will carefully studied their positioning. Kyle and Bison remained in their places, which was perfect.

Suddenly, Will lunged to his left, grabbing the outstretched arm and pistol of the Bader who had the loud voice. He whipped the man around, smashing him into the man next to him while at the same time kicking his right leg backward into the gut of the man in the center. He didn't expect the other armed man to be foolish enough to fire into the cluster of bodies.

Disengaging himself, Will unleashed a punch to a Dorset still standing, and suddenly his father rushed past his left, Bison to his right. The rest of the fight was brief, since after one more punch, Will scrambled back and grabbed the phase pistol. He backed far enough away to get them in a single sweep if need be.

"Enough!" he bellowed, causing everyone to look his way. As soon as Kyle saw the situation, he let go of the man he held and dropped him to the ground. He bent and picked up the other pistol, which had been lying, forgotten, in the dirt. Bison was entangled with his own opponent, and it took him a moment to free himself and stand.

"I think we've all had enough!" The men picked themselves up and moved over, one rubbing an elbow, another trying to stop a bloody nose.

"We'll be leaving now," he said. With a jerk of his head, he indicated for Kyle to take Bison toward the flyer.

"Son, you do know that ship isn't going anywhere," Kyle said softly.

"We have to get away from them, it was just a direction," Will said.

"The woods, then," Bison suggested.

"They know these better than us, don't you think?" Will asked sarcastically.

"Actually," Kyle started, "we have nowhere else to go. Our transport is dead and they don't seem to have any. They must live nearby, which means they probably have friends. Going deeper into the woods makes the most sense."

"Any particular direction?" Will asked.

"You went to school for navigation. Look up."

Will did as instructed, momentarily feeling as if he were eight again, and then shrugged it off. He looked at the day sky, estimating the sun's path and position, remembering their heading before they were blown out of the sky. For a moment he used his senses, ignoring Bison's muttering. The wind rustled the trees, moving north to south, slowly so it would keep them cool. The sun was heading west and there was a distinct lack of animal noise. The crash and subsequent fight chased everything away, but that wouldn't last. They had to get started.

"That way," Will said, pointing in a northwesterly direction.

Without a word the men began hiking. Quickly, Will ticked off what they had and did not have. No communicator, no rations, no water. Given their relative physical condition, they would need frequent rests. He'd have to find them something to drink along the way and also sustenance. Well, most forests had something to offer; they'd just have to be on the lookout.

"I don't suppose you know which berries or fungi might be edible," Will asked Bison after several minutes.

"I'm an economist," Bison said glumly.

"Lot of good that's going to do us out here," Kyle grumbled. "Looks like it's up to you and me to get us through this."

Will didn't reply and kept marching, keeping in the lead.

"Nice fighting," Kyle finally said nearly half an hour later.

"Thanks," he said and was amazed at the ease of the compliment, something that rarely came from his father in years past. "This changes nothing," Will added several moments later. "We still need to contact the captain."

Kyle nodded slowly, eyes ahead.

Will couldn't help but feel apprehensive about their random flight around Delta Sigma IV. He'd feel much better with the capital in sight. Until then, all he felt was the sense of disaster looming over them.

"You used your head," Kyle continued. "Guess you did learn a few things along the way."

And Kyle was right, but Will wasn't ready to admit it. One of the things Kyle had drilled into him during fishing trips, hikes, and even housecleaning was the need to anticipate, think, and then act. Will had been doing so ever since, and not once had he given his father credit for teaching him. And even now, he couldn't bring himself to admit his debt. After all, learning to think didn't erase the resentment he felt for being manipulated or abandoned.

"You've been right since you found me," Kyle suddenly said sometime later. Will had been letting his tired mind drift, short of getting sleep, so he almost missed the comment. What attention he had was directed toward finding them water. If Bison had gotten himself that thoroughly drunk, he'd be needing rehydration more than either Riker. But eventually, all three would need it.

He turned and looked at Kyle, who set his jaw and stared ahead.

"This is mostly my fault, my doing, and I can't hold a crumbling world together in just my hands."

Will wasn't sure he was hearing the man properly. The earlier tone of guilt was missing from the voice, which was clear and matter-of-fact.

"Doing all that flying, and now hiking, it's given me time to think. Seeing you has also made me think of the years gone by, the opportunities lost. I wish I could explain how I can help wage a war but not stay in touch with my own son."

"Or sons."

"Thomas. Right. When Ann died, my hope for a second child died with her. And then to have you come in out of the blue with that preposterous story, well . . . well, I acted badly."

"You took the news horribly, and that was the last time we spoke," Will reminded him.

"Have you seen him?"

"Not since he was taken captive before the war."

"They must have freed him by now from Lazon II." Will was startled by Kyle's knowledge of exactly where Thomas was imprisoned, seemingly for life, for his actions as a member of the Maquis terrorist group. His father was more aware of the situation than Will ever gave him credit for. Had he tried to have Thomas released to the Federation? As far as Will was concerned, his "twin" could remain on Lazon II.

"If so, then he's kept to himself, and to be honest, I think that's for the best. Everything he did leading to his arrest goes against everything I ever learned. Everything you taught me."

"And taught him, right?"

"He shares those memories," Will said tightly. Thomas's impersonation of Will and his theft of the *U.S.S. Defiant* to aid the Maquis still didn't make sense to him. Was being trapped on Nervala IV for eight years enough to make Thomas turn against all his ideals?

"You and he didn't agree on things, did you?"

"No. We both wanted Deanna, and he resented my promotion."

"And you and I didn't agree on much," Kyle added softly.

"No."

"I've made some mistakes over the years. Big ones, ones that cost people their lives. But letting our disagreements keep us apart, that has to be my biggest mistake. I didn't know what to do with you after a while . . ."

"So you left," Will finished. "Left me to finish growing up on my own."

"And I regret that now, although it's too late to change anything."

Will felt uncomfortable, not only with the frankness of the conversation, but with the fact that Kyle was willing to engage in it with Bison silently listening behind them. But his father was being open and honest, something that hadn't happened in a Will's memory. They talked about walls on Kyle's one visit to the *Enterprise*, and no sooner was there a crack than the wall was repaired. Now it seemed to be all tumbling down. Wasn't that what he wanted? Longed for during the loneliest years?

Before speaking, Will heard something. He put up a hand and they stopped, feet shuffling in the dirt. Turning on a heel, he moved in a circle, making sure he wasn't imagining it. A tinkle of sound. Water. Kyle had caught the noise, too. Their eyes met and it was Kyle who pinpointed the direction.

Within minutes, they found a small stream. Will bent low and cupped his hands in the cool, flowing water. It was chilled but felt terrific. He sipped some and it was refreshing. No doubt filled with minerals that might cause him trouble later, but for now, they all needed refreshment.

Each man rinsed his hands and then drank his fill. The rest did them well but Will didn't want them taking their time. The sun was heading for the horizon and he didn't relish the notion of being alone in the dark forest. He hadn't read up on natural predators but he knew they existed. Now was not the time to make their acquaintance.

They resumed their walk and Will was gratified to see their pace had picked up.

"A lot of it has been my fault," Will finally admitted once they were under way. "After you came aboard, we finally started to talk and then I never followed up. Kept letting duty get in the way."

"Chip off the old block," Kyle said sardonically. He adjusted their angle and he was silent for a time, concentrating on flying.

Will finally agreed. "True, but one of us had to change the pattern and it should have been the younger dog learning the new trick."

"So, now I'm an old dog."

Will wasn't sure, but thought he saw a smile cross his father's face.

"I'm not sure what you're looking for in a father,

Willy," Kyle began, nodding in agreement. "I'm not sure what kind of a father I can be at this stage, but we can try."

"We'll never agree on everything. Nor should we," Will added. "But that hasn't kept people apart. You should see some of the fights Deanna has had with her mother."

There, Kyle was actually smiling at the name. He hadn't seen his father this loose before, actually enjoying a conversation. Will wasn't certain what had changed between them, but the tension in his gut was also evaporating.

"Ah, the bewitching Lwaxana. A force of nature, that woman."

Will's eyes widened. "Have you two met?"

"Once or twice. You don't do my kind of work without coming across the daughter of the Fifth House . . ."

". . . Holder of the Sacred Chalice of Rixx . . ." Will added.

"And heir to the Holy Rings of Betazed," they completed together, and both let out a chuckle.

"You know, Deanna says the chalice is really a moldy old pot, although I've never seen it for myself," Will added between laughs.

"I'm sure she's exaggerating," Kyle said.

"Who, Deanna or Lwaxana?"

"Deanna, I think."

"Sounds like some woman," Bison offered.

"Shut up," Kyle said.

They walked along in silence until Kyle asked, "Still mooning over her?" For the first time in a while, Kyle stopped looking ahead and gazed seriously at his son. And it didn't bother Will.

"I wouldn't call it mooning. We've sort of started over again."

"For real this time?"

"It's always been real. But this time I think it's for good."

Kyle's brows knit together as he pondered that. "You let duty get in the way last time, didn't you?"

"How'd you know?"

"Because it kept me from marrying again. Kept me and Kate Pulaski apart. You're more like me than you'd ever admit," Kyle said, a touch of wistfulness in his voice.

"I've heard that."

One of the aides walked over and handed a councillor a glass of water. They leaned their heads together and exchanged a few words before the aide departed the room. Watching from a corner of the cramped office, Deanna Troi suspected the aide was off to share information with the opposing office. With a satisfied smirk, she concluded that not every member of the Council agreed with Jus Renks Jus's decision to split the body along racial lines.

On the other hand, she grew concerned that with every passing hour, the contagion was more likely to find its way to every Bader and Dorset in the building. She shuddered at the notion of a ruling body that was already fundamentally divided along racial lines giving full rein to their aggressive natures.

Still, it was going to be some time before Crusher was ready to deploy her cure. Personally, Troi sided with the captain, but she sympathized with her friend. It was a terrible decision that had to be made under severely adverse conditions. She admired Picard for at least having the debate and airing the issue before rendering a decision. He always welcomed input, regardless of circumstance. It was just one of the many reasons she appreciated her job aboard the *Enterprise.*

Naturally, her mind was tugged toward the future after Beverly told her she might pursue the soon to be vacant position of surgeon general. When Deanna was alone, she pondered her own career. After Beverly had gotten some command experience, Deanna too had passed the rigorous command tests. A few years back, during the gateways crisis, she even briefly commanded a much smaller ship, the *Marco Polo,* and had come to enjoy the work. Since then, she had considered where she wanted her career to go. She certainly didn't want to work on a planet or a space station; she enjoyed being aboard a starship and encountering the unexpected. She wasn't sure if she got that from her father's experiences in Starfleet or her mother's wanderlust. Probably both, she concluded. Still, the day was coming when Starfleet would succeed in breaking up Picard's command crew. The first chip was the posting of Worf to Deep Space 9. Since then, they tried again in the wake of the Dominion War, arguing that experienced command personnel were in short supply, but Picard called in favors and kept everyone together. But if Crusher left for Starfleet Medical, that was only going to encourage Command. And Will should be getting his own command at last.

Will. Her *Imzadi* had always wanted a ship of his own, but he had turned down offer after offer because he was learning so much by working alongside Picard. Yet lately he had been posted to temporary commands, first the *Enterprise,* then the *Excalibur,* and most recently the *Enterprise* again. He was ready—she knew it and she knew Command knew it. Deep down, she knew he'd take that next offer, and then where would she go?

Their relationship ended the first time because Will put duty and desire for command ahead of love. Would he do that a second time? They were older, different people today, and she privately hoped they would remain together. But would there be a place for her on Will's new ship? As counselor or even—dare she ponder the possibility?—first officer? Was that the track she wanted? She felt ready for new challenges, but the next step after first officer was usually captain, and starship captains were more distanced from the crew. Was that something she desired?

Too many possible paths to properly consider at this moment. Instead, she had to tuck her aspirations away and concentrate on the here and now. The councillors continued to do little more than direct relief efforts and try to find ways to assign blame. They all had their own pet concerns, and the strain of the chaos was taking its toll as they made fewer decisions and dithered more.

With a cure coming, there wasn't any more she could do until Picard broke the news to them. Then she could help with the healing. She had remained in a static situation for too long and needed to do *something.*

Picard had quietly entered the room, and she hadn't even noticed until he walked right into her line of sight. She gave him a small smile and he nodded in return. The strain was having its effect on her friend too, she realized.

"Deanna, there's nothing more for you to do here," he began quietly. "Instead, I'd like you to contact Lieutenant Vale and begin a more intensive hunt for Will and his father."

Deanna's eyes widened and she said, "You must be developing telepathy."

He gave her a tight smile but didn't pursue the comment.

"We know that Will has found his father and they are together. The lack of bio-signs suggests as much. You can both start at the location of his last signal and see if you can pick up a trail. It would be too much to hope that he's still at that location."

"It's more likely his combadge was destroyed, which explains that brief signal," she answered.

"I agree," Picard said. "You're both to be armed, and I suggest you carry an emergency medical kit. I hope he won't need a doctor's services."

She checked her own mind and feelings and didn't sense anything amiss. "Not right now, anyway." Troi brightened a bit when she saw the look of relief in the captain's eyes. "Where will you be?"

He sighed heavily and looked around the room. "Here. Once we know the timetable for releasing the new strain, Beverly and I will speak with the councillors. Hopefully together."

Deanna nodded and then turned to contact Vale. Her relief at finally doing something useful was mixed with a thread of fear: what would they find when they did manage to locate Will?

He was alive, and that comforted her. But what of

Kyle? And were they working together, or were they at one another's throats?

A province where the Bader were dominant was being harassed by its Dorset neighbor. As best Vale could understand it, they were arguing over which province controlled the water rights to the river that formed the natural boundary. In the past, both used the river, but maintenance was handled by the Dorset. Suddenly, the Dorset claimed the right to charge shipping tolls, which brought about Bader protests. And right now, just about every dispute on the planet was quickly escalating into a fight, and just about every fight was becoming a riot.

Vale didn't care. Left to her own devices, she'd anesthetize the planet worse than the liscom gas. Starfleet frowned on that approach, so she continued to direct her people the best she knew how. But she was beginning to worry about them. Even with twelve hours off between planet shifts, they were fatigued. Most were unused to missions of this scope. Hell, she wasn't used to anything this size either, and while she appreciated the captain's unwavering support, this was rapidly becoming a no-win scenario. No one liked the no-win scenario, especially in Starfleet, where people often had to face one. She'd never taken the infamous *Kobayashi Maru* test, and couldn't begin to imagine how she'd handle it.

Right now, though, as she stood on the riverbank watching columns of dark smoke rise from a burning dock on the opposite side, all that mattered was stopping these people from killing each other until the cure was introduced. The last time she checked with the ship, they were still synthesizing enough to seed. Data and La Forge were working out schedules, but nothing was approved yet, so the holding actions would continue.

She had beamed down a few minutes earlier and was being briefed by Almonte, a short, stocky ten-year veteran. His bloodshot eyes and untended scrapes told her much before the briefing had even begun. He had been trying to mediate the dispute when there was an explosion and then a fire. Almost immediately, the opposite shore had been lined with Bader who accused the Dorset of trying to destroy their way of life. As expected, the Dorset had taken to the shoreline and matched insult for insult. Vale half expected them to start throwing rocks at one another despite the width of the river.

"I don't want to split my team in two, so I'm trying to herd these fine folk away from the river. If I can get them out of earshot, maybe they can be distracted," Almonte said, with a trace of a soft accent.

"And we're outnumbered." Placing her hands on her hips, she surveyed the scene, looking for inspiration.

Troi had called a few moments after she arrived, and while the notion of hunting the Rikers had an appeal, she needed to settle this first. The counselor had agreed and was going to gather the supplies she thought they would need. That bought Vale some time, which she needed to put to good use.

On her side of the river there were over three dozen Dorset, screaming insults and waving fists. They were near a landing pier, complete with ropes, hydraulic ramps, and ODN connections for the incoming ships. The usual antigrav units were strewn about, waiting for the next time something needed to be loaded. Behind them were warehouses of varying sizes, ship repair facilities, and even a cafeteria. Nothing she could use to calm things down, but also nothing the rabble could really use as weapons. If all they were going to do was yell, she'd leave Almonte and head out.

But someone on this side had managed to launch something that started the fire. If it could be done once, it could most likely be repeated, and it was her job to stop that kind of escalation.

"What's in the warehouses?" she asked.

"I have Nikros checking now," Almonte replied. They both looked over in that direction, finally spotting the broad-shouldered, gray-haired woman from Rigel. With a tricorder in one hand and a phaser in the other, she was scanning buildings before entering. Vale estimated she had three more to check before finishing.

Nikros tugged on one wide door and found it locked. She consulted the tricorder and tugged again. Vale narrowed her eyes in suspicion at Nikros's trouble. Several Dorset also seemed to notice the security guard's situation, and they started toward her.

Without hesitation, Vale withdrew her phaser and began walking toward her subordinate, trying to match pace with the Dorset. As they hurried, she broke into a jog and yelled for them to stop.

Only one obeyed, but in stopping, he swiveled and aimed a weapon of his own at her. Vale recognized it as a wrist-mounted pulsed energy weapon, and she dove to the ground as the man snapped his wrist, activating a blast. It sizzled overhead and she looked up, took aim, and fired off one phaser burst, which found its target.

The others hadn't hesitated and continued toward Nikros, readying their own weapons. Vale looked to Almonte, who was already yelling for the rest of his squad. A twist of her head, and she saw Nikros alert and taking aim at the approaching men. Vale jumped to her feet and also took aim, coming at them from a different angle so as not to put her own officer in the way.

Three shots went off simultaneously. Vale and Nikros had both targeted the same man, who jerked like a puppet as he got hit from opposing directions. He slumped heavily to the ground. The third shot was from a man who fired at Nikros, aiming low. Vale watched the shot burn into the woman's leg. She saw a spark of flame and then Nikros crumpled, her hands beating at her ruined knee to put out the fire.

Behind her Vale heard shouts and then the sound of feet. The Dorset were rallying behind their fallen comrades. Scattered among the approaching throng were Vale's people. She spotted the tall, gangly Glavine, the heavily muscled Wigginton, and the lean form of the Vulcan Stenik. All were running, phasers at the ready.

It was about to become a full-scale riot, and Vale mentally calculated how many reinforcements she could summon. There were two squads that had beamed up just before she arrived here, and they could be recalled, but one team looked fairly banged up. Well, one more team was better than none. She made the call, and then broke into a run to get to Nikros before the man who had already winged her. The man had gotten closer but didn't fire again. Vale wasn't about to let him. She took aim and got off one shot that got him in the back. He fell to the ground, and she exchanged relieved looks with Nikros.

The sound of approaching footsteps had Vale whirling about, phaser gripped in both hands. Her field of vision was filled with approaching men, women, and, surprisingly, children, none of whom seemed anything less than in full fury. Tapping her combadge, she called out, "Vale to security team Delphi! Break them apart. Slow them down, and maybe we can get out of this!"

Without waiting for acknowledgment, she rushed forward, putting herself between Nikros, who remained down, and the mob. Something was worth protecting inside the warehouse, but she didn't dare speculate until things were under control. Five people converged on her, and Vale set her feet, her left shoulder out, right arm with phaser tucked against her belly. As they hit her, Vale whipped out her right arm and knocked down one of the women. A roundhouse leg sweep knocked down two more, and a left jab landed on another.

As one of the Dorset ran away, Vale grabbed another by the shirt and yanked him forward into her upraised knee. One managed two quick punches into her ribs, forcing her to exhale. With cries of rage, they converged on her once more, and this time she dropped into a squat to prevent them from getting a good grip. Quickly holstering her weapon, she balled her hands into fists and propelled herself upward, fists and elbows making contact. The cluster broke apart and she kicked out, knocking one boy over another man.

Sparing a glance, she spotted Stenik applying a nerve pinch to a woman while neatly ducking another's punch. Almonte was flailing with his fists, a veritable punching machine, keeping attackers at bay. The recalled squad, Gracin's as it turned out, were in the rear, doing what they could to pull Dorset back and away.

A man ran at Vale with a tool in his upraised fist, one end sparking. She didn't have time to grab her phaser, so she reached out as his arm came down, grabbed it, and spun the man around, kicking him in the backside to propel him away. Then a woman jumped on her back, and Vale reached over her head to break the hold. The woman tugged at her thick hair and wrapped her legs around Vale's waist for greater support. Vale finally forced herself over, letting the woman's weight carry them crashing to the hard ground. The woman's hold broken, Vale was able to quickly disengage herself and got back on her feet.

She looked around and saw an older man pummeling Nikros. The Rigelian kicked back with her good leg and fumbled for her phaser, which had been knocked aside. Vale rushed over, but she didn't get far before being tackled by someone she hadn't seen. They tumbled to the ground, Vale striking her right shoulder hard, and grappled. She couldn't get her hands free, and she was too entwined with her attacker for her feet to do any good. With little choice, she reared back and smashed her forehead into the man's nose. She heard cartilage break and the wet sound of blood. He screamed in pain and let go, his hands flying to his injured nose. Vale scrambled to her feet and looked for Nikros. What she saw made her jaw drop.

Nikros was a bloody heap, her injured leg at an unnatural angle. Her attacker was standing with his back to the warehouse door.

Vale didn't hesitate. She withdrew her phaser and fired at the man. Then she dashed to her colleague's side and saw that her breathing was shallow.

"Vale to *Enterprise.* Emergency beam-up for Lieutenant Nikros directly to sickbay."

"Acknowledged," came Nafir's voice.

As Nikros's broken body dematerialized, Vale uttered a short prayer.

Turning, she saw the mob had broken into clusters. In horror, she watched as her people were overwhelmed by sheer numbers. Olivarez had fallen and was about to be trampled until Wigginton bodily picked up and body-slammed her attacker.

This was getting out of control and had to be stopped. Now.

"Vale to security teams Beta and Delphi! Commence stun fire. Put these people down!"

Within seconds, bright beams of coherent light scattered the Dorset. Vale took aim and knocked down those on the periphery. It didn't take long at all for most of the Dorset to become slumbering heaps, bodies in a tangle.

Several of her people looked the worse for wear, and Vale sympathized as she rubbed her own sore right shoulder. She signaled to Almonte that all was fine and then turned back to the warehouse door. She wanted to see what was worth fighting for.

Her phaser made quick work of the lock, and she shoved the wide doors apart. Automatic lights snapped on as her body tripped a sensor. The vast space was filled from floor to ceiling with identical boxes. One of them had been dragged down and cracked open, its cushioning spilling out from beneath the top. Vale lifted the lid and saw that this box and probably all the others in the warehouse contained explosive devices. That made little sense to her, since the planet was known for its peace. There was a data chip affixed to the underside of the box top below the printed words Ree Packan Ree Construction. Suddenly it made sense. These devices were for demolition, probably for tunneling.

But the Dorset knew. They had used them to start the fire on the other side of the river.

The riots were now on the verge of becoming a race war, and Vale realized they were quickly running out of time.

Chapter Eight

"CAN'T YOU LET ME GO? I won't be a bother to anyone again. I promise."

Both Rikers turned and looked at their unwilling companion and then exchanged glances. It was clear to Will that his father was uncertain as to what path he should follow. Now that they seemed to be communicating, he hoped to be able to guide his father toward a reunion with Picard once they reached the capital—whenever that would be. They had been hiking through the dense forest for hours now. Twice more they encountered the running stream and were glad for the water, which seemed to be agreeing with them all. On the other hand, they had found nothing to eat and Will's stomach was beginning to rumble.

From what Kyle could determine from their flight plan before being forced down, they might be finally nearing the edge of the forest. Neither Kyle nor Bison knew what might be on the other side, but Will was hopeful they made it out before the sun set, which was not far off.

The two Rikers were talking and it seemed there were more issues to cover, but that would have to wait for that promised drink in Ten-Forward. Between the hike, their exhaustion and the presence of the ever-complaining Bison, neither felt like getting into the heaviest issues that remained between them. Whereas Kyle might be fine with that, Will was not. He had to tread carefully so as not to ruin the mood. Will did admit to himself, things hadn't felt this relaxed with his father since their fight on the *Enterprise*-D so many years ago. And those feelings didn't last, did they?

"Excuse me, I'm asking a question here!"

"We heard you," Will said harshly. "You're coming with us to the capital."

"Swell," Bison said grumpily.

"My thoughts exactly," Kyle added.

"When's supper?" Bison complained.

"When we're hungry," Kyle said.

"Well, I'm hungry now."

"Shut up."

"It's more like when we find something safe to eat," Will said with waning patience. He thought that would keep things quiet for a while but less than a minute later, the former test subject spoke up.

"They going to execute me?"

The question caught Will off guard. He knew nothing about the judicial system on Delta Sigma IV but was fairly certain, given what he knew of these people, that capital punishment was practiced.

"They should, you know," Bison continued, sounding dejected. "Unoo was a bitch, but she didn't deserve to die. Not like that."

The trio continued on in silence, with neither Riker certain of what to say.

"I'm asking, do you think they will want me to die for starting all this?"

"No, I don't think so," Kyle said. "It's not something you did consciously. Someone had to be first and fate picked you."

"Me and not one of the four other poor fools," Bison said. "Me, the Federation's lab rat."

"Okay, if it wasn't fate, then the Federation figured you had it in you," Kyle said testily.

"That's not a lot of help," Will replied.

"Are we still on course for getting out of this godforsaken jungle?" Kyle asked.

"More or less," Will said.

"More or less?"

"Is there an echo in here?"

"Shut up," Kyle said to Bison. To his son, he added, "Explain please?"

"I'm judging from the way the trees grow that things are beginning to thin. But the shadows also make it tough to tell. Shouldn't be much longer."

"You keep leading the way," Kyle said.

They continued to march.

Finally, Will could see something other than leaves and trees. He spotted the beginnings of twilight peeking through the limbs. The forest was ending and they were emerging just when it would have gotten too dark to manage much farther. They were dirty, tired, and hungry but they had made it through the forest alive. Bison continued to complain about everything, mostly hunger and his fate, but Will managed to tune him out.

As they cleared the last tree, the trio paused and took stock of their situation. In the near distance, over a rise, were lights indicating a village or city. There were sounds of machinery, even a voice or two. That was clearly their direction, even if it was farther west than Will would have preferred. Still, they'd find food and hopefully a means of reaching the capital and the Council. Along the way, Will imagined only the very worst possibilities, not daring to hope they'd return to find a cure in effect courtesy of Beverly Crusher, M.D. and miracle worker.

"Something's wrong, son," Kyle said, breaking the moment.

"What do you mean?"

"Look at the way that light is moving. It's flickering like it's alive."

"Like it's on fire," Will said, alarm in his voice.

"We better hurry over there."

"How do you see us helping?"

"Extra hands, I guess. We don't have any emergency aid equipment but we have to be there."

"I know," Will said. "Because you fix things."

"Damn right," Kyle said and set out at a strong pace. It didn't take long for Will to follow and he never turned back but was gratified to hear Bison's footsteps behind him.

Within twenty minutes they had cleared the rise and saw the outline of a small city. Boxy, squat buildings—no surprise there—but these didn't look like homes. This part of town had to be the business district, and to the right were the flickering lights. Then a tongue of flame rose above as if to beckon them closer.

And drawn like moths, the men moved closer.

Will forgot all about eating. As they neared, it was clear the building in flames was populated. He saw emergency workers helping people with blankets and even oxygen masks. A few more minutes and the figures became more distinct.

"My God," Kyle muttered.

"Children," Will said.

"It's a school," Bison said. "I'd know those markings anywhere. Primary school. Had some terrible times there . . ."

"Shut up," Kyle said. "Willy, we have to go help. My God, children are in there. My fault . . ."

Will turned on his father, grabbed his shoulders and shook the older man once. "Look at the fire! Study the pattern. What do you see?"

Kyle did as he was ordered and was silent for over a minute. Finally he began speaking. "Pattern burns are even on the south wall. East wall is clean. No fire on the ground. The fire's moving from one side to the other. Given the elevation of the fire, it didn't start on the ground or in one spot."

"Arson," Will concluded for him.

"Most likely. And no surprise given the madness we've seen elsewhere."

"Someone threw the bomb," Bison said.

"Point to you," Kyle agreed. "If they're still around, we might be able to put an end to their threat."

"Spoken like a good tactician," Will added with a grin. "Okay, let's go play hero."

His father's features darkened. "We're neither playing nor heroes. We're responsible for this carnage."

"Thought so," Bison said.

"Shut up," both Rikers said in unison.

"Definitely an echo around here," Bison said and then, looking at Kyle's expression, shut his mouth.

As they neared the school, everyone studied the damage that continued to spread. The rooftop was aflame and windows on two sides had been blown out. People were running back and forth, their movements appearing aimless from the air. Firefighters were present, as were other emergency service workers, but they were no match for the ferocity of the flame. Barricades kept most of the onlookers a safe distance away, but again, there were too few peace officers to ensure they remained on the proper side. Will imagined that many of them were worried parents.

"Do we have anything to protect us?"

"The cold weather gear is heat resistant, or so I'm told," Kyle said.

Will eyed the outer clothes he wore. "It will have to do, I suppose."

He was already closing up the coat, ensuring every fastening was closed and used a scarf to act as a mask. "Dad, you can scan the perimeter while I go inside."

Without looking back, his father agreed. "Each to our strengths."

Will nodded, more to himself than to his father. Before moving closer to the burning building he looked over at Bison. Narrowing his eyes, Will said, "Stay put. Don't complicate this any more than it needs to be."

"Save the kids," he said quietly. Will was surprised by the compassion in the man's voice. Within seconds he could feel the heat generated by the fire, amplified by the winter gear he wore. Moving quickly, he worked his way past gawkers and panicked parents. The security cordons were fine for those trained to obey the rules but had the crowd wanted, they could have overrun the scene, slowing up relief efforts. Whatever had happened to these people, at least all their common sense hadn't fled.

Since the school was aflame mainly on the south side, he chose to enter from the north. The heat grew worse with each passing step, and he felt sweat form on his chest and a trickle run down his spine. He hadn't eaten a proper meal since the one at Seer's house over a day ago, and sleep had been a series of catnaps. Hc was pushing his limits of physical endurance and realized that soon he'd be at less than peak performance—probably already was.

The windows on this side were still intact, and he quickly pushed one open and stepped through. Like the other buildings he'd visited, the school was a series of boxlike rooms and connecting hallways. He stood in the classroom, amid overturned chairs and tables, and computer terminals flashing error messages. Listening, he tried to determine where the flames were, where the children might have gone to await rescue. There was the telltale crackle of fire overhead and in the distance a stream of water, but no cries from children. He longed for a tricorder.

He placed a hand against the classroom door, which someone had wisely closed. It didn't feel particularly warm, so Will gingerly cracked it open and paused. No rush of heat or flame, so he was safe. Carefully, he opened it all the way and then looked up and down the hallway. He tried to imagine himself a frightened child. Where would he go? A sound of breaking glass to his right decided matters for him, and he headed in that direction.

The hallway was littered with dropped belongings, padds, data chips, articles of clothing, even some old-fashioned paper. The fire hadn't reached here yet but it would. The building was a loss, just waiting to be consumed as a sacrifice to the problem unleashed by the Federation.

Will worked his way carefully toward the end of the hall, where he suspected the sound came from. All the doors he passed were closed, and he looked for any signage to give him a clue where children might be found. Finally arriving at the last classroom, he tested the door and then opened it.

No one was inside, but Will cracked a smile anyway. It was a science lab, with all manner of tools and equipment on the worktables. There was some form of communications device half assembled on the middle table. A quick glance told him it was a person-to-person device, the kind families would use. It didn't have a lot of range, but it might still be useful. Pulling off his gloves, he knew he had only a few minutes at most.

Will hadn't worked with chips, wires, and soldering equipment like this in some time. Still, the relatively simple nature of the device made his job easier. He took two power supplies and connected them, allowing him to boost the signal. Then he used a small stylus to adjust the frequency, one he hoped the *Enterprise* would be able to pick up. Riker then pulled out pieces of the device and found some adhesive tape. He unfastened his coat and found a seam. Using a sharp edge of the stylus, he ripped open the seam and quickly taped the power supply and pieces of the communicator to the upper chest portion of his jacket. With luck, someone on the starship would pick up the signal and then track his whereabouts until he could be contacted or beamed up.

Finished, he used more tape to repair the seam and then closed the coat. Turning, he quickly plotted a course of action. He jogged down the corridor, back in the direction he had started from, and opened each room, shouting for children. The smoke was thicker now and turning black, so he knew the fire was approaching. Running while breathing smoky air through his scarf wasn't easy, and he felt himself getting a little winded. With each empty room, Will grew more and more concerned that there were still people in need of help and that but he was in the wrong part of the school.

Children would know enough to run away from flames, so he was in the right half of the building; he just wasn't in the right room. They would not go up where the fire sounded closer but . . . Will wondered if the school had a basement.

He found a T-shaped juncture and turned, heading closer to the fire. The heat had risen, he sensed, as more perspiration ran down his brow and neck. Halfway down the hall, he spotted a door that had an emergency graphic. It was wider than the classroom doors and painted a dull gray, in contrast to the muted colors of the other rooms.

He yanked open the door without checking for heat and shouted down.

Within seconds, voices answered. Scared, young voices all pleading for rescue.

"I'm coming," Will yelled as he bounded down the steps.

The basement room was well built for any disaster. Light panels were affixed to the walls and ceiling, and there were emergency medical kits every ten feet as well as a locker full of rations. A communications unit sat unused alongside one wall, and Will lingered over that for a moment before focusing on the center of the room.

Three children, two boys and a girl, huddled together, tears running down their faces. They looked about six years old, but because of their accelerated aging, Will could only guess.

"I'm here to help," he said, making certain his smile was wide and reassuring. "The fire isn't entirely on this side of the school, so we can get out safely. Are you ready to go?"

Three nods.

"Okay. First of all, I'm Will. I'm trained to help, so you have nothing to worry about. Now, I need to go first and make sure the way is clear. All right with you?"

Three more nods.

"Then let's get started. We'll go single file up the stairs. Once we're all up, I'll show you the path we'll follow. Here we go."

He turned and started up the stairs and then paused, making certain they were following. All three had stopped crying and were following, although they seemed petrified at the notion.

"How'd you get separated from your teacher?" he asked as he climbed the stairs.

After several seconds of silence, the girl spoke up in a tiny voice. "Addie here insisted we go back and get his art project. We followed one way, the teacher kept going the other way."

"It was my for my da's birthday," one boy said defensively.

"Do you still have it?" Will asked.

"No, the hall was too full of smoke."

"Well, the smoke is still there, and it's probably thicker. You need to cover your faces with your shirts when we come out. I'm going first." With that he stepped out into the hallway that was now dark and thick with smoke.

"Hurry," he urged them and in a burst they stepped into the hallway. Immediately they all began coughing, and one of the kids began crying again.

Will shepherded them toward the large window he had entered through. The air would be clearest there, and he could signal for help if necessary.

The classroom was dense with soot and smoke, but it was fire-free. Will walked the children to the window and hoisted them one by one through the opening, placing them gently on the grass. Within seconds, they were all clear.

Will doubted he'd be able to get back in and free others—if there were any—before the fire reached every foot of the school. He was inordinately pleased about having saved three innocents, but more than that, he finally had a way to get back in touch with Picard.

He walked the children toward the barricades, and an alert peace officer spotted the ragtag group approaching. She hurried over, muttered thanks to Riker, and ushered the children away for medical attention.

His duty done, Will unwrapped the dirty scarf from around his face and sucked in huge lungfuls of clear air. He coughed a bit and then breathed normally. The air carried the stench of the fire, but it was cool and felt great. He unfastened the top of his jacket, letting the cooler air refresh him. He was tired and he needed a shower, but more than that, he missed Deanna. She wasn't far from his mind the entire time they were apart and her absence was a constant ache.

He trudged back to the edge of town and spotted his father leaning against the hull of a purring flyer. Kyle looked a little the worse for wear. His pants were ripped, and a small streak of blood was visible above his brow. Will worried for a moment and then shoved the thought aside. Kyle Riker was more than capable of taking care of himself. He certainly didn't look like he needed any help.

"You find whoever fired the bomb?" Will asked as he got within earshot.

Kyle nodded slowly. "They won't be bombing any more children."

Will looked sharply into his father's eyes, trying to read into the sentence. All he saw was guilt, pain, and steel, the same things he had been seeing since they first met up several hours and more than a few continents before. He wanted to ask his father for details, but he knew from his expression that there would be no answer.

For the moment, that would have to suffice.

"So now we owe someone else for yet another flyer?"

"You want to get back to the capital or not?"

"I don't," Bison piped up from the doorway.

Will gave him a look, too tired to yell at him.

"Can we leave now?" Kyle asked his son. Will nodded and together, they entered the new, cleaner craft. Bison remained where he had been, nothing out of place. For once, Will thought the tide of circumstance was changing in his favor. Carefully, he put his jacket on the deck, threw the scarf and gloves atop it and walked back to his seat.

"Did you save them?" Bison asked.

"Ycah."

"Good." The tenor of his voice changed and he practically growled, "Okay, we can go to the capital so they can try and execute me and we can end this nonsense."

Kyle told the man to be quiet and busied himself with preparations for lifting off. Will sat, trying to wash the exhaustion from his mind and body, but he felt he was failing at it. He knew he would need to remain sharp and seize any opportunity there was to gain control of his own situation.

Father or not, there was much Kyle had to answer for, and his time was rapidly approaching.

They were getting nowhere fast.

Vale and Troi stood at the edge of a forest and looked for clues their tricorder might have missed. The sun was starting to set and the fall air was cooling rapidly.

"The signal came from right here," Troi said, perplexed.

Vale finished walking a circle around the clearing. She finally put her hands on her hips and looked at the darkening sky.

"They were above us when the badge was smashed. It's the only explanation, Deanna."

"And we don't even know which way they were headed," Troi said glumly.

Vale walked over to the other woman and paused, taking one final look around. She shook her head and stopped to think of the next step. Troi wanted to be patient, but she'd spent way too long just waiting and liked the notion of acting.

"Will would have put up a fight before the badge was disabled," Deanna said. "So who broke the badge? His own father?"

"Never met him. You have. So, tell me, is this something Kyle Riker is capable of?"

Troi pondered the question and admitted, "I don't know. If he's still as desperate as he appeared on the lab recording, then anything is possible."

"Wish your senses could work like the sensors," Vale said.

"Me too, but we're not that lucky."

"Okay, I'm going to do some old-style detective work. I want to look through these reports from my teams, see if I can find a correlation. Maybe that will help."

She began walking away from the trees, her features highlighted by the tricorder's glowing screen. After a moment, Troi followed behind her, happy to at least be moving.

"So tell me, if you don't mind, what's up with you and the commander?"

Troi shrugged. "I know what you're asking, but I don't know the answer myself."

"Wasn't always like that, I gather."

"True. We spent most of our time on the *Enterprise* as colleagues and friends."

"Not lovers until the Briar Patch," Vale said. Not once had her eyes left the tricorder, but she managed to keep a conversation moving and avoid tripping over dead branches and small stones.

"Not really," Troi said. "That really was earlier."

"Oh? I knew there was something in the past, just never knew the story."

"It's not something we usually post for casual consumption," Deanna said.

"Sorry if I'm intruding. I'm really a romantic and I think there's a good story."

Troi hadn't expected that, but she enjoyed talking about Will to an unbiased listener. And it did pass the time.

"Well, we were naked when we first met," Troi began.

Vale lowered the tricorder and turned to stare, her mouth agape. "That certainly must have helped things along."

Troi laughed, happy to have the attention. "It was at a wedding. Will was a young lieutenant. He was assigned as Starfleet liaison to the Federation ambassador on Betazed. His first duty was to represent the ambassador at my girlfriend's wedding. I was her maid of honor, and he couldn't keep his eyes off me."

"That's right, your planet doesn't hide a thing, mentally or physically. Security personnel take special courses when posted to your world. Did you look back at the commander?"

Troi chuckled at the memory, although at the time it wasn't funny. "No. Not really. I grew up sheltered, despite having a human father. My mother wanted me to be a proper lady of Betazed, so Will's look and thoughts, well, they were so alien to me."

"So nothing happened at first?"

"He pursued me, I'll give him that. And I was intrigued. I had never seen anyone so focused on the primal, physical needs or so confident in his abilities."

That earned Troi a raised eyebrow from Vale. She ignored it.

"We finally met a few times, and I needed him to slow down and learn who I was and what I wanted from a relationship. It took some doing. A lot of doing. And to be honest, that was when I sensed there was something special about him. Our minds touched, a first for me. Being only half Betazoid, I thought I was unable to communicate telepathically with anyone but my mother, who is especially powerful. So, to have another voice in my head . . ."

"Creeped you out?"

"No, but it took getting used to. And then he told me he heard a word in his own mind, *Imzadi.*"

"Wait," Vale said, once more giving the counselor her undivided attention. "I've heard you use that word. It's something special."

"More than that, Christine. With some people it can be an endearment, like 'beloved.' But what Will heard, and what I meant, was the purer meaning. It means 'first,' and we were each other's first true, deep, meaningful relationship."

"But not your, you know, first . . . ?"

"Actually, he was," she said. And she sensed Vale's embarrassment, which amused her. "Ever since then, there was always going to be a connection between us, regardless of time or place."

"Which is how you sense he's still alive," Vale continued.

"Yes."

They were silent for a moment, and Troi sensed a touch of unease from the other woman. To help keep the conversation going, she went on to tell of being a hostage during a botched Sindareen attempt to steal precious Betazoid artwork and how Riker was the one who rescued her. The story certainly appealed to the security officer side of Vale.

"Wow. Wish I found someone like that for me."

The two continued to walk, Vale once more intent on the tricorder.

"Hasn't there been a great love in your life?"

"Maybe. I mean, there was no telepathy, no word exchanged between souls. But we had one glorious year during my first posting. I was just an ensign, recently assigned to the *U.S.S. Al-Batani . . .*" And Vale went on about her experiences while Troi just listened. And thought about Will and the jungle, about Maror holding her life in his hands until Will arrived.

"Wait a minute," Vale said, interrupting her own story and Troi's thoughts. "Found it. A pattern, that is. We've been getting reports of humans coming to hot spots, helping out and then vanishing."

Troi smiled at that, knowing it had to be the Rikers.

"It took a while to piece together, considering these were buried eyewitness reports in a mound of other information. But there's a pattern emerging. Jim has been helping coordinate the pattern."

"Jim?"

"Jim Peart, my number two. He's at tactical and says a rough chronology would have had them pass this way. We have a direction."

"Where are they heading?"

Vale cracked a smile and gestured to the west, toward the last remnants of the setting sun. "Thataway."

"This is getting tedious," Vale grumbled sometime later as they arrived at a site where there had been a riot. Indications were that two men had waded into the middle of the fight and broken it up. She suspected it was Kyle and Will Riker, but they only had hearsay to go on.

"Well, what choice do we have?"

"None, since they're eluding our best sensor scans. They're not making this easy on us."

"I think that was the idea," Troi noted.

"True, but it's a pain in the ass."

"Also true."

The two saw that there were small clusters of people still talking among themselves. Troi equated them with embers waiting for a stiff breeze to fan them back into an inferno. She decided to keep a watch on them, adjusting her empathic abilities so most of the feelings passed over her. She was emotionally spent, having been surrounded by the strong feelings of a planet full of people who were experiencing them for the first time. It made her both mentally and physically tired.

"If only there were a nice restaurant nearby," she muttered.

"Hungry? I have ration packs."

"I've had more than enough of those, thank you."

Vale shrugged and took a drink of water from her canteen. "You get used to them after a while."

"Maybe you do in security. The rest of us much prefer even replicated meals."

"I'm just real practical, you know," Vale replied. "So, you never told me. Why'd you guys break things off?"

The two walked around the small town with its broken shop windows and overturned containers of foods and fabrics.

"Will told me he intended to be the youngest ever to be named captain. All he had was his career as a goal. There didn't seem to be a place for a lady of Betazed."

"You mean, you joined Starfleet to follow him? Haven't I heard that before," Vale said with a knowing tone.

"Actually, getting to know Will truly opened my eyes

to the possibilities beyond my own world. It made sense to put my empathic skills to work, and Starfleet was just establishing its counselor program."

"The stars were in alignment then."

"I guess you could say that," Troi admitted. "It never occurred to me we'd be posted to the same ship. When I learned who Captain Picard had selected as first officer, I kept the fact that I knew him private. The look on Will's face was, I have to admit, priceless."

"I can only imagine. And that opened up fresh possibilities, didn't it?"

"Yes, but as you know, it took us a while before we took advantage of them."

"Too long, if you ask me."

And Troi couldn't argue with that assessment. They continued to walk along in compatible silence.

The riot, reports indicated, had flared quickly and spilled over a three-block area before it was broken up and peace officers managed to restore order. It was one of the few places they had visited that had not required assistance from the *Enterprise.*

"Gracin to Vale."

"Go ahead."

"We have the Huni port secure. It's just about all wrapped up."

"Casualties?"

"Nothing to mention."

"Good. We were due for one like that. Okay, check with Data and see if you're needed. If not, get your squad back up. Vale out."

Vale shrugged apologetically to Troi, but the counselor was well aware that the security chief was needed to coordinate the massive efforts of her teams. Even supplemented by personnel from other departments, her teams were stretched thin. Every stop they made required constant communications with squad leaders. And every time Vale apologized.

"You don't need to do that, Christine."

"I want to help find the Rikers. These just feel like distractions."

"Necessary ones, so stop apologizing."

Vale's next words were cut off when five hulking men rounded a corner and stopped in front of the women. They assessed the women with insolent eyes, deciding if the two would cause trouble or would be easy prey. The security chief shot Troi an exasperated glance before concentrating on the men.

"What have we here, Noraa?"

"Entertainment," the man farthest back said.

"Or not," Vale said, withdrawing her phaser with complete nonchalance.

The men paused, looking at the weapon, and then the man called Noraa laughed. At that, all five rapidly withdrew their own weapons, ranging from some form of energy pistol to a multibladed knife.

"It doesn't have to get ugly," Vale said casually. "I don't want to hurt you."

"Hurt us?" And the men laughed.

"Five against two, all with weapons. I like our odds," Noraa said.

"I'd like things a lot better if you'd just let us leave."

"And miss out on your engaging company?"

"Well, yes, now that you mention it." Troi watched and saw that, as usual, Vale kept things casual, but it was all a facade. If someone looked carefully enough, they'd see muscles tensing, eyes sizing up the situation, and a body carefully moving into optimum position. Whatever happened, Troi was clearly there as backup, and her biggest task was not to get in the other woman's way. While Troi was fully trained in and even excelled at the Klingon martial art of *mok'bara,* she was nowhere near as good as Vale.

The nearest man moved to flank Vale, blocking her escape route to the right. Another stepped forward, shifting his knife between his hands, a little too eager for something to happen.

He tossed the knife from left to right and back again, trying to intimidate them with his ambidexterity.

With split-second timing, Vale kicked her left leg, catching the knife when it was between hands and sending it high into the air. She then threw herself into a backflip as the knife man skidded backward to avoid being struck by his own weapon. Her move also served to confuse the men on both sides. As she smoothly landed on her toes, she fired first to her left and then the middle.

Troi took aim and let go one shot that went wide and then a second that struck the man to her right.

Noraa, farther back, dropped to one knee and aimed his huge, gaudy pistol directly at Vale. His shot was loud and bright, and an orange beam sliced toward the women. Vale managed to dodge the beam, but her movement caused Troi to lose her balance getting out of her way.

That allowed one of the others to rush her. He grabbed her around the middle and dragged her to the ground. One hand held her right wrist against the dirt; the other was hooked under her left knee as he tried to wrestle her into submission.

Instead, Troi brought her right leg around, caught him in a scissors hold, and then squeezed, using her free hand, the one holding her phaser, to club him against his ear. He howled in pain and she squeezed tighter. With one arm pinned between her legs, he used his free arm to punch her weakly in the shoulder. She had all the leverage, and he was flailing. Not that the punches were ineffective—Troi knew she'd be bruised come morning—but they weren't stopping her.

Finally, he seemed to weaken and she used the butt of the phaser to smack him right between the eyes. He seemed to go limp, and she squeezed one final time.

As she disengaged herself from her attacker, she looked up carefully, wondering where the rest of the fighting was taking place. Instead, she saw Vale disarming the fifth and final man.

"Have fun?"

"Not especially, no," Troi replied with a tired grin.

"Admit it, it felt good to just let go and get all that tension out of your system. I bet you've wanted to bash one of these guys since the problems began."

"That's not a very enlightened view to take," Troi said, trying to sound calm and professional.

"No, but it *is* very human."

"Well, I am only half human," Troi reminded her.

"That's why you only managed one to my four,"

Vale said with a grin. "You were far too much in control."

Enough was enough, Picard thought as he rematerialized between the Council chambers. He caught Carmona's eye and gestured for him to approach. The guard appeared alert, but the captain saw the exhaustion in the man's eyes. In addition to his work with the Council, he had to be concerned for the crew, too. Everyone was going above and beyond, which Picard had come to expect from his crew but didn't take for granted. Much as he needed to continue to earn and retain their respect, he in turn was especially conscious of the need to show his own respect and appreciation for the work done by the hundreds of souls under his command.

And right now, they were tired.

"Mr. Carmona," he began. "Please use whatever resources you need to gather the councillors in one place. Have their chief medic, Wasdin, available as well. You can pick the site you feel will best protect them."

"Aye, Captain," Carmona said, and turned to sprint off.

Within five minutes, Carmona returned and with an off-kilter smile announced they were convened and ready for him.

Tapping his combadge, Picard summoned Crusher and Morrow to beam down and join him. Within moments they arrived, and he looked over at the ambassador. Morrow's health had improved, but he moved with a slight stiffness that indicated pain.

Picard, Morrow, and Crusher followed Carmona into the building, turning right, away from the Bader headquarters. At the end of a hallway they entered an office Picard had not been in before. The series of rooms implied some sort of suite arrangement. Deep in the back was a conference room, with a table more than large enough for all the councillors. It was windowless and totally secure. Carmona and Williams positioned themselves on either side of the door, with Carmona, the senior man, inside the room.

The councillors for a change were not speaking among themselves, but sitting with grim, expectant expressions on their faces. All eyed Picard as he entered and went to the head of the table. He surveyed them for a moment and then nodded to them. He noted the presence of Seer of Anann, their protocol officer and the last man to have seen Will Riker. Picard worried about Will, hoping that Troi and Vale were making progress on the hunt.

But for now, he was on his own and it was time to begin.

"We have identified the problem and the solution," he began. "What I am about to explain will be difficult for some of you, but it's the truth. When we're finished, I can make all the medical findings available to Wasdin." He paused and looked directly at the older woman, who he would have sworn had aged five years in the past twenty-four hours. Her face was more deeply lined; the dark smudges under her pale green eyes had deepened to black.

"What Starfleet Medical discovered was that a natural agent in the atmosphere was causing a chromosomal change that was resulting in the premature aging. They managed to find a cure for this, but they made a fundamental error. They were so concerned with repairing the damage, they neglected to fully study the changes in body chemistry.

"As best as I can explain it, liscom gas, which has always been part of the ecosystem, has been acting like a narcotic, depressing certain functions within the brain. The result is that every one of the original settlers was, over time, effectively drugged into cooperating with one another."

He paused, letting that sink in. Sure enough, several members of the Council began objecting, talking among themselves and gesticulating. Some things never change from planet to planet, Picard assured himself. Seer and Wasdin, though, did not object or comment. They seemed ready to hear more.

"If I may continue," Picard said loudly. He waited a moment to see that people were once more turning their attention to him. "What the medical treatment did was screen out the liscom's effects on your brain chemistry. You will now live your normal life cycle in another generation or two. However, you are all experiencing your true natures for the first time. Without a set of moral codes and experiences, the people on this planet are suddenly feeling extreme tendencies for the very first time and don't know how to handle them."

"That's the madness?" Wasdin asked incredulously. "Ourselves?" She looked at Crusher, who nodded sadly, a wan smile on her face.

"Yes," Crusher agreed, "you are all reverting to type, and since both the Bader and the Dorset tend to be aggressive, there have been outbreaks of violence. Your media has made this out to be a form of madness, which has inflamed public opinion against the Federation."

"What about El Bison El's murder of Unoo of Huni?" Seer asked.

"Something agitated him, we don't know what," Picard admitted. "He was the first to truly exhibit these feelings and acted out. He had no true sense of how to rein in the new emotions. Unoo's death was the first unfortunate consequence of this condition."

"Unfortunate is too mild a word, Captain," Seer replied.

"Do you have a cure?" Wasdin asked.

"Yes, Dr. Crusher has come up with something. But before deploying it, we want you to understand the full implications of our actions."

"Unlike last time," Cholan of Huni muttered.

"Indeed, Councillor, we have made mistakes in this matter," Picard continued. "My chief medical officer has worked around the clock to find a way to stop the violence. Her solution is not perfect, but it gives your people time."

"What do you mean?" Seer asked.

"We can introduce a plant hybrid into your ecology and let its natural effects work much like the liscom. It will provide you with a normal life cycle, but it will continue to depress your brain chemistry, returning you to a peaceful state."

"Not enlightened, drugged," Jus Renks Jus said, more to himself than to others. Looking at the captain, he spoke up. "You want to drug my people."

"And our people, too," Cholan added. Picard saw that the solution needed to be introduced quickly. The Council was only going to fragment further if this persisted.

"Everyone will be like they were a week ago," Morrow interjected. "The difference is, you know there's a problem to be fixed. And by living your normal life cycle, you have the time to determine for yourselves how best to chart your planet's future."

"I wish you never tried to fix the problem in the first place," Cholan muttered. "We were fine."

"No," Seer said from across the room. "We were dying. That's not how I define 'fine.' "

"How do you introduce this new cure?"

"We have shuttles standing by, Wasdin," Crusher said. "An entire timetable has been worked out that will seed every continent and major island. A mist of the synthesized concentrate will also be introduced into the major population centers. Our expectations are that it will help calm people down, or at least slow down the current problem's spread."

"Your people spent a year testing five of us, and it was a disaster. Now you want to introduce a cure based on what? Simulations?"

"Your concern is a valid one, Wasdin," Picard answered. "Had we the time, we would have tried this in stages. Trust me: aggressively introducing something like this into a planetary environment is not how we normally do things. My senior staff and I discussed this at length. Ultimately, as I have told first Chkarad and then Jus Renks Jus, a leader must act. Right or wrong, something has to be done. I do not say these things just to inspire, but they are words we need to live by. As the Federation's representative assigned to deal with the problem, this is what I have decided is the best course of action for your planet."

"Do we even get a say?" Renks asked.

"Several of you on the Council are exhibiting signs of the current problem. As a result, you are either in a drugged state or an extremely agitated state that robs you of clear thought processes. Therefore, I am informing you of our actions. Once the planet has been stabilized, you and your scientists can take the time to study and plan. Right now, I feel your world is out of time."

"I thought you said you never ran a planet before," Renks challenged.

Picard looked at him, a tight expression on his face. "I never have. And trust me, this is not running a planet. I'm just trying to stave off its death."

"Seems pretty dictatorial to me," a woman challenged.

"Actually," Morrow said, standing beside Picard for a show of support, "by asking for our help, you have triggered a mechanism clearly laid out in the Articles of the Federation. A problem that threatens life must be dealt with if a solution presents itself. There's little choice, I'm afraid. I'm fairly certain the Federation Council will back the captain's actions."

"Have you signaled the shuttlecraft yet?" Seer asked. Picard was happy to have the conversation back on a productive track, and he appreciated Morrow's official backing.

"No, I wanted to inform you all of this and explain myself. I want you to understand that the violence and problems will not end immediately. Just as the current problem spread like a virus, so too will this cure. Your emergency services people will have to continue to do their jobs."

"And Captain Picard's people will continue to provide

assistance," Morrow interjected. "The Federation is not abandoning one of its member worlds. This has been an extremely difficult mission, and I concur with the captain: your world needs immediate help."

There was a pause, as everyone in the conference room considered what had been said and what was about to happen. No one spoke, although the captain watched exchanges of expressions. Body language told him more than enough; his plan would proceed without more than token objections from these people.

"What do you need from our people next?" Seer asked, earning him a reproving stare from Renks.

Picard thought about that for only a moment before responding. "You need to keep your people focused on providing aid and comfort. You need to do damage control. My people can handle the riskier concerns."

"We still have cities without water or power," Renks complained.

"My people have provided vital services only to watch them be sabotaged again," Picard said, fighting his temper. "They will continue their efforts, you can be assured."

"Thank you, Captain," Renks and Cholan both said, which prompted some chuckles from around the table.

"I'd like to suggest that in the name of our common goal," Morrow said as the laughs died down, "you work together. Not apart. I gather nothing positive happened because of your division."

"Thankfully, the people never found out," Seer added.

"I agree," Picard said. "I'm going back aboard the *Enterprise* to monitor the progress of the plan. I can be back in moments if required."

"I'll be staying, though," Morrow said, looking at the captain. Picard saw the confidence on his face and then cast a glance toward Crusher, awaiting confirmation. She nodded in agreement, so it was settled.

"Excellent," Renks said. "Cholan, can you please ask An Revell An to have everything reconfigured once more?"

"Of course, Speaker," Cholan replied, although to Picard's practiced eye, the Bader councillor seemed none too thrilled with being given orders. This was the room that needed Crusher's handiwork sooner than most, but he wouldn't insult them by walking in carrying a hypo. Besides, Data had already arranged the flight paths, and the capital was going to be the first city to receive the treatment.

Picard nodded to the group and withdrew from the room, nodding in appreciation to Carmona on the way out. Once in the courtyard, he signaled the ship.

"Mr. Data, you may dispatch the shuttles."

"Aye, sir."

Troi and Vale were tired of the wild-goose chase. The security chief was ready to hunt down and shoot the goose, any goose, just so they could stop running around the planet. Instead, they continued to check out each report that implied the Riker men were involved. Sure enough, unidentified people had been stopping fights, repairing damage, and just recently, rescuing children at a school fire.

But they remained hours behind the duo. The two women were tired, and Troi had to admit she was pretty hungry, too.

The two were catching their breath at the site of the school fire. The building had collapsed in on itself, and emergency workers were hosing down the remains. The crowds had dispersed earlier, but some people lingered, talking about a man in odd, heavy clothing who rushed in and saved three children. Troi heard a woman mention that the bodies of four people had been found nearby, with incriminating equipment by them.

"The commander never would have done this," Vale said as she stood over one of the bodies. The man's neck had been snapped, the head lying at an unnatural angle.

"This was a brutal fight, not at all disciplined," she observed. Troi would take the security chief at her word since the details were too subtle for her.

"Could Kyle Riker have done this?"

"Interesting question, Deanna. I know the man's a trained specialist, and I gather he trained the commander as a kid. Could be. If Commander Riker saved the kids, his dad could have been here."

"I only met Kyle once, and he certainly seemed fit enough for the task."

"That was more than ten years ago, you said," Vale added.

"True. If you're right, this was something I never would have expected from him."

"If it was Kyle Riker, he has to answer for this." And the words hung between them. The notion of Kyle committing a crime like this, so brutal, so cold, made her shiver.

"You're right, of course," Troi finally said. "Where would they have gone from here?"

Vale pulled out her tricorder and began entering information. She paused, waiting for a result, tucking a stray lock of hair behind her left ear.

"They're on an erratic but definite course back toward the capital."

"Erratic?"

"They keep stopping to do things, like help with the fire."

"It seems that Kyle Riker may be in control of their situation. He may be the one to have them stop and get involved. I would say he is exhibiting signs of a profound guilt."

"What's he guilty of?" Vale asked. "Other than this?"

"It's all vague, but I have the notion that he feels responsible for what has happened here."

"But he's tactical, not medical. How could he be responsible?"

"A very good question, but I'm without a very good answer," Troi admitted.

"Right now, he's got some more immediate questions to answer for if you ask me," the other woman said. "All right then, they're headed for the capital. Maybe we can predict their next stop based on flight paths and reports on the local security net."

Troi nodded and was about to respond when her communicator signaled.

"Data to Counselor Troi."

"Troi here, Data."

"Counselor, we have verified that the Enterprise *is receiving a signal we believe may be from the commander."*

"Explain, please."

"While performing a routine diagnostic, communications reported we were receiving a recurring position signal that seems aimed directly at the ship. Delta Sigma IV's communications arrays do not use any Starfleet frequency."

"But this signal does."

"Correct. It took some time to identify it, and we have determined it matches a signal unique to personal communicators used by the populace. However, it is merely a positioning signal, and we cannot communicate directly."

"Where is it coming from?"

"It is moving, currently on a direct line toward the capital."

"Ah ha!" Vale exclaimed.

"What was that?"

"That, Mr. Data, was Lieutenant Vale feeling vindicated."

"I see," Data replied.

"Thank you for the information, Data. We'll need to be beamed directly to their position as soon as they stop."

"The transporter room is already standing by."

"Good, Troi out."

Vale was grinning and Troi had to appreciate the moment. They were both feeling that things were drawing to a conclusion. Standing amid the dead bodies, though, Troi wasn't feeling particularly sanguine about how this would play itself out. In fact, she was beginning to fear for Kyle Riker's, and by extension Will's, safety.

Crusher stood in the courtyard at the Council's makeshift headquarters. She had Nurse Weinstein beam down a device filled with the concentrated form of the synthesized compound that was used for the new plant life. Using her tricorder, she verified that everything was intact and the dosages were properly preset.

Before Picard returned to the *Enterprise,* she had suggested that she supervise the release of the compound near the councillors and stand by just in case. He approved the plan and then twinkled out of existence. Minutes later, the device arrived.

Wasdin entered the courtyard and looked at the squat metal object, noting its winking red and yellow lights.

"Our salvation is in something so . . . ugly."

"Form over function," Crusher said, making a final check.

"I don't like the notion of being doped up."

"I don't like it either," Crusher admitted. "I was opposed to this, but I can see the captain's point. You need the time to address your future. I'm just providing you with that time."

"But can my people make a decision when we're not in our right minds?"

"Actually, you're finally going to be in the enlightened, peaceful minds you've always considered natural to you. Now you understand why you cooperate. You can build from there." She didn't necessarily believe every word, but she needed to convince Wasdin that the starship crew was united behind the captain. She owed him that much loyalty.

They stood in silence for a moment and then the two doctors exchanged looks. It was time.

Crusher set a timer for thirty seconds and then stepped away from the device.

"It'll emit the spray in five-second bursts until it's empty. Based on the current weather, it should drift along the wind currents and spread," Crusher explained.

"Will it be like a virus, spreading upon contact?"

"Eventually," Beverly agreed. "These concentrated doses will actually be absorbed through the pores and immediately enter the bloodstream. The pass-along rate will happen once the new plant forms take root. We're sort of kick-starting the process to bring some order back to the people."

"So senseless," Wasdin said.

"And we're ending it . . . now," the starship doctor said. A pink haze surrounded the device and then dissipated. With her tricorder, Crusher recorded it and nodded in approval. Moments later, another pink mist appeared, this time at a different angle. And then another.

Wasdin took in a lungful of misted air. "When will I feel something?"

"When you stop feeling like you want to hit me, you'll know."

"I certainly hope so, because I really don't like that feeling."

"Me either."

Chapter Nine

"WHOEVER KNEW REBUILDING a power plant would take so damn long?" Vincent Porter grumbled. The engineer had been coaxed down to help supervise the reconstruction of the power plant on Tregor. The work was slow because outdated systems had to be replaced and damaged work controls had to be reconstructed from the ground up.

Taurik and Anh Hoang had both been present from the beginning of the repair work, but it was more than the two could handle efficiently. Taurik recognized the need for assistance, and Porter was the logical choice. The dark-skinned man had been at work for an hour straight, rewiring power conduits while Taurik concentrated on the actual generator and Hoang worked on the consoles. She liked working with the circuits, making neat connections, watching indicator lights wink back to life. *Too bad all work couldn't be so simple,* she thought.

Clemons and Studdard, the two large, beefy security guards, had recently arrived and remained on guard.

Weathers continued to patrol the perimeter, complaining good-naturedly that the sights left something to be desired. The people had stayed away, which meant the work could continue unimpeded.

Studdard, as squad leader, periodically had to check in with Jim Peart back on the *Enterprise* and get updates. Hoang was resetting one panel back in its housing as she heard him do the routine check. There was a longer than usual exchange that she couldn't make out, but the man's voice, on the high side to begin with, seemed to rise. She tensed, anticipating more problems.

"There's a cure in the air! The shuttles have completed two orbits of the planet, seeding something sickbay discovered."

"Excellent," Taurik said. "How long before it is effective on the populace?"

"Peart says it'll take a little time for it to spread, like the first problem. But they're seeding it everywhere, so it should be faster."

"Wahoo!" exclaimed Clemons, exchanging some complicated hand gesture with Studdard. Hoang smiled but continued to work, not even bothering to look up and share the moment. After all, the city was without power and sooner or later people would come to vent their frustration. It would be too much to hope that the cure would take effect soon enough to prevent that. Help always seemed too far away when she really needed it.

She continued to make her neat connections, concentrating on each conduit, each optical line, and tried to force images of Starfleet rescue craft coming to her devastated apartment too late to save her family. So intent was she on the work at hand that she failed to notice that things had grown eerily silent.

"Studdard?" she asked in a soft voice. He should be nearby and should reply immediately. Instead, she received no response.

"Clemons?" Still nothing.

"Taurik?"

"Here."

"Where are they?"

"Lieutenant Weathers heard something, and they went to check," he said without coming out. He continued to work in his area, and she tried to get back to the circuits, but she was finding it difficult to concentrate. Minutes ticked by slowly, and she finally realized that she had slowed down further with each passing moment, which was not helping the situation. When neither security officer returned, Hoang grew anxious.

"Should we go look for them?"

"I think we should do our work and let them handle matters on their own," he replied.

"Here, here!" added Porter. He had finished work for the moment and was approaching her with a canteen. Sweat dripped from his grinning face. It was obvious that he had finished a complicated portion of the assignment. He took a long drink, then handed her the canteen. "Haven't handled anything like that in a lo-o-o-ong time," he commented. "Nice to get your hands dirty every now and then. Not that I'd like to do this every day, but it's certainly a nice change from getting ready."

"Ready?"

"Haven't you heard? The big brass is doing an inspection tour and you know we're gonna be on the list sooner or later."

"Of course. We haven't been under the microscope enough as it is." She worried all over again about the cracked injector and the work it required.

"Guess not," Porter said with a laugh. "Well, none of us have failed an inspection yet, so I doubt it'll be an issue."

"Even with the extra attention?"

Before he could reply, there was a roar of sound, the crack of wood snapping, and then a phaser firing. Porter whirled to face the entrance some twenty meters away while Hoang capped the water and let it drop. Both grabbed their phasers, and Porter called for Taurik while Hoang carefully sealed a connection before disengaging herself from a console.

"Clemons to Taurik, get your people out here to help. It's a mess!"

Without acknowledging, Taurik looked at his charges, both of whom nodded ready. Not that Hoang felt ready or even willing to wade into a battle, but she had to aid her colleagues.

In a tight cluster, the three walked toward the entrance, and with every step the shouting grew more distinct. People wanted power, wanted to be able to see in their homes, wanted to know why Starfleet was depriving them of their routine. The people were whipping themselves into a frenzy. The storage units near the building had been overturned, and tools and raw materials were suddenly being turned into weapons.

Anh looked for Studdard's massive form and found him surrounded by at least a dozen people, all screaming at him. Clemons was several feet away, being attacked with something heavy. He ducked under it and swept a leg to tackle his opponent. Weathers, who had come at a run, was firing at people who were hurling stones from the nearby rooftops. Shattered concrete made running tricky, as did the lack of lighting, since the nearest light pole had been bent at something like a forty-five degree angle.

"Hoang, assist Studdard. Porter, come with me," Taurik said as he took off at a run toward Clemons, who was now being pounded with fists.

Anh jogged to the crowd surrounding the much larger Studdard. His eyes seemed sympathetic, his hands patting the air as he tried to answer their harangues. She was worming her way through the people, trying to get close to the security guard, when someone ran a hand into her hair and yanked her off her feet. She fell to the ground and tried to get back up, but a booted foot found her hand and ground it against the concrete.

"We'll deal with you in a minute," the old man snarled and then turned toward Studdard. He withdrew a thin obsidian stick on which he pressed a hidden release. A gleaming steel blade emerged, long and thin but very deadly.

Anh reacted instantly. With her good hand, she aimed and fired a burst. The man jerked spasmodically and fell to the ground beside her.

Few had seen the man attack Hoang. They only knew that one of their neighbors had been felled by a Starfleet officer. That was enough to touch off a fresh round of violence, and people began pounding Studdard with their fists. A woman, her child in a carrier on her back, reached for Hoang. Grateful, the engineer accepted the hand, but when she was halfway up, the woman's foot kicked out, smacking her in the belly and propelling her several feet away.

Shock and anger replaced the stab of pain, but Anh only gripped her phaser more tightly. She did not want to fire out of emotion, but from need. Studdard certainly had need of her. Fists drove him to one knee, and he swung wildly to protect his head. Hoang took aim and fired in a wide arc with the hope of dispersing the crowd. As expected, some fell, and others ran. The security officer flashed her a smile and then reared back and planted a punch on an oncoming attacker. The man was knocked back and over a fallen form.

For the next several minutes, the fighting was artless, with the starship personnel doing what they could to contain the violence and keep people out of the facility. The last thing they needed was to lose all the repair work they had already done. Every so often, Hoang saw Weathers or Taurik handle a crowd of people, but she concentrated her attentions on Studdard, as much to use his bulk as a human shield as to provide backup.

At one point, they were back to back, watching people regroup. "Crazy, huh?" he muttered to her.

"Not something they really trained us for," Hoang admitted.

"Guess not. I got my riot training after the Academy. Guess engineers skip that course."

"Well, you get to skip warp theory in exchange," she replied with a tired smile.

"Good thing. Way too much math for me. Hey, look over there!"

Hoang turned her head to see a crowd of people run away from Weathers, who had knocked down several with a phaser shot. They were running blindly, and in their panic they didn't notice the woman who had kicked Hoang, the one with the baby, lying on the ground. She had one arm around the infant, still in his carrier, and was holding her ankle with her other hand. She had obviously twisted her ankle.

She was going to be trampled.

Hoang began to run toward the crowd but judged she was too far away to reach the woman in time. Instead, she raised her phaser, eyes glancing over the setting to be safe, and then fired. She had hoped to divide the crowd, sparing the woman. At first, people ran right or left, away from the beam, although it struck two immediately, and they fell. One man leapt over one of the fallen bodies, but he caught his foot in some loose clothing and went sprawling. He fell right on top of the woman and the infant, and all Hoang could hear was the combined scream of man, woman, and child.

The man was scrambling to his feet, ready to keep running, ignoring the woman and child. Hoang was already there, her legs spread to prevent the man from going anywhere. She turned her attention to the woman and saw her cradling the child, who did not appear to be breathing. When the engineer reached toward the woman to help, the gesture was greeted with a snarl. Hoang recoiled, then stood for a moment, watching. All other sounds receded, and her field of vision was limited to the bodies in her immediate area.

"Is the baby hurt?" Hoang asked in a quiet voice.

The woman did not respond. The man, though, tried to break away, but Hoang grabbed his upper arm and whipped him about, forcing him to look at the woman. Silently, they watched as the woman cuddled the baby, listening for any sign of life. As the woman whimpered, Hoang strained her hearing for any sign from the infant. No cry of pain, no sound of any sort.

"Dorset bitch," the man said to himself.

Hoang snapped. She punched the man in the midsection, knocking the air out of him so that he doubled over. Viciously, she kneed him back up and then struck out again with her fist wrapped around the phaser. The man was quickly turned into a punching bag, the recipient of the bottled-up hate and fear that had never truly found its release since the Breen attack. Every hit, punch, and kick was payback for the death of her family, for the war that claimed countless lives, and for the foolishness of the disease that had driven a planet to the brink of madness.

The man was long past being able to defend himself and soon was not even able to call for help. He was limp, taking the beating without any hope of a swift ending.

Hoang reared back for another blow, but her small fist was caught in Studdard's much larger hand. She squirmed for a moment, then went limp herself, her lean body falling against his comfortable bulk.

"I think he's paid the price," he said soothingly.

"Is he breathing?"

A pause as he looked over her head at the body on the ground. "Yes."

"Then maybe he hasn't paid the full price," she said between deep breaths.

"I'd say he has. His fall killed the baby, but it wasn't intentional."

"Children . . . they shouldn't . . . not out here . . . no one should be hurt," Anh said incoherently.

"No one's innocent here, no one's blameless," Studdard continued, his hand stroking her short hair, providing unexpected comfort. Hoang heard his heart thumping loudly in his chest, his words softly overlapping the now distant sounds of the riot. She didn't notice that most of the people had been run off or stunned into silence. Nothing seemed to sink in other than his heartbeat. Steady, rhythmic.

"Heard you lost your own family," he said hesitantly. "I can see how this would make you more than a little nuts. But you can't take it all out on this man. He's done nothing to hurt you."

"But, but . . . he hurt the baby . . . the baby," she stammered.

"The baby isn't the first innocent to die today. I'd like to think he's the last, but I don't know. We won't know for a while, I guess."

"She tried to hit me before, blame me for taking away her power," Anh managed to say. She took several deep breaths, forcing her body to calm down.

"No one was in the mood for logic. Must have been very hard on Taurik," Studdard said.

She had to smile at that, and then she looked up at Studdard. His smile created dimples in his cheeks, his white teeth showing through his lips. He held her gently, letting her body regain something approaching normal.

"I have to let go now, check on my people," Studdard said after another few moments.

"Of course. Thank you . . ."

"Aaron."

"Thank you, Aaron."

The big man let go and walked over to Weathers, who seemed to be nursing a sore shoulder. She watched him, feeling a great sense of gratitude. After another moment, she looked down at the body of her victim and was flooded with a sense of anger and mostly of shame. She looked up again, watched Studdard wander off, and realized the sight of him gave her comfort—a feeling she hadn't had in a long time.

"Third orbit's complete," Peart reported from the tactical station. Data, who had been sitting in the command chair, acknowledged the report, and then watched telemetry come in on the screen directly before him.

The turbolift doors opened, and La Forge walked onto the bridge. The chief engineer came directly to the command section and took the chair normally used by Counselor Troi. Data watched, measuring his friend's speed, rate of breathing, and level of distraction.

"I'm tired," La Forge admitted. "We're short-handed up here and stretched to the limit down below. My people just got attacked at the Tregor power station."

"Injuries?"

"Nothing serious, according to Taurik," La Forge replied. "How're we doing here?"

"Fourth orbit has just begun, so one-third of the planet has now been seeded."

"Any sign of improvement?"

"I am still awaiting word from the medical staff on the planet."

"Things getting any worse?"

"Not that we can tell."

"Well, I'll take that for the moment."

"Agreed. How goes your own operation?"

"Dex is due soon with the new plasma injector. But first I had to cut some new deals. Seems the *Hermes* was short some vital ODN parts, so he had to first pick up spares from the *Magellan* and that delayed him."

"But you are in control of the entire network?"

"Makes my head hurt to remember it all, but we're doing some real good here."

"I believe we will have to inform the captain of this when he next returns. Sooner or later he will learn of this, and I conclude it is better he learn from us than from another captain."

La Forge had a shocked look on his face, but then nodded. "You know, all this time I've been dealing with fellow engineers and it never occurred to me that a captain might be in touch to complain . . ."

". . . or, more likely, offer congratulations," Data finished.

"I suppose so, but you're right, better he hear it from us. In fact, I can only imagine what would happen if he learned of this from someone like Captain Conklin."

Data studied the face La Forge made and catalogued it as a sour one. He knew this was considered an undesirable feature. La Forge leaned back in his chair, watching additional information come in from the shuttles.

"Mr. Peart," Data said, "any deviation in flight paths?"

"None, sir," Peart said. "You have the best flyers out there."

"Who've you got?" La Forge asked.

"Lieutenant Perim aboard the *Jefferies,* Lieutenant Hras on the *Chawla,* Lieutenant Copern on the *Keuka.*"

"Wish we'd had a chance to finish repairing the *Ballard.* We're still awaiting some components, but that's low on the wish list," La Forge said. He was, in fact, the one who had crashed the shuttlecraft a few weeks earlier.

"Understandable," Data said.

"Commander Riker will be insulted you didn't list him among the best," La Forge cracked.

"I would have if he he'd been available. Lieutenant Vale and Counselor Troi are still searching."

"Well, that's something," La Forge said, and looked over at Data. The android was calculating whether or not having Commander Riker pilot a shuttle would have made a difference in their completion schedule, and the conclusion, which took .00356 seconds to reach, was that at best that shuttle would have completed its work thirty seconds sooner. He was about to offer that opinion but chose not to say anything as a subroutine reminded him that such information, while accurate, was not always welcome.

"Ever since the doctor started talking about leaving . . ." La Forge began, then hesitated.

Data gave him a penetrating look.

"It's nothing, really," La Forge said. "There's gonna

be an opening at Starfleet Medical and she's thinking about taking it."

"Does she believe she will enjoy the experience more than the last time?"

"Maybe. I'm not sure. I think seeing Wes got her to thinking about the future and where she wants to be. While we're weathering this storm with Starfleet right now, it's clear we won't be together forever."

"No. In fact, Captain Picard's ability to keep the senior crew intact has defied all probability."

"That's because of the incalculable role politics and dumb luck can play with expectations. But she's right, we won't be together for that much longer."

"That thought first crossed my mind when we lost Lieutenant Yar at Vagra II."

"That was a long time ago, Data."

"Indeed. But since then, as various department heads have come and gone, I have assessed the comparative strengths and weaknesses of the command staff and weighed that against Starfleet's desires for continuity versus their need to staff ships with seasoned officers."

La Forge let out a low whistle. "Do you think about that often?"

"Of late it has occurred with greater frequency, which is understandable in view of our last several months of duty. The doctor would make an excellent surgeon general, given her field experience as well as previous tenure on Earth." He paused, cocking his head to one side, which indicated deeper computations were taking place.

"I do know that her absence will be felt," he continued. "Her lessons have been most helpful to me in assimilating myself with the crew."

"Well, she hasn't said yes. I think she's still thinking about it."

"She will no doubt make the decision that best serves Starfleet as well as her personal ambitions."

The flyer neared the capital city and Will thought things were about to be settled one way or the other. By now he figured the *Enterprise* should be finding his signal and sending help. He hated to admit it but he had dozed for a while as Kyle flew them in silence. Even Bison had the grace to stop complaining.

No one had eaten, everyone needed a bed and some serious rest.

And he needed Deanna. The feeling continued to grow with every passing minute, which helped him crystallize his thoughts and also gave him the strength to keep moving.

His wandering thoughts were jarred when the flyer banked and headed for a small town.

"What are you doing?" Will demanded of his father.

"We're low enough I can see a mob," his father explained. "We have to break this up."

"No, Dad, we don't," Will said with as much patience as he could muster. "We have to get Bison to a hospital. We have to tell Captain Picard and Dr. Crusher everything you know."

"What he said," Bison chimed in. "Really, if I can help, fine. If I'm to be executed, fine. But I don't need another stop on my way."

"Shut up, both of you," Kyle said. "We'll stop, contain the fight, and move on. It's what Starfleet does, right, son?"

Will just shook his head. His father had the controls and he didn't want to fight for them in case things got out of hand.

"This has to be the last time," Will said slowly.

"That's the Willy I know."

"And you really have to stop calling me that, Dad."

Kyle ignored the comment and set up for landing. Within minutes they were on the ground and the hatch was sliding open.

"You have the phase pistol, Willy, so you have my back. We just break this up, send everyone on their way and then we can go to the capital."

The trio strode out of the flyer, assessed the situation and the Rikers moved forward as one. Before them were at least two dozen men and women, mixed races, and no one was saying anything intelligible. The fight could have started over anything and Will was too tired to begin speculating. He wanted to end this quickly and move on. A part of him also recognized he was doing this to help his father's guilty conscience but unlike the school, this seemed trivial. And that was the main reason that this had to be the final interruption. Kyle was clearly losing the capacity to judge when it was appropriate to get involved.

Kyle and Will were two meters from the closest body and they stared at the tangle. They looked at each other and shrugged simultaneously. As one, they reached forward and grabbed whatever limb they could latch onto and pulled. The tangle was quickly separated but no one seemed happy about it.

"We really have to stop doing this!"

Kyle glanced over his shoulder to watch as Will grabbed a rifle from an overweight, older Bader, and used it to trip the assailant to his right. Will grimaced at the strain on his right shoulder. Here they were, in some small, out-of-the-way community, charging headlong into a melee without bothering to understand the nature of the fight. By now, these people were probably fueled by enough fear and anxiety that it could have been sparked by spilled milk or a man looking the wrong way at another's wife.

All Kyle wanted to do was separate enough people so that emotions could burn themselves out and things could settle down. The town was too small to have peace officers stationed nearby, which put the onus on Kyle.

Will gritted his teeth, jammed an elbow into a charging woman, and swung the rifle like a propeller to keep others away. He needed to pause and take a look around him. Wherever they were, it was in the late hours of the night. Dawn would be breaking over the horizon shortly.

People were mixing it up on the main street and several side streets. Kyle was using his hands to literally lift fighters off one another and push them aside. Women, teenagers, and men were in the fight together, creating odd-looking combinations. Will started to lower the rifle when he saw one man approach his father from behind, a deadly looking piece of metal in his hands. Quickly, Will adjusted his arms and released the rifle, letting it spin. An instant before the man could swing, the rifle smacked him in the back and caused him to cry out in pain. Alerted now, Kyle turned and used the man's off-balance position to knock him down.

Father and son exchanged satisfied glances and then resumed their efforts.

"Where are these weapons coming from? I thought this was a residential community."

Kyle shrugged and reached into a mass of people to pull several apart. He smiled and reached in again.

He's enjoying this, Will realized. His father was actually getting some perverse sort of pleasure from doing something that was merely providing a short-term solution. While Will never shied away from a battle, he certainly didn't go looking for one either.

A young girl watched as her father got clubbed to the ground. She shrieked and leapt onto the attacker's back, trying to pull out his hair. A man came to the attacker's defense, reaching to roughly pull the girl off. The father, from a kneeling position, reached out, waving a knife to protect his daughter.

Will realized this was never going to end without some form of planetwide intervention. Still, he felt compelled to save as many lives as he could. With a deep breath, he ran over to the crowd, kicking out to push the intended victim away from the knife. He then reached down and with a judo move forced the man to release the knife. His booted foot stepped on it, preventing anyone else from reaching it.

"Take your father and go home," Will ordered the girl. She nodded once and reached to help the man to his feet.

Will was absorbed in the moment, unaware of the sounds around him.

He didn't see men rushing from both sides to come to the downed man's aid.

He couldn't see that one man was aiming a phaser directly at his head.

He didn't hear the warning cry.

All Will Riker saw was a girl comforting her father as they staggered away. Then all of a sudden he was being pushed to the ground. As he fell backward, he heard the familiar whine of a phaser firing. Then there was a limp form on top of him.

Then all he heard were footsteps receding and screams in the night air.

Riker struggled to move the body off him, concerned that there was someone out there with a phaser, unable to reach his own. His nose wrinkled at the odor of seared flesh as he rolled the body off his legs.

And only then did he recognize his father's body. In a flash, Will understood that Kyle had seen his son endangered and had acted, sacrificing himself.

It wasn't supposed to happen this way.

His father's vacant eyes were dull. There was no peace in those eyes. Just a look of anguish.

Will tried to control his breathing, assess the circumstances, and act like an officer. But his eyes were wet, blurring his vision.

Boys don't cry. His father told him that endlessly in the early years after Ann died. And since then, Will had not allowed himself tears. He blinked them back, but one escaped, trickling down his cheek and disappearing into his gray-flecked beard.

Will stood, withdrawing his phaser and looked about. People struggled here and there, but clearly the worst was over. None came near him, and that was just fine by Will.

Imzadi.

If he ever needed Deanna by his side, it was now. With his father dead at his feet, no way to contact the *Enterprise,* and far from the capital. He stood lost and alone.

Looking down at the body and the black sear that ran from Kyle's left shoulder blade down his back, a part of Will analyzed the phaser setting. Part of him wanted to look away.

We never resolved this crisis, Will thought. *He'll never know how this plays out.* Kyle's strategic expertise was now lost to the Federation and no doubt would be needed. The galaxy was far from stable and people like Kyle had to look at the big picture. His father was always looking to the stars, reading something in their alignment that no one else could fathom. That skill was gone.

A future that might have been was snuffed out in an instant. After so many years of estrangement, the wall between them had started to crumble and let light seep through. Will had dared to hope. Now it was gone.

He was lost.

Will was so mired in his own thoughts that he didn't register the sound of a transporter beam. It was only after arms wrapped around him from behind that his mind registered a warmth.

"Will," Deanna said.

He turned, despite being squeezed tighter, and somehow his lover was there. He needed her and she had come and he rested a tired head atop her own. They stood together in silence.

Beside them, trying to give them privacy, Christine

Vale knelt by Kyle's body and studied it. She focused on the injury and then checked his body for potential weapons or boobytraps. All she found was a piece of technology she didn't immediately recognize and put it aside to study later.

It was time to return to the *Enterprise.*

Chapter Ten

TROPP RAPIDLY RUBBED his hands together, generating some friction to warm them. He couldn't wear insulated gloves since he needed his fingers to reach inside the Dorset woman's chest. When he had received the call from Gracin, Tropp had just settled down with his first real meal in two days. Things had calmed down enough for the duty personnel to be given time off, and his first thought had been of a nice, hot meal.

Which was why Gracin called. Tropp was sure of it.

A building partially collapsed, killing some people and stranding others in their rooms. Tropp figured the place was either a large inn or a small hotel. Regardless. When he materialized by the rubble, Gracin told him the old structure had been the victim of a natural disaster. There was nothing sinister, based on tricorder readings.

Starship crew were busily pulling debris away, creating openings to allow rescue staff to enter. Gracin saw to it that medical personnel were each assigned a security officer so they could work unimpeded.

No sooner did an entrance appear than Tropp was through it, his wrist light casting eerie shadows. The hallway was filled with bodies, torn paintings, random clothing, and unidentifiable debris. His tricorder found the first life sign five meters to his left. He moved gingerly over cracked paneling and quickly looked ahead to make certain there were no exposed circuits.

When he found the woman, her saw her chest had been crushed by falling objects. She was breathing raggedly, but there was still hope.

And here he was, carefully reaching into her wound, gingerly removing dirt and bits of debris. He paused every few moments to use an antiseptic spray to keep the wound clean. The work was slow, but she continued to breathe shallowly and her pulse remained steady.

As he concentrated on his work, Tropp heard a great deal of noise behind him. He shut it away, thinking only of the woman. The doctor took comfort from the notion that he had a guard watching his back.

The noise grew louder and finally, he used the spray and looked up. The guard was relaxed, his phaser pointed down, and he was watching down the hall, the way they had entered. Tropp twisted around and dropped his mouth open in surprise.

A motley collection of Bader and Dorset people were pulling away debris, others shoring up the entrance with fresh-cut wood. They were smiling and working hard, but with purpose and pleasure. Tropp shook his head in disbelief. Crusher's formula had worked. The people were shoving their natural tendencies back into their private boxes and were once again calm and cooperative.

He returned to work on the woman, smiling through the entire procedure.

Picard had fallen asleep in the Council chamber while waiting for reports to arrive from around the globe. The chairs weren't particularly comfortable, but cxhaustion had finally caught up with him.

Carmona, somehow still on duty, gently prodded the captain awake. He was instantly alert and grinned a little sheepishly for letting himself nod off.

"It's the *Enterprise,* sir. They've found the commander."

Picard's eyes widened at the good news, but the security officer's face didn't seem to match the good tidings.

"Kyle Riker, though, is dead. Both are back on board."

Picard stood up and went to a corner for privacy. He contacted Data and was quickly filled in on what had happened only an hour's flight away. A part of him was pleased that father had saved son, but it was still a tragic and needless loss. He wondered briefly what reaction this would bring from Admiral Upton. Well, they had discussed what a mess of a mission this was likely to be, and now the prophetic words rang true.

Riker was sleeping, Troi was staying on board to be nearby, and Crusher was tending to the body. He'd talk to them all later.

"What of the cure?"

"Reports from the capital show that people are calming down. There are fewer outbreaks being reported."

"Well, that's something. With Dr. Crusher occupied, please see to it Dr. Wasdin receives all our data."

"A link has already been established."

"Very good. I'll remain here for a little while. Picard out."

He saw Morrow and Seer enter the chamber, chatting. Neither looked as if he had slept, but they were certainly animated about something. In fact, the protocol officer seemed downright excited, and that piqued the captain's interest.

"Something of note, gentlemen?"

"Seer has already outlined the beginnings of a repair program for the entire planet, and it makes remarkable sense," Morrow said.

"You're surprised?" Seer smiled wearily.

"Let's just say that our experiences with the Council didn't lead us to expect such energetic activity."

"Ah, I can see that, having served in the past. Well, without my normal duties to perform, I just used the time wisely. Captain, what's wrong?"

"Wrong? Oh, I just received news from the ship. You'll be happy to know that we've found Mr. Riker and he's back aboard. However, his father was killed while saving his son."

"That's terrible," Morrow said, shock crossing his youthful features.

"The final duty," Seer said solemnly.

The three men discussed the circumstances, and talking about it made the captain feel a little better.

The next few hours passed quickly. Reports were finally coming in from a number of peace officers and medical personnel that matters were finally settling down. In fact, since the shuttles began orbiting the world, no new fires, explosions, or acts of sabotage had been recorded. Picard took cold comfort from the news.

"Captain, we have begun tallying the damage," Jus Renks Jus told him at one point.

Picard put down his cup of *coolar,* the closest thing the planet had to tea. He looked a question at the tall Speaker. The Dorset man spoke quickly, droning on about pipelines, power grids, public and private property losses, and other damage that would need attention in the coming days and weeks. The captain concluded that the planet sounded like the rest of the Federation. Even four years after the Dominion War's end, the rebuilding was continuing. This world had not been caught in the conflict, had in fact prospered because it had much-needed food supplies. And now they were as damaged as the others.

"Actually, Speaker, I believe Seer has already outlined repair programs that are quite promising," Picard told the man.

Genuinely surprised, the Speaker looked around the room until he spotted Seer speaking with one of the women councillors. He nodded to Picard and hurried over to the protocol officer.

Progress, at last, Picard thought. He wondered what would have happened had the leadership actually started preparing the populace sooner. How much damage could have been avoided?

He watched Seer hand over a padd with the information and then walk away from the Speaker, who studied the results. Picard sought out the protocol officer and offered him a fresh mug of *coolar.*

"How did you manage to assemble the information so much faster than the Council?"

"Cainam, one of the aides, has been bringing me quarter-hourly reports. It was easy for me to assess continent by continent what needed doing."

Picard shook his head in amazement.

"Will Renks follow your plan?"

"I honestly believe he will. He's always been one of the more rational councillors I've dealt with."

"The Council has to rebuild, I agree, but then they need to plan. Delta Sigma IV will not always be able to avoid conflicts with other races."

"Will and I discussed a lot of that while we flew. And your ambassador and I have also been chatting."

"Sounds like you want to have a more active role."

"Maybe it's my own aggressive personality coming to the fore. Maybe not. Still, I never wanted to leave the Council. And now that there's a vacancy, I find that I want to take a more integral part."

"Your planet needs you. I applaud the decision."

Seer smiled at the vote of confidence. "Now I just have to share the news with Dorina."

"Will that cause a problem?"

"I intend to have the conversation before the ambassador leaves, just in case I need help," Seer said with a laugh.

Picard smiled. For the first time he felt a glimmer of hope that the planet would survive. It would have the time it needed to rebuild and then decide its fate.

His thoughts were interrupted when he saw a form

materialize near the center of the room. Years of experience told him it was Beverly Crusher, and he smiled in preparation.

"How's Will?" Picard asked immediately.

"Still sleeping. I checked in with Deanna before beaming down," she replied.

"Good. What news?"

"It's working," she said simply. "It's spreading, although about thirteen percent slower than the simulations indicated. But I think we can live with that."

Picard nodded. "So do I."

"Good. If you'll excuse me, I want to go over the findings with Wasdin."

"Of course. I'll be here if you need me." He watched her walk off. His confidence in a successful end to the situation was rising rapidly.

Crusher quickly left the compound and headed directly for Wasdin's office, each step bringing her closer to concluding the mission. A moment too late for Kyle Riker . . . and possibly for the entire planet.

When she had received the signal from Vale, her heart had dropped, but she had immediately switched to her professional mode and personally met the body in the transporter room. Nafir had had the good grace not to say anything and mutely watched as Deanna helped Will from the platform and Vale waited with the body. Kyle was placed on the antigrav pallet, and Nurse Weinstein carefully walked it back to sickbay. No one had said a word; there really wasn't anything to say.

As expected, her sensors had told her exactly what she

expected: death had been caused by a phaser blast. However, her exam had also revealed numerous fresh cuts, scrapes, and abrasions, so whatever Kyle had been doing, he had certainly been active. She had raised her eyebrows at the number of older wounds and broken bones. She had always thought Kyle was a thinker, but his body told her otherwise. Crusher never got to know him, and now her curiosity would never be satisfied.

Entering the medical facility reminded her all over again about the possibilities of having similar research equipment at her disposal should she choose Earth over the *Enterprise*. With things winding down, the time was coming when she had to organize her thoughts and make a decision.

"Dr. Crusher, I'm thrilled you came in person."

With Wasdin's words, Crusher put her own issues aside and smiled at the worn, older woman. She handed over an active padd.

"Everything is there, from my research to the telemetry from our sensors. You can follow the progress further from your own satellite network."

"At least the fighting couldn't reach them," Wasdin remarked.

"Small favors. How are things here?"

"Ah, not so bad. Those high doses you sprayed here have certainly taken hold. I certainly don't feel like hitting anyone anymore."

"That's comforting to hear," Crusher said. Inwardly, she winced at the notion that Wasdin, like millions of others, were being drugged back to peace. She reran the arguments in her head again and again, and no doubt would for some time to come. While things had improved for the people, she remained uncertain that effectively drugging a world would be well received by Yerbi Fandau, or by the Federation itself.

Those were going to be debates for another day.

"Hand me the scope," Hoang asked.

Porter nodded and gave her the device without comment. Hoang appreciated the silence; it gave her a chance to concentrate. Things had calmed down over the last few hours, and she had worked straight through the night to help repair the power station.

Taurik wanted to make sure the station would work for the long term, so every circuit, conduit, and isolinear chip would have to be checked. Porter had regulated much of the power flow, and Taurik followed both of their accomplishments with diagnostic checks.

Studdard and Clemons volunteered to remain on hand to watch them while other members of the security detail had rotated back aboard the ship for rest.

Hoang took comfort in seeing Studdard's broad, smiling face every time she emerged from behind panels. She actually caught herself wiping some grease off her cheek before standing up to accept the scope from Porter. What she was feeling, she knew, was good, yet she wondered if it was all right for her to feel good over a simple smile.

She knelt down once more and checked her final series of connections. Green lights flashed back at her.

The smile this time was deserved. Everything was in place and would last.

She popped up again, barely containing her grin.

"Green?"

"All green, Lieutenant," she replied.

Porter's smile matched her own.

Porter and Hoang walked over to the completely rebuilt master control panel, and Hoang and Taurik flanked him. Everything was in standby mode; amber lights dotted the board. Hoang knew that Taurik's work was exacting, but she worried just a bit about her own. She had been so distracted of late, it was screamingly apparent she really did need to take Counselor Troi up on her offer to help.

"Lieutenant, I believe the honor should be yours," Porter said, stepping aside.

Hoang looked at him for a moment and then took two steps forward. Looking over her own handiwork, she nodded. Everything seemed right. Her left hand reached out and entered a command code. Four lights flashed confirmation. She then placed both hands on the board and began to enter the start-up sequences.

Seconds passed and she studied the board. Lights moved, indicators rose, and then finally, the welcome sound of a deep thrum.

"Power's up," Porter said with a whoop.

"As expected," Taurik noted.

Hoang stepped back and watched. Things were definitely looking up. Finally.

One of the security officers, a Gallamite she did not know, came running through the main entrance. With a grin, he jerked a thumb over his shoulder. "You did it!"

The various officers walked behind the Gallamite out into the fresh air. Hoang was amazed to see the sun was starting to come over the horizon. She watched the golden light against the sky, which was filled with billowy clouds. Dotting the horizon were the squat buildings of Tregor, and she saw they were filled with light. Light powered by the plant.

"What's that?" Porter asked, cupping his ear.

"Cheers, sir," Studdard said. "That's a city full of people expressing their appreciation." He flashed Hoang a grin.

Hoang nodded in agreement. Things were definitely starting to look up.

Chapter Eleven

WILL RIKER ADJUSTED the collar of his dress uniform. He looked in the mirror, liking the way it draped over his chest.

He didn't like the reason for wearing it.

Troi was right behind him, handing him the decorations he had received over his career. Absently, he accepted each one and affixed it over his left breast. She remained silent, letting him take things one step at a time.

"Not bad for a career man, don't you think?" he asked Troi.

"I'd say there's room for a few more," she replied.

"Thank you," he said gently. He looked once more in the mirror, ran a hand through his hair, and nodded in satisfaction.

"Ready?"

"Just about." Riker paused, looking around his cabin, uncertain why.

"You don't have to speak if you don't want to," Troi said in a voice full of sympathy.

"I have to. No one else on board knows him as well. Knew him. Dammit." Riker paced the cabin.

"We didn't speak a lot, but that doesn't mean I'm ignorant of his accomplishments. They add up to one thing: he died as he lived, making sacrifices to secure the future. These people now have a future. And I . . . I have a future because of him."

Troi walked over, wrapped her arms around him, and hugged. The warmth felt good to him.

"Remember when I said the other day how much I hate unfinished business?"

She made an affirmative noise.

"I never got to finish business with my father. And I don't like that feeling. I don't want to feel that way again."

"Marry me."

"I can't bear the thought of not having you in my . . . what did you say?"

"Marry me, Will. Please."

They broke the clinch and looked at each other; Will's eyes were filled with astonishment. She took his hands and continued speaking.

"Every moment you were searching for your father, I was thinking about you. I missed you. I watched so much loss of life here, saw people lose their futures. I don't like unfinished business either, and it's about time we completed what we started on Betazed. I want to be married to you, William Riker."

"I was thinking the same thing," Will said. "About the need to build my future with you. You're too important to me to let slip away. I so very much want you to be my life mate, to share the time we have left."

"We were meant to be together from the moment we met. Your desire for a career put us on hold for a long time," Troi observed.

"Too long."

"You see that now. You didn't always."

"I don't know what to say."

"Well, the answer better be yes."

"Yes." He smiled.

She returned the grin. "Good. There, doesn't that feel better?"

"You don't propose to all your visitors, do you?"

"Of course not. On Betazed it's strictly one spouse at a time."

Will nodded, squeezing her hands.

"You have to promise me one thing."

"To love, honor, or cherish?"

"No, after that. Seriously, I've thought about this a lot. The men in the Riker line aren't all that easy on their women. Or children. You have to promise that the moment I act like my father toward the children—or you—you must hit me. Hard."

She giggled for a moment and then straightened her features. "Absolutely. You have my word that I'll beat you to a pulp."

"Good."

Will took Deanna into his arms, all thoughts of the upcoming service banished. All he saw was her beautiful face, all he smelled was the herbal soap she loved, all he heard was her breathing, and all he felt was the rapid beating of her heart.

He leaned down and kissed her.

"When this is over, we should go look for a ring," Troi said long moments later.

Will's eyes twinkled and he put up a forefinger. Quickly he turned and reached into a drawer. A moment later, he held out a small wooden box, etched with an intricate design. He dropped to one knee, and offered her the box.

"You've been planning this long enough to find a ring?" Her voice was filled with admiration and confusion.

"Truth to tell, Deanna, it's only been seriously on my mind these last few days. But when Seer and I were looking for my father . . . we passed a jeweler in a small town. This caught my eye, and earlier today I asked him to secure it for me. He had it beamed up only an hour ago."

She looked at him, eyes glittering, happy. Carefully, she weighed the box in the palm of her hand and smiled. Then she used a fingernail to pry open the hinged lid and studied the contents.

She smiled broadly.

"It's gorgeous!"

Quickly she withdrew the emerald and diamond ring, studying the setting. The jewels were set in a three-toned golden metal, artfully intertwining.

"And you knew my ring size?"

Riker grinned. "A good first officer knows all pertinent details about the crew. It should fit. Go ahead."

Deanna slipped the ring onto her left hand and then admired it in the light. Will stepped forward, took her hand in his, and inspected the ring.

"I think it fits just fine," he finally said.

She didn't reply, just looked up and kissed him.

Picard sat in his ready room, already in his dress uniform even though the service was hours away. He figured it was best this way, just in case he was summoned by Starfleet Command or the Council. To his right sat a stack of padds requiring his attention. He had asked Data to send him everything that normally required Riker's attention. There was no doubt giving his first officer time was paramount.

Since rising, he had seen to the communiqués from Starfleet and begun wading through the personnel reviews that had been completed by Troi and Riker before arriving at Delta Sigma IV. He was surprised, but not that surprised, to see the number of transfer requests. He knew some of the names better than others, and noted that Riker had amended Kawasaki's request. He'd found the time to talk with her before they reached orbit here, and she had changed her mind about leaving.

Riker strikes again. Picard nodded in approval.

His door chimed, and he invited his guests in. Data and La Forge, still in duty uniforms, entered and were waved to seats before the captain's desk. During all the troubles below, the starship had run smoothly, and he began by thanking them for their efforts.

"We were just following your orders," Data said.

"And most ably, as will be reflected in my mission report. The last thing I needed was a distraction up here. Now tell me, Mr. La Forge, what's wrong with the plasma injector?"

La Forge explained about the manufacturing defect and the need for a brand-new injector. It was something that could not be replicated.

"What did the sector quartermaster say about that?"

Geordi shifted a bit in his chair. "Well, I didn't ask him."

Picard's eyebrows rose a bit.

"I would have, but after my last few requests, I began to get the sense that he's really stretched thin."

"I gather resupply, especially this far out, has been a problem."

"Yes, sir. We haven't usually spent this much time out in the farther reaches these last few years."

No, we haven't, but we are getting a taste of that now, thanks to the admiralty, Picard thought. "So, what solution have you devised?"

"I've actually devised more than a solution, sir."

The eyebrows rose a bit more.

"It's an elaborate network of trading with other ships in the nearby sectors."

Picard nodded thoughtfully. "And how do you propose we get supplies from one ship to another. By shuttlecraft?"

"Er, not exactly."

"How then?"

La Forge looked at Data, who remained impassive. He looked back at Picard and swallowed. Whatever was coming was going to be unorthodox, Picard concluded.

"A Ferengi named Dex has been contracted to act as courier between ships. He'll be here tomorrow with the injector."

Picard was nonplussed. He quickly mulled over the elaborate network that had been erected and the notion of using someone outside of Starfleet to act as agent. No doubt that would gain all manner of attention when he filed his reports.

"A Ferengi? And he can be trusted?"

"Actually, Captain," Data interjected. "This is exactly what the Ferengi specialize in. Geordi learned that the Ferengi's craft was in need of repair as well as protection in this portion of space. They live by their commercial codes, and in this case Dex ferries the supplies for a variety of Starfleet ships, receiving repairs and our goodwill in return. Should something befall his ship, he will have a large number of starships predisposed to come to his rescue. He does gain much profit from this, although much of it is intangible."

"Dex's vessel actually appreciates in value with the repairs," La Forge added. "*That's* tangible."

"I see," Picard said, mulling over the plan. "How long has this network of yours been in operation?"

"Since before we made orbit, sir. I needed a new quad and the *Nautilus* had one and, well, one thing led to another."

Picard was already several steps ahead of his chief engineer. He knew his crew, he trusted them, and he continued to value their judgment. The captain knew exactly the tangible and intangible benefits this program would bring the *Enterprise*. The goodwill La Forge and, by extension, Picard were earning at a time when goodwill was hard to find at Command.

"This has the makings of something rather unusual,"

Picard finally said. "And I can't say I particularly approve of using a Ferengi courier without the knowledge of Commander Riker or myself."

"Under the circumstances, sir, we believed this to be an efficacious and sound program that we were certain you would approve."

"And I do approve it. A bit late, but this was fine thinking. However, in the future I would appreciate it, Mr. La Forge and Mr. Data, if you would make every effort to keep me apprised of such activities earlier so there are no surprises."

La Forge looked relieved and settled back in his chair. "It serves a lot of ships and keeps us in fine form. And when the *Enterprise* is added to that inspection tour, well, I don't want to give them any cause for complaint."

Picard had pushed thoughts of the inspection out of his mind, but it bolstered the need for La Forge's plan all the more.

"Do we know when we will be added to the list, sir?"

"Not yet, Data."

"In the future, we might look forward to Dr. Crusher as an ally."

Picard frowned and looked directly at his second officer. "What do you mean?"

"Should Dr. Crusher accept the position of new surgeon general, she might come on future inspections tours."

"Yes, of course," Picard said quickly.

He sat back, stunned. While he knew that Dr. Fandau had made a written offer to her—per regulations, the doctor had to inform Crusher's CO before making the offer—Picard had assumed by her silence on the matter that Crusher turned it down. But clearly she was considering it if she would discuss it with La Forge and Data. Why hadn't she mentioned it to him?

He put himself in her place. She had just seen Wesley, she had watched the ship and crew placed under unfair scrutiny by Command, and she had to be aware of time passing. It made some sense that she would consider the opportunity. *And why not?* he mused. She was qualified for it, even more so now than when she had held the post a decade earlier.

All of Starfleet and the Federation would benefit from her taking the new position. Well, all save the captain. He felt the loss of family quite deeply, and disliked the notion of another loss. He'd lost crewmembers all the time, but not often from his senior staff. There had been Jack Crusher in the waning days of his *Stargazer* command. There had been Yar and Worf and Daniels. And now, maybe Beverly.

He'd be happy for her. If this was what she wanted, he would not stand in her way. Privately, he wished her to stay. In so many ways she was a comfort, and he dreaded the notion of losing her.

Chapter Twelve

ALL BEVERLY THOUGHT about on the walk from her cabin to Picard's was that now was the time to tell him about Starfleet Medical. After getting some sleep, she had finally looked at her private communications, and there was a draft of Yerbi's formal retirement announcement. It was dated three weeks hence, which meant the rumor mill would be in full swing within the next week. She had that much time to make a decision. Crusher knew Yerbi had wanted to leave his post sooner, but delayed while she was preoccupied.

Beverly had to weigh and balance her professional wants against her personal needs, and even though she had received feedback from Troi and La Forge, she still had not reached a decision. As she rounded a corner before arriving at the captain's door, she felt a longing she normally ignored. But this time it continued to draw her, probably because a part of her mind was already imagining a life apart from the *Enterprise* and its captain.

Picard bade her enter, and she saw the usual breakfast table set for just two. He seemed refreshed, although she suspected he was still strained. After all, the last few days had been hard on everyone, and there was still mopping up to do. She knew he was trying to handle some of Riker's work, letting the man deal with his loss. Rather than assign the work to Data, he took it on himself, his way of showing respect for his first officer.

They had all lost so much over the last few years, starting with La Forge's mother going missing. Picard lost his brother and nephew to a fire. Worf lost his wife on Deep Space 9, Data gave away a part of himself by surrendering his emotion chip. And now Kyle Riker was gone. And once again she felt the conflict between fleeing a stressful situation and the benefits of a fresh start.

"Beverly?"

She realized that she let had her mind wander, and Picard had noticed. With a smile, she took her seat and placed the linen napkin in her lap.

"I'm fine, Jean-Luc. Just a lot of things to think through."

"No doubt," he said. The tone got her concerned, subtle as it was. Only someone who had known him for decades would have picked up on it.

"In your dress uniform already?"

"Well, I needed to tend to some things, and I didn't want to have to take the time to change later."

She poured herself a glass of juice. "What's the word?"

"The galaxy is quiet this morning. The afternoon, well, that's another matter."

"Oh?"

"There's no knowing when something will go wrong. Or when we'll be given our next assignment."

"Of course. Well, I'll take peaceful for the morning. That way, we're less likely to be interrupted later." *Tell him,* she scolded herself.

"My decisions are never easy ones," Picard said, catching Crusher off guard. He poured himself tea, placed a pastry on his plate.

"Of course not," she said, just to say something.

"And once they're made, I have to live with the consequences. Between assignments I can either brood and reflect or keep moving on. Sometimes those choices are easy, other times less so."

"Are you saying the seeding of my cure is one you will brood over?"

He took a plate of fruit and studied it. "Actually, I meant giving you that order, forcing you to do something against your better judgment."

"All your reasons were valid ones, and you certainly won't be alone in the brooding department."

"No doubt. But Beverly, this could fester and make our next disagreement more difficult. I value your counsel too much to let that happen."

Tell him!

"The crew will never always be in total agreement with the captain's decisions. We're hundreds of people from dozens of worlds, so there are going to be times when we disagree. But still, you're the captain; you get to make the hard decisions. I have to do the same on the operating table. Sometimes, I have to choose between letting a patient live or die. Of all the crew, I understand best."

Picard chewed thoughtfully and then nodded.

"Friends, then?"

"Always." *Now.*

A chime sounded, and Picard's eyes darted to the door in surprise. "Come."

Riker and Troi entered. Both were grinning, not something she expected from a man who had just lost his father. *Well,* she thought, *at least it seems to be good news.*

"Will, good to see you," Picard said, rising. "Join us."

"We're not staying long," he said. "We need to finish getting ready." He paused, soaking in the moment, and Crusher was getting a flash of insight into their news. She was already beginning to smile.

"Sir, we'd like to inform you—"

"Don't be so formal," Troi said, jabbing him with an elbow. "We're engaged!"

Beverly jumped from her chair, letting her napkin fall to the floor, and enveloped Troi in a long hug. Picard was already pumping Riker's hand and offering congratulations. The captain then gave Troi a hug while the doctor gave one to Riker.

"Well, when did this all happen?"

"A few minutes ago," Riker said. "It was time."

"It was time years ago, if you ask me," Beverly said.

"I keep hearing that," Riker said.

Crusher then noticed Troi was already wearing an engagement ring and gave it a close look. "Well, this was certainly fast."

"Will had it waiting for me," Troi said.

"The smoothie," Crusher said, giving him a pleased look. "It's amazing."

"From Delta Sigma IV, too," Deanna added. "He arranged for it to be brought aboard."

"I didn't think Betazed traditions included engagement rings," Picard said, taking his turn to study the ring.

"Usually they don't," Troi agreed. "However, this certainly honors my fiancé and my father's culture."

"How true," the doctor said. "Are there any plans?"

"Not yet," Troi said. "That will come in time. Obviously, we want you both involved."

"Absolutely," Riker agreed.

Picard smiled. "Well, later today we shall return here for a proper celebration. Does anyone else know yet?"

"No," Riker said.

"We were going to tell the others after . . ."

"Of course," Picard said with a nod.

A whistle interrupted something Troi started to say, and Picard looked at his desk. His screen was announcing an incoming call.

Crusher grabbed a piece of bright fruit and ushered the others out. "We'll see you at the service," she said.

No sooner had the others left his cabin than Picard swiftly moved behind his desk and sat. The good feelings seeped away quickly, and he arranged his features in order to deal properly with Starfleet Command.

As expected, he was greeted with the visage of Admiral Upton. The man flexed his bushy gray eyebrows once, then twice, and finally spoke.

"Captain, I understand from your reports that a cure has taken hold."

"That's right, Admiral," Picard said.

"Am I to understand that this all stemmed from incomplete work at Starfleet Medical?"

"That is one way to look at it, but I wouldn't," Picard argued. "What happened here was unique and not something you'd find on a routine checklist."

"I told you this would be a lousy mission," Upton said, still looking dissatisfied.

"And it was. It took a higher toll on my crew than expected."

"So I see. Nine dead, forty-five seriously injured. And you actually had non-security personnel swarming over the planet."

"I wouldn't say several hundred volunteers constitutes a swarm."

"Volunteers?"

"Yes, Admiral. When it was clear we needed help to contain matters, I asked for volunteers. The response speaks for itself."

Upton made a coughing noise, which Picard couldn't interpret as a positive or negative assessment. Perhaps the admiral didn't know, either.

"Riker's a loss to our future planning," Upton said, changing the subject.

"He made a choice, and sacrificed himself for his son. It says a lot about the man's character."

"It will complicate some of the brewing problems elsewhere."

"Anything we can do to help?"

"No," Upton said bluntly.

"Admiral, with all due respect. We've taken the assignments, and paid our dues. I would like to think this ship and its crew deserve better. We're scrambling for proper supplies and support, and our morale has been shaken."

"At least you didn't bang up the ship, for a change," Upton said. Picard recognized he was going to get nowhere with the admiral.

"Sir, the offhand way in which you're talking about my crew's sacrifices diminishes their contribution. Ever since the demon ship, we've all been suspect. And time and again, my people have risen to the challenge and excelled. They have exhibited superb competence, and my senior staff has kept them working toward our common goals. We prevented a world from destroying itself. I lost people along the way, people who believed in the mission. They, if not I, deserve your respect and consideration. It's time for us to return to more strategically vital missions."

Upton just stared at Picard, eyes smoldering. He was either going to give in or bust Picard back to ensign. Rather than prolong the argument and incur the man's temper, the captain wisely thought it was time to back off.

An hour later, Picard exited the turbolift and began walking toward the conference room that had been refit for the memorial service. It was the largest one on the ship and would be used for the subsequent services to be held for the crew that had died. But first, the Federation's tactical envoy was to be memorialized. As he walked, he felt a mix of unease from his conversation with Admiral Upton and joy for Riker and Troi.

In fact, coming from an adjoining corridor was Troi,

escorting Seer of Anann, who towered over the counselor. He was dressed in some form of formal attire in muted yellows and oranges. They were chatting amiably, followed by Data and La Forge, both in their dress uniforms, as befit the occasion. Both nodded in Picard's direction, and he returned the look.

"Protocol Officer, it's nice to have you aboard."

"My first time on a starship, actually," Seer said.

"If you can stay, afterwards we can arrange a tour if you like."

"That would be most gracious of you, Captain. I have meetings scheduled with Ambassador Morrow for after the service, but maybe we can work something out."

"How are things below?"

"Calming down. The Council saw fit to use my plan, and it seems to be working. I suspect, though, we will be petitioning the Federation for some additional help."

"Fortunately, we have an ambassador on hand to expedite things for you. I must say, I am glad your family was spared the worst of it."

Seer nodded gravely. "My family, yes. My house, no. I will be devoting quite a number of days to roof repairs and repainting. At least, that's what Dorina tells me."

Picard grinned and was about to say something when Seer continued.

"May I ask, Captain, how did Riker elude us for so long?"

"Ah, yes, the great mystery. As you know, Kyle Riker was one of the Federation's top tacticians. He therefore had access to the top-of-the-line equipment for all manner of work. He used a bio-signal inhibitor. Very sophisticated and usually used when conducting field work on potential first contact worlds. The range was expanded to include the commander as well."

"Amazing," Seer said, clearly impressed.

Picard gestured for them to follow him. They walked a short distance and then entered the conference room. A podium was erected in the right corner with a small spotlight, the Starfleet crest affixed to its front. Beside it was a coffin that gleamed in the light. A Federation flag was draped over most of it so the ends seemed to twinkle. Above the coffin, on a wall-mounted screen, was Kyle's current service photo. The features were stern, the eyes slightly blurred because they had moved. He had clearly been uncomfortable having the picture taken. Row after row of chairs were being filled with crew, most of whom had served with Will Riker over the years. Picard's eyes drifted over the assembled bodies, and he was pleased by his ability to name the vast majority of them. They were good people, and he took justified pride in their actions.

Seer took a seat at the side, beside Colton Morrow, who looked fully recovered from his injuries. *At least one of the Federation's envoys will make it back alive,* Picard mused. The front row was for the senior officers with La Forge, Data, and Crusher all seated. Vale entered the room and seemed uncertain of where to sit. Picard beckoned her over, gesturing to a chair up front. She had more than earned her place with the others.

Finally, after another minute or two, Will entered. The happy glow on his face was gone, replaced with the mask of the mourning son. From what the captain gathered, they were just beginning to speak once more when the tragedy occurred. No doubt this severely complicated how Will now saw his father.

He tugged his uniform jacket tight across the chest and then strode to the podium. All eyes turned to him, ready to begin the memorial.

Chapter Thirteen

PICARD KNEW ENOUGH about Kyle Riker from their one meeting and from the legends to understand that he wouldn't have appreciated a long, ceremonious event. As a result, his son provided a streamlined service.

He spoke about the man's accomplishments, a slightly longer version than Kyle's service record, keeping personal observations to a minimum. Periodically, Picard glanced at Kyle's image on the screen and frequently turned his attention to Will. The first officer sat stone-faced and solemn. His hand was wrapped within Deanna's and she seemed to be shedding tears for them both.

Finished, Picard paused, letting his final words sink in. He then looked over at Will, who nodded and then slowly rose. Stiffly, he walked over to the podium and replaced Picard, who took the empty seat in the front row.

"As most of you know, my father and I didn't always get along. That wasn't always the case. My father worked hard in the years after my mother died. He was juggling his difficult career with the Federation along with trying to properly raise a young boy who couldn't accept that his mother was gone.

"I probably made it unnecessarily hard on my father those first few years. But he stuck it out, teaching me to fish, camp, hike, and appreciate our home in Alaska. What I didn't come to appreciate until he was gone was that he was also teaching me how to be alone. I became self-sufficient, able to accept responsibility for myself and my surroundings.

"He was gone by then, doing the Federation's work. As you heard from his record, Kyle Riker threw himself into the middle of conflict after conflict. At the time, I was too angry feeling abandoned to understand that not only did I need him, but so did the quadrant. And he couldn't be in two places at once. He had stayed home when I needed him the most, and when he saw the job was done, only then did he return full-time to the stars.

"It took me a long time to understand all that and appreciate his contributions. Truth to tell, it wasn't until these last few days that I really understood his dedication. Or fully understood that the bond between father and son . . . was unbroken.

"The Federation owes Kyle Riker a debt of gratitude it can never fully repay. And I owe my father my life, and I intend to take that life and honor his memory with continued service to our goals of peace and exploration.

"He wasn't easy to talk with or easy to live with, that's for sure. But we feel his absence more keenly as a result of those precious few years we did have.

"Good-bye . . . Dad."

Will looked down at the coffin and then returned to his chair. Picard vacated it immediately, placing a fatherly hand on Will's shoulder, and then returned to the podium to conclude the service.

Once it was over, people rose as one, acknowledged the coffin, and then turned to file out. Picard knew most would seek Riker out in the coming days to offer their personal condolences. Already, the communications buffers were filling with notes to Riker from member worlds and unallied planets. Deanna had told him there were notes from people Riker barely knew to those who served alongside, from Captain Klag of the *I.K.S. Gorkon* to Elizabeth Shelby, captain of the *U.S.S. Trident.* He hadn't read a single one yet, but he would.

Seer walked up to Riker and extended a hand. Will grinned at seeing the man he had befriended on the hunt for Kyle Riker. They spoke briefly, Will taking the time to thank his friend for arranging to have the engagement ring purchased and brought to the starship. Data then escorted the protocol officer to another venue for his meeting with Ambassador Morrow.

Finally, La Forge, Crusher, Vale, Troi, Riker, and Picard were left in the room. The captain knew crew would be by soon to remove the coffin and ready the room for the subsequent services. He would need time to consider the lives and careers of those who had died, and decide how best to honor their memories. It was not a task he looked forward to at all.

"That was nice, Captain," Riker said. "Just like my father, straight and to the point."

"You're welcome."

"Sir, I'll be ready to return to duty tomorrow."

"If you're certain you're ready. We'll be departing orbit in twelve hours, and we'll have plenty of time before our next assignment comes through. I seem to have left Admiral Upton with a few things to consider."

That earned the captain a few curious stares, and he met them all evenly since he had no idea how the last conversation with the admiral would affect their future. He needed to remain positive, if not for his own spirits then for the crew's.

"I'll be fine, sir," Will said.

"Make it so," Picard said.

The doors slid open, and Riker was once more back in his cabin. Normally he never paid attention, but right now it felt empty. He was alone and it didn't sit right with him.

Troi had told him of the people who wanted to offer their personal comments both in person and by com and he would no doubt need to be alone after all that, but not now.

Now he sat in his cabin and felt uneasy. He had just ended one part of his life by saying good-bye to his father, minutes after beginning a new part with Troi. As he transitioned from one feeling to the next, he knew he would remain happy and dedicated to his work.

Unfastening his dress jacket, he took a deep breath, letting his chest expand, enjoying the feeling of freedom. Letting the jacket hang open, he sat on the corner of his bed and just breathed.

His thoughts were interrupted by the chirrup of the com system. He rose and walked to his desk, moved aside several padds he had been trying to focus on earlier, and activated it.

Vale's face greeted him. *"Sorry to bother you, Commander, but you're receiving a private communication from Starfleet Command."*

Riker's brow furrowed. Was this to do with his father's death or with the brass being unhappy with Picard again? There was just one way to find out.

"Pipe it down here, Lieutenant."

"Aye, sir."

Vale's face faded away, replaced with that of a woman he hadn't seen in many years.

"Admiral Janeway," he said, quickly closing his jacket.

"Dressing casually, are we, Commander?" She smirked at him.

"I just got back from my father's memorial," Will said.

Janeway's face expressed her sympathy. He looked at the handsome features and realized she had aged quite nicely since their Academy days.

"I was sorry to hear of Kyle's death. He was a good man."

"He was at that." Will knew it was true, but it still felt unusual to hear it in his own voice.

"Will, I asked to be the one to discuss this matter with you. It's somewhat delicate, and I thought it best if you heard it from an old, well, acquaintance, I guess."

He frowned at that. "What's up?"

"As you know, not everyone here at Command is a big fan of the Enterprise *or its captain right now."*

Riker's mind was racing. Were they replacing Picard? Were the political intrigues on Earth going to destroy a career after countless enemies had failed to achieve that goal?

"However," Janeway continued, *"you do have your fans here. Your record is exemplary, and I'm amazed you haven't taken your own command by now."*

"It's never been the right time."

"How about now?"

Riker blinked at the screen. Janeway remained serious, and he knew not to reply with a joke.

"What do you mean?"

"The Titan *is in need of a captain. It'll be ready to fly within a few months."*

His own ship? Riker had wondered if the opportunity would ever come again. But how could he leave Picard? And Deanna? Would they be married and then assigned to different ships? He hated that notion and immediately wondered if he could bring her along. How fully staffed was the *Titan* to date, and how much of a change would Command allow him to make?

"The timing is . . . complicated. Both personally and professionally, things are a bit of a mess, to be honest, Admiral."

"It's just us, Will, call me Kathryn. What's going on?"

"Won't I be seen as abandoning my captain when his reputation is besmirched?"

"Some might see that. We're a big organization, and you will find unanimity on precious few things. That was my first lesson when I got back from the Delta Quadrant.

"What I see is a man who has stood by his captain through thick and thin, someone we have come to rely on when we needed capable officers. I also see a man

whose career, on paper, has stalled. Few who turn down an offer of command are asked again. You have been asked more than once, and honestly, Will, this may be your last offer."

Riker nodded and thought further, growing somewhat excited at the notion. But he also began imagining how Picard would act if he lost his first officer. They had served together for many years and often thought and acted as one. Where would they find another person able to mesh as well? Or was that Command's goal?

And then his mind was already turning over the *Enterprise* roster to see whom he might want to bring with him. Kell Perim at helm? Vale at tactical? He'd never get Crusher to come along, and he didn't know Tropp well enough. In his heart, he wished Worf were an option, but the Federation's ambassador to the Klingon Empire had his own life to lead.

"Do I give you an answer now, Kathryn?"

"If you want."

"Not exactly."

"I thought as much. You have a little time. But we're going to need a captain in place in a few months to begin finalizing the crew selection and do the shakedown."

"I won't take too long to decide. Promise."

"Good luck, then, Will. You'd be a fine first captain. Hope to see you in that center seat."

She winked out, and the screen filled with the Federation insignia.

Riker sat back and let his jacket fall open. He took several breaths, uncertain who to discuss this with first—Picard or Troi. Each would tell him to take it, he knew that much. But what would each say about the repercussions of such a decision?

And then, to his surprise, he wondered exactly what his father would say.

He put his head in his hands and sat for a long while.

Koll Azernal sat in his office reviewing reports from Starfleet Intelligence. He began each morning, well before the sun rose, with these reports. The middle-aged Zakdorn absorbed and digested huge amounts of information far faster than most of the people who served the Federation president.

The door to his office opened and Admiral Upton entered, blinking a few times, clearly trying to be alert. Azernal preferred meetings with Starfleet officers at times of his own choosing, keeping things on his own terms.

"What have you learned from the *Enterprise* reports?" Azernal asked without even greeting the admiral.

Since he wasn't offered a chair, Upton remained upright, a scowl permanently etched onto his features. The admiral outlined the medical branch's confirmation that Crusher's work would succeed.

Azernal nodded once and picked up a padd. He thumbed it to life and read something from it before speaking.

"We need to place the original research and cure into a top-secret storage facility. It should be placed under voiceprint access only, limited to you and myself."

"Yes, sir," Upton said, and looked as if he was about to ask a question.

"Admiral, we are still recovering from one war, and others are ready to flare up at any moment. We're far from safe and secure. Starfleet is still rebuilding. If I need soldiers in a short time, we can manufacture the original serum and use it on the Delta Sigma IV adults. I can give you an instant army. That was the original goal during the Dominion War when the problem first came to light. We solved it, but too late.

"But there will be another war. There always is."

Acknowledgments

These books cannot possibly be written in a vacuum. It all starts with an idea and in this case, John Ordover called me with the pitch barely a month after *Star Trek Nemesis* opened. Fans had filled gigabytes online debating how this happened or why that person was at the wedding and not someone else. Clearly there were stories to tell and after research showed how much time existed between *Star Trek: Insurrection* and *Star Trek Nemesis,* John knew he had an event.

These two books of mine would not be here without the contributions, advice, cajoling, and friendship of my fellow authors. Our latest doc, Tropp, came from Dayton Ward and his barbecue-lovin' partner, Kevin Dilmore. Jim Peart and Chief of Staff Koll Azernal are the creation of David Mack, who will spotlight them more in the following volumes. There are other little touches you'll see from the works of John Vornholt, who kicked this whole thing off, and Keith DeCandido, who tidies everything up at the end. Keith actually does more than that in so many less obvious ways and he gets a special salute.

The actors who brought the characters to life clearly must be acknowledged, especially Jonathan Frakes and Marina Sirtis, who made us want Riker and Troi to stay in love despite all their duties and other distractions. Being the author to finally write the proposal was a privilege.

A tip of the hat to my colleague Jeff Mariotte, who provided a good look at the Rikers' relationship in his *Lost Era* novel, *Deny Thy Father.* And no book about the romance of Riker and Troi would be complete without referencing the events depicted in Peter David's superb *Imzadi Forever.* Thanks for the inspiration, Peter.

At Pocket Books, I couldn't ask for better assistance and support than from publisher Scott Shannon, editor Ed Schlesinger, and assistants Elisa Kassin and John Perrella. And at Paramount, a big thanks to Paula Block and John Van Citters for keeping me on the straight and narrow.

A tip of the hat to the Malibu Gang for being there; to the readers at PsiPhi.org (the best online *Star Trek* book website around) and the Trek BBS for their support and kind words. Special thanks to Jim McCain, who tracked down an elusive name or two for me while I was in the middle of a paragraph.

The support isn't all online, either. Shore Leave and Farpoint, two of the best fan-run conventions you could ever ask for, continue to support the authors and provide priceless opportunities to speak directly with the fans.

And there are my supporters at home. Deb understands my passion for the material and my need to write, exercising muscles I do not get to use in my current editorial job. She's more of a fan than she likes to admit in public, and I couldn't ask for a better partner. My kids have grown up watching television and movies with us, and have turned into their own creative selves, able to quote obscure movies or song lyrics at the drop of a hat. They've sat at my side as I've written through the years, supportive in so many subtle ways. Kate's about to leave home for college, so the next project will be different, written without her daily presence. I get two more years with Robbie, which is nice since he's more overt in his support—he actually makes time to watch *Enterprise* with me, giving me someone to chat with for instant feedback.

And a nod to Dixie, the loving wonder dog who usually is at my side or underfoot as I write.

Without friends and family, writing these books would be so much more like a job than a pleasure.

About the Author

Robert Greenberger wishes he were the last son of the doomed planet Krypton or was bequeathed an emerald power ring. Instead, he was born in a more mundane manner, surrounded by a loving family on Long Island. His parents encouraged him to pursue his dreams, which first led him to SUNY-Binghamton for his Bachelor's in English and History and then into the world of publishing.

He has spent the majority of his adult life at DC Comics, joining them after a three-year stint at *Starlog* Press. At DC, he began as an Assistant Editor, rising to Manager–Editorial Operations prior to taking what amounted to a two-year sabbatical in the grown-up world.

After ten months as a Producer at Gist Communications, he was lured back to comics, spending a tempestuous year as Director–Publishing Operations at Marvel Comics. He returned to DC as a Senior Editor in their collected editions department in 2002, where he continues today.

Along the way, he has written quite a number of articles, interviews, reviews, and a smattering of comics before turning to prose. He has collaborated with Peter David and Michael Jan Friedman on several *Star Trek* projects. Additionally, he has written several solo novels, including the one you have hopefully just completed. He has written two eBooks for *Star Trek: S.C.E.* and short works found in *Enterprise Logs, Star Trek: New Frontier: No Limits,* and *Star Trek: Tales of the Dominion War.*

He has also written many young adult nonfiction books on a wide variety of subjects. Coming this fall, he contributes essays to *You Did What?,* a look at decisions throughout history that must have made sense to someone at the time.

He makes his home in Connecticut, joined by his patient wife, Deb, and his way-too-old children, Kate and Robbie. When not writing or working, he wants time to read and watch too much television, and prays for the day the Mets win another World Series.

The saga continues in August 2004 with

STAR TREK®

A TIME TO KILL

by
David Mack

Turn the page for an electrifying preview of *A Time to Kill*. . . .

Worf clutched the inner edges of his bronze stole, which was draped evenly across his shoulders and down the front of his bloodwine-colored cossack robe. "Our request of an escort for our flagship is not an indictment of the Empire's sovereign interest, but an urgent appeal for the support of our trusted ally."

"Don't insult me, Worf," Martok said, his voice underscored by a low growl of contempt. "Zife wants our ships to be the *Enterprise*'s lackeys." Worf admired the ragged patch of crudely grafted skin over Martok's left eye socket. The chancellor bore the old wound with the pride it deserved. He closed his right eye for a moment. When he opened it again, it burned with contempt. He bared his teeth and grunted. "Worst of all, he tries to bribe us—as if we were Ferengi!"

"The Federation's offer of the Mirka colonies is unrelated to its request," Worf said. He was simply repeating what he'd been told by Koll Azernal, the president's chief of staff. Worf couldn't be sure how much of his diplomatic briefing was actually true, but even he was galled by this transparently callous attempt to buy the Klingons' favor. Unfortunately, he didn't have the luxury of admitting it aloud. He had to relay the message as it had been given. "The current economic crisis in the Federation has made the sustenance of those colonies untenable," he continued. "For that reason, the Federation Council has approved President Zife's petition to remand the colonies to Klingon jurisdiction."

"Does Zife really believe he can buy us so shamelessly?" Martok pounded his fist on the arm of his chair. "Am I supposed to believe the timing of this resolution was a coincidence?"

"Regardless of what you believe," Worf said, "it is done."

"It makes no difference," Martok said. "Tezwa's threats are a matter of record. Its fleet is preparing to launch. The Empire cannot—will not—permit this challenge to go unpunished."

"Their challenge can be withdrawn."

Martok shook his head angrily. "Not good enough. We will not be seen as weak, Worf. . . . I will not be seen as weak." He lowered his voice. "You know as well as I do, this is a dangerous time for the Empire. The war cost us dearly, but the Empire must continue to grow. . . . Mercy is not an option."

"But prudence is." In defiance of protocol, Worf took two steps toward Martok. "The honor of the Empire can be preserved without the risks of war, if you permit Captain Picard to negotiate."

"Why should I put my trust in him?" Matrok said. "How do I know he doesn't have an agenda of his own?"

"I served with Captain Picard for many years," Worf said. The words came out a bit more defensive-sounding than he would have liked. "He has always shown the deepest respect for our laws and traditions—and you of all people should know he has proved more than once that he is a true friend to the Klingon people."

Martok let out a contemptuous guffaw. "Why? Because he installed my predecessor? That incompetent narcissist Gowron? That act of friendship nearly led the Empire to its doom."

"Gowron's sins were his own," Worf said. "But if not for Captain Picard, the Empire would be in the hands of traitors."

"If you pledge to me that Picard's a good man, I'll believe you," Martok said. "But his first loyalty is to the Federation. If he's forced to decide between its best interest and ours, whose welfare do you think he'll favor?"

"Captain Picard is an honorable man," Worf said. "He will negotiate fairly, and honestly. And he will not let the Empire be betrayed—not by Tezwa, not even by the Federation. Of this I give you my word—as the Federation's ambassador, as your kinsman . . . as a Klingon."

Martok simmered for a long moment. He glowered with his one eye. Then he got up from his chair, stepped down, and stood in front of Worf. He flashed his jagged, sharp-toothed smile. "Your word was all I needed," he said. "Our fleet will escort the *Enterprise* to Tezwa." He reached out and grasped Worf's forearm. Worf returned the gesture, sealing the agreement. "*Qapla'!*" Martok said.

Worf nodded. He had faith that the crew of the *Enterprise* would defuse the crisis on Tezwa. And considering the situation's incendiary effect on Federation-Klingon politics, he knew he was the best person to help the two allies reconcile their often incompatible foreign policies. But he couldn't deny that he missed the days when he was able to solve problems with actions instead of words. He did not regret becoming a diplomat, but he was still a Klingon; the time he'd spent living on Qo'noS had reawakened the long-dormant fire in his warrior's heart.

And though he couldn't say so, had the decision been his to make, Tezwa would already have been destroyed.